Blood on the Water

Simon Phelps

Published by Forward Thinking Publishing

First published 2023

Published by Forward Thinking Publishing

Text © Simon Phelps 2023

The information given in this book should not be treated as a substitute for
professional medical advice; always consult a medical practitioner. Any use
of information in this book is at the reader's discretion and risk. Neither the
author nor the publisher can be held responsible for any loss, claim or damage
arising out of the use, or misuse, of the suggestions made, the failure to take
medical advice or for any material on third party websites.

A catalogue record for this book is available from the British Library.

ISBN: 978-1-916764-01-9

Place Names

I have used spellings as close to the time the novel is set as far as possible to create a flavour of the times. My sources are various and spelling at the time varied from writer to writer so accuracy is impossible. Regions and Earldoms, even nations had different boundaries from today so names that are similar to modern ears do not necessarily correspond to present day mapping. Towns usually are where they were a thousand years ago.

Abergafenni – Y Fenni	Abergavenny
Afon Guoy	River Wye
Al Qayrawan	Kairouan
Cathures	Glasgow
Caer Went	Caerwent
Caerleon	Caerleon
Corebricg	Corbridge
Deverdoeu	Chester
Dùn Breatainn	Dumbarton Rock
Dyflin	Dublin
Geddwerde	Jedburgh
Genoa	Genoa
Glowecestre	Gloucester
Hereford	Hereford
Ircingafeld	Archenfield
Lundenburh	London

Jorvik	York
Papia	Padua
Pentwithstart	Land's End
Porthsgiwed	Portskewett
Scone	Scone
Temese	Thames
Wincestre	Winchester

Blood on the Water

*In 1054 England is at peace but beyond its border's life was far from
calm. The great northern Earl, Siward, leads a large force across the
northern border to attack the Scottish King we now call MacBeth.
Both sides call in their allies thus provoking one of the fiercest contests
of the times.*

*Meanwhile in Wales, one ambitious man, Gruffud ap Llewellyn,
aims to claim the whole country as his own. He too, schemes to create
a powerful alliance in an attempt to unite his nation, for the first
time, under one ruler.*

*Not far across the waters the Irish and the Norse settlers they've assim-
ilated are poised to help, or hinder, those who can offer advantage,
wealth or reputation.*

*One young man, caught in the eddies of the powerful, while
following his own destiny, is a witness to these events. This is his story.*

Simon Phelps

Part One

Chapter One

The tanner, you could tell he was a tanner by his slimy clothes and the stench that went with them, slowly got to his feet. He swore at us then spat, sloppily, through blackened teeth as he pulled out a short, plaited leather whip from his belt.

'Here we go,' I thought, 'another drunken twat who doesn't know when he's beaten.'

He flicked the whip back and forth in front of him, swaying slightly and burbling some crap about boys who think they're men. Then he lurched forward, straight at Gyric as I knew he would. No-one ever saw skinny me as a threat. I quickly side-stepped, then, as he passed, thwacked him across the back of his skull with my blackjack. He went down like a stone.

I grinned at Gyric then saw the flicker in his eye. Before he could speak, I whipped round to find the tanner's mate coming at me and saw a glint of silver in the moonlight. A knife. Now this was serious. To his obvious shock I stepped in, grabbed his arm, pulled him into me and swung him round. His mouth opened, screaming, as Gyric struck him hard across his back with an axe-handle. His foul breath filled my nostrils as I pushed him down on to the muddy, cobbled road. Gyric struck him again across his back while I gave him a couple of hard kicks between the legs. He writhed onto his side to clutch at his crotch and the knife fell from his fingers.

I picked it up and, after shoving it into my belt, knelt and spoke to the groaning man, 'If Earl Siward knew you'd used a blade on the streets of Jorvik you'd greet the dawn with your neck in a noose.'

I kicked him again in the head, then stamped on him. Gyric pulled me away, 'Back off, Sar, he's out cold, done, alright? You kill him and you'll be the one hanging. Harold's man or not.'

We rummaged through their clothes but, as usual, by the time they were this drunk they never had anything of value left on them. I looked up at Gyric, 'What on earth are we doing Gy? Here we are, Earl Harold's men, trained warriors. Well, you are anyway, throwing out drunks from a tavern.'

'We're getting by till Siward lets us leave,' he replied with his usual easy-going grin. He winked, 'and life with Hilda isn't so bad.'

I grinned back. We both shared Hilda's bed from time to time as well as looking after her inn while her husband traded over the sea. Exciting stuff for Gyric and me. I might be sixteen and Gyric was seventeen but we'd become killers before we'd been lovers. Hilda was fun and warm and we had much to forget behind the hanging curtains around her soft warm bed.

We turned the drunk's faces out from the sticky mud so they'd not suffocate or drown in their own vomit and left them where they lay. We wanted no corpses here. Siward's justice was hard and its products hung by their necks, legs dangling, above the Mykla Gata Bar.

Jorvik was a hard city under harsh law. The dark logs of the town's buildings brooded over its slippery streets. Endless drizzle dripped off the thatch covered workshops with their open fronts, where chilly craftsmen and women blew into their hands. The sharp stench of burning hoof, horn and hair cut through the background pungency of smoke, urine and pig shit. The winter had been long and followed by a wet, stormy spring which had kept the fishermen on the shore. The hungry gap had come early this year. There were no grains, no wheat, no rye nor barley, to be found in this forlorn city while the crops were still green in the fields. Harsh law meant robbers were hung, so when they robbed, they killed. It left no witnesses. I had long dirtied up the hilt of the honed down seax that had become my mother's knife. The richly decorated weapon that the father I'd never known had looted from the grave of an ancient king. I'd used it to kill my mother's murderer. His son, Oslaf, had used it to carve me from ear to chin. The scar still itched. I'd killed Oslaf's brother, Osric, to avenge the murders of my aunt Ealhid, my sweet young cousins and my warrior friend, Toki. I wasn't done yet. Oslaf still lived. I hunted him while he, he hunted me.

Back in the inn we asked Lodin about the takings for the night. His huge forearms opened to reveal the usual mixed bag of glass beads, leatherwork, combs and cheap jewellery and the odd cut penny. It never ceased to amaze me what men would trade in for the privilege of getting drunk on stale beer and sour wine. Hilda would string the beads into necklaces and bracelets to sell to the guilty or love-struck, to placate unhappy wives or seduce easy women.

Lodin dragged himself out from behind his table heaving his way across the floor on crutches. 'Got a couple of smokies here as well, Saint Stephen in his church might know how old they are. I can tell you there's little mould and no maggots,' he said nodding towards a couple of withered looking wind-dried smoked fish.

I squinted at them in the firelight but could not really see them, maybe that was just as well. I took the skillet and placed it on the embers. Old fat sizzled as I flaked the fish into it. Gyric dropped some eggs into a pail of water. Then, after throwing the floaters into the fire, he cracked the others into the pan. Attracted by the smell of frying Hilda came down the ladder from above. 'Do you need salt, my lovely lads?' she asked, 'Eggs without salt make a poor supper.'

Lodin pulled out a fish flake and tasted it, 'No ta, the fish is salty as well as smoked. You joining us?'

'After I've put away the takings,' she answered as she rooted through the bits and pieces. After picking out anything of real value she climbed back up to hide it away.

Gyric cracked another couple of eggs into the pan and I stirred it all around. Hilda came back down and we sat around the pan each taking turns to dip our horn spoons into the scrambled mess.

'Iesu Mawr achub fi,' I cursed in Welsh, as I did when I was particularly pissed off.

'Speak English, Sar,' said Gyric.

'Or better still Dansk,' added Hilda.

I wiped my spoon off on my once fine tunic and spat into the dusty straw, 'No offence Hilda, but last year I was eating meats from an Earl's table. Siward won't give us leave to go or to serve in his court. Even Grim don't come and see us anymore.'

'Northumbria is a vast Earldom and Grim is away on the Earl's bidding as trusted housecarls often are. You know this Sar, he will come for us when the time is right,' answered Gyric, 'It is as God wills.'

Grim Haldorson was Toki's brother. He, with a Frisian pirate captain, had led the raid on Oslaf's mother's hall which we had burned to the ground. Once we had escaped from the hostile ships of Earl Aelfgar's East Anglian navy into the endless maze of the Fens it was decided, to Grim's delight, that we had no choice but to come north. After an arse blistering row, we had finally found our way to the Humber and up the Ouse to Jorvik. Earl Siward had welcomed Grim back with open arms. Bear hugging him with those arms so powerfully as to make Grim look small.

I'd seen Earl Siward before and instinctively liked the rough old Viking warlord with his grizzled beard and blunt speech. He didn't feel the same about us. He stared down on us from his high seat of black ancient wood, carved with polished entwined, writhing wyverns and declared. 'Hmmm, Harold's men, eh? Never cared much for Godwin's silver tongue. Slipped far too easily into Cnut's trusted circle,' he chuckled at his own wit while Gyric and I exchanged startled looks. 'Not sure I care much for his over-dressed and over-mighty children either,' he continued, sniffing and glaring at us while spitting into the rushes on his mead-hall floor.

I had shuffled uneasily, curbing my tongue. Gyric politely asked for horses to allow us to return home.

'Thegn Scalpi's son, aren't you? Now there's a man I respect. Proper Dane, but no, you can't have a horse. You and that red-haired streak of piss next to you will stay in Jorvik until I decide otherwise.'

At first it hadn't been so bad. Jorvik was a big town with lots going on. We ran and wrestled every day outside the town walls to keep fit. Gyric would practise with his sword while I cast my remaining spear over and over again until eye and arm became one. I also learned how to throw the wickedly sharp little axe the Frisian captain had given me before they rowed away.

'Fulk will pay my family well and you fought like a man,' he had said, 'though I won't tell you my name, I will give you this.' As he brought out the axe a memory flashed into my mind. Now I knew how he had stopped a charging man in his tracks against the flickering background of a burning hall.

'That's how you did it!' I breathed excitedly.

'Aye, my ancestors fought with these. Though they have long ceased to be the fashion my grandfather taught me their use. You have this, I can get others made.'

I liked throwing weapons. I struggled to fight in a mailed byrnie while carrying a heavy shield like the Saxon housecarls who'd been meat-fed from childhood. I had to rely on speed, agility and my cold killer's heart when I fought, or killed.

The winter had dragged. We'd traded away anything of value we were willing to let go of. Neither of us would sell our weapons. For Gyric that was his sword and a knife. We'd not taken mail or war shields on the raid. Me, I had my long knife of course, my little wood and bronze targe and the throwing spear I liked to fight with, as well as the axe. We'd both had arm rings which we'd traded away while Gyric had sold his fine metal cloak clasps. I kept my silver wire torque that Faelan oi Airtre, an Irish warlord, had given me after

7

the battle at Porloc, and the silver spoon I had found in the ashes of Ealhild's hall. Gyric had a ring of his father's he had sworn to keep. With nothing else left, we wound up working for our lodgings in the tavern Grim had found for us. Hilda's warm bed was a welcome comfort though Gyric's Christian principles had worried him.

'She's not a real wife though, not church wed,' he'd fretted, 'not really adultery.'

'Oh yea, so you'd shag Earl Harold's Edith and say, sorry sir, but she's only wed Danish style,' I laughed at him.

He blushed at the thought. Who didn't fancy the beautiful Edith? Then he shook his head as he imagined Harold's vengeance.

'Look at it this way Gyric, she's the one good thing that's happened in this stinking town and you'll know how to keep your wife happy when your father finds you one.'

He had smiled at that and we pushed to the back of our minds the thought of what would happen when fine weather brought the traders back from over the sea.

Coming back into the present I returned to my grumbling, 'We must go to Siward again, ask him to give us some real work and some proper food or let us go home.'

Lodin said, 'There'll be work on the docks soon enough for willing hands.'

'I meant work for the Earl, not labouring for merchants.'

Lodin was offended at this. His legs had been smashed when he'd slipped under the keel of a newly built longboat as it launched down the slips. 'Get over yourself you poncey little runt,' he growled then, after dragging himself to a bundle of blankets and old furs, he bedded down for the night.

Hilda laughed and with a swing of her yellow hair and a flounce of her ample skirts she headed for the back door. 'Now, you boys stay in here while I go and do what even a lady such as me must do from time to time.'

She had a laugh like silver bells and always seemed cheerful so despite my sour mood I grinned back at her as she left.

No sooner had I put the skillet into the fire to burn it clean when the street door banged open. Without looking I could tell they came from the docks and had recently been at sea. I could smell the salt. 'Fuck off,' I said, 'We're closed.'

Gyric spoke, 'Excuse my friend, but we are shut.'

A gruff voice said, 'Sit down boy, I'll decide if we're shut.'

Five burly seamen, two of them carrying a large sea-chest stood behind me. Their leader shook off his dripping fur cloak. As he turned into the glow of the firelight, I could see that he had a huge nose that at some time had been badly broken. If his eyes were looking to the prow of a ship then his nose was pointing firmly to the steerboard.

'I don't know who you young men are but, I am Einvar Crook-Nose and I own this tavern.' He stared round the room strode to the nearest bench and sat. 'So where is my wife?'

Gyric jumped to his feet, even in the firelight I could see that he was blushing violently, 'You mean Hilda. You're Hilda's husband?'

Einvar stared at him, hard, 'Yes, what of it?'

Gyric started to stammer. I didn't like the way this was going. 'Oy,' I said, 'Crook-nose! Why they call you that then?'

Einvar leaped to his feet, if Gyric's face was red, Einvar's had gone deeply purple. Swinging a fist as big as a badger ham at my face he charged at me. I ducked under his arm and dove straight into the boot of one of his men. Grabbing the boot hard I tipped the sailor on his back and jumped up onto a table daring Einvar to come at me.

'Want me to straighten that for you, eh?' I shouted, lashing out at his nose with my foot. As my right foot smashed into his nose, my left was wrenched out from under me. I crashed down between the benches to find Lodin's powerful shoulders holding me down to the floor, his forearm pressed against my windpipe.

'Get off me you fucking cripple. What are you doing?' I said, choking my words into his hairy face.

'Saving your stupid life, now stay down.'

9

Behind the noise of the benches being dragged aside I could hear Hilda pleading for Gyric's life. Then one of Einvar's boots thudded into my side, another kick deadened my thigh. Lodin grunted as a third kick slammed into him while we thrashed about on the floor.

'Stay still, you skinny git.'

I wriggled sideways and got my lower half out from under only for Einvar to stamp on my belly. Vomiting chunks of fish into the straw, badly winded, I gasped for breath. Lodin rolled off me as Einvar landed another kick to my ribs.

From the corner of my eye I could see Gyric held up against the wall with a knife to his throat while Hilda was pulling at Einvar's clothes and pleading with him.

'Let them go, husband, they have been helping here this winter. One of Siward's men lodged them here.'

Einvar drew back, 'Siward's man?' He paused, thinking slowly, still scowling while breathing heavily through his mouth. Hilda tried to dab at his bleeding nose with the end of her shawl which soon got sticky with blood and snot.

'Yes husband, Grim Haldorson, he left them here in the autumn.'

His eyes narrowed, 'Grim eh?'

As he pondered, I began to breathe again, sucking air in with shuddering gasps. 'Yes, Grim,' I said, 'he brought us to Jorvik.'

Einvar made his mind up. 'Throw them out,' he said. Then turning to his wife he kissed her, 'you glad to see me darling?'

I missed her reply as Gyric was given the bum's rush then I too was dragged along the floor and thrown out into the mud and rain of Guthrums Gate.

'Christ, Sar, what was that about?' asked Gyric as the door slammed shut behind us.

I lifted my hand out of a fresh pig turd and sat up, 'You were blushing like a little girl. I thought next thing you'd be defending Hilda's honour.'

'Oh what? You were saving me? Were you worried that we might get a beating and get thrown out into the street,' retorted Gyric ruefully. He was standing now, vainly trying to rub clinging street slime off his clothes.

'Would have been worse if he'd have guessed the truth.' I became aware of strange snuffling grunts. 'Ha, ha Gyric, would you look at that!'

Just up the street the filth covered tanner was struggling to get to his feet from under the weight of an enormous sow. Her frantic litter of piglets squealing excitedly all around. Gyric and I waded in, laughing helplessly as we kicked the sow away. The tanner rose to his feet and looked around for his mate, seeing he was gone he scuttled off into the darkness of the alleys.

Gyric and I looked at each other, breathing heavily and giggling gently.

Suddenly Gyric stopped, 'Sar, our weapons and our cloaks, they are all in the inn.'

I shook my head, suddenly despondent. Without good clothes, with no weapons and no lodgings, we were nothing but vagrants.

Chapter Two

We spent the rest of the night sheltering miserably in the lee of Saint Olaf's church before heading back to the inn at dawn. We woke Lodin by gently tapping on the door. As it opened we could hear the snores of sleeping seamen.

'Not a chance lads. Even if I could carry your weapons, which I can't, I'd not get them past that lot,' he whispered. 'I'll get Hilda to hide your things in the loft. If you want them back, bring Grim with you.'

We nodded and slunk away. 'We're going to look a right pair of fools pleading with Grim,' I moaned to Gyric.

'Got to find him first,' Gyric replied.

'Siward's hall, let's try there.'

On getting to the hall we were firmly turned away. We had the wrong clothes and the wrong accents. For the next two days we watched the comings and goings from up the street.

On the third day, cold, wet and very hungry, we were close to giving up when a group of housecarls strode down the street. Using their long spear-shafts they pushed the crowd back against the walls and into the tradesmen's booths.

'Make way for the King's thegn, make way,' they yelled at the curious crowd.

Coming up the slight rise was a long procession of heavily armed men on horseback. They were led by a huge man carrying a large red and yellow standard.

12

'By Saint Cuthbert,' breathed Gyric excitedly, 'I know that banner.'

He started pushing through the crowd as I wriggled after him. Being Gyric, always polite, he was saying, 'sorry, excuse me, sorry,' as he pushed the people aside, gently but firmly.

Coming up against the spear-shaft barrier we saw a richly dressed man with the thick paunch of well-fed middle age riding beside the standard bearer.

Suddenly Gyric was bellowing, 'Thegn Burgric, it's me, it's me, Gyric.'

The nearest housecarl pushed Gyric away from the street. 'Get back man, what are you doing?'

Gyric pushed back with all his youthful strength while yelling, 'Foster-father, Thegn Burgric, stop, please stop.'

I had no idea what he was on about but I grabbed the housecarl's spear and pulled. As the man let one hand go to push me away, Gyric leaped through the gap and grabbed Burgric's reins.

'Get this vagrant out of my way. Is this what you call discipline in the North,' Burgric shouted, barging his horse into Gyric's chest.

A group of Siward's offended housecarls rushed over to grab Gyric when he shouted again, 'Burgric! How is the Lady Agatha?'

By the time Burgric raised his hand and the whole column came to a sidling, snorting halt, Gyric was firmly held by two of Siward's men. I hung back to see which way the wind blew.

Burgric leant over his horse's withers, who sidestepped at his rider's movement, to peer into Gyric's face, 'Who are you to call my wife's name in the street?'

'Do you not know me, foster-father? Gyric. Skalpi's boy?'

'Skalpi's boy serves Earl Harold,' replied Burgric, his voice now uncertain.

'And so I do, sir. I've grown since we last met, grown a beard too,' said Gyric, his grin broadening into a wide smile.

'Ha, it is you! Gyric, by God, I'd know that smile in the dark despite that ugly scar on your face. Let the boy go, he'll do me no

13

harm,' said Burgric alighting from his horse. 'Come here foster-son, come here.'

They embraced delightedly, thumping each other on the back before heading on up the street with Gyric leading Burgric's horse. Dodging the bemused housecarls, I ran up to Gyric's side figuring I'd be welcome now.

Burgric glared at me, 'Who is this? Some gutter bred mongrel by the look of him.'

'I'm Gyric's friend, also Harold's man,' I retorted, offended.

He ignored me and asked Gyric, 'Your 'friend' speaks like a barbarian. Who is his father?'

Gyric grimaced apologetically, 'Well he is a bit Welsh and has no father.'

Burgric sniffed and spat, 'A bastard eh? Can't trust a bastard, or a Welshman, come to that. Still he can serve you I suppose.'

'Just shut up Sar, alright,' hissed Gyric, 'just for once, hold your tongue.'

He meant it. I could tell. So I did.

By now we were approaching Siward's great hall. Before its massive dragon carved doors stood the mighty Earl himself. He strode forward, his arms wide open, 'Welcome Thegn Burgric. Welcome to my city and my hall.'

Burgric raised his hand and we all stopped. He stepped forward, 'Earl Siward, the King sends his greetings and,' he waved at his column of warriors, 'many of his men. We are just the vanguard.'

'My soldiers will show them where to camp. Meanwhile bring your leading men to my hall and we shall eat and talk,' replied Siward.

About ten of Burgric's men dismounted while others took their horses. As Burgric and Siward walked together into the hall Gyric and I followed them in, our mouths already watering at the thought of food.

Just as we walked through the doors we were pulled roughly aside. 'Come here lover-boys. We need to talk,' said a well-known voice.

'Grim, how good to see you,' I said, genuinely pleased.

He did not look so pleased to see us, 'Seems like I can't leave you two for a moment.'

'Moment! It's been weeks since we've seen you!' said Gyric, laughing.

'I've been busy up in the North,' replied Grim, 'while you, I hear, have been straightening Einvar's nose.'

I shuffled my feet. 'Well that was me,' I said, avoiding his eyes.

'Rumour also has it that you've been looking after his wife as well.' Grim looked searchingly at Gyric who blushed to his roots.

'One look at him and I know the truth, while you Sar. You can lie like rushes on the floor,' said Grim.

'I'm not lying when I tell you that we need you to come to Hilda's tavern with us,' I grimaced wryly, 'to get our weapons back.'

'Your weapons? You've lost your weapons. What has happened to you two?', his voice was thick with disgust.

We squirmed with shame under his steady glare, unable to answer.

He stroked his beard thoughtfully, 'Well if you want my help, you'll have to wait. Meanwhile you can't be in the hall tonight. Go straight through, there's a kitchen in the back. Tell them I sent you. I'll find you in the morning.'

We ate in a small side kitchen behind a hall from which we could hear no singing, no boasting and there were no girls serving food or drink. I leant back against the roughly daubed wattle wall behind me and nodded towards the door, 'Some feast that, no fun at all. What do you think is going on?'

Gyric answered, 'This must be serious business as Grim said. Burgric is one of King Edwards most powerful and loyal thegns. He's from one of the few remaining old English noble families.'

I remembered something, 'You called him foster-father. Why?'

'Because he is. I was fostered with him at the age of ten.'

'But you've got a father.'

Gyric looked at me frowning, 'I forget how little you know. All the better families foster their sons to other noble households.'

'Your families send you away?'

He nodded in agreement and poured himself a drink.

'When you are still children?' I persisted.

Gyric nodded again.

'Sent away from your mother and sisters,' I said appalled.

'Yes, it creates alliances between the families,' he answered staring off into the shadows.

I could see his eyes welling up. I thought it best to take another tack, 'So when we faced the King last year, your father was on one side and Burgric on the other?'

'Yes, that's right. Thing is Sar, if it had come to a fight that day and we'd lost. Then, if Skalpi, my real father, had survived to be tried and put to death by the King, Thegn Burgric would protect me and the rest of my family from the King's vengeance.'

'In exchange for what?'

'Skalpi would do the same for his family and so would I.'

'Doesn't that just encourage fights?'

'More often than not it ties us together peacefully. I'm fostered by a King's thegn. One of my sisters will marry one of Earl Leofric's thegns. I now serve Earl Harold so my family has links with many other powerful people.'

'Like Toki and Grim serving different earls?'

'Yes Sar.' Gyric had had enough, 'Worked out well for us today, didn't it? Now shut up and eat.'

I'd eaten plenty so I got up to tug the cloth hanging over the door aside. 'They're all up the end of the hall round one table.'

'Don't spy, Sar. It didn't work out too well last time,' said Gyric.

I shuddered, remembering Harold's wrath, but just as I was turning away the guards let another party in through the hall door. When their leader came into the light of a burning torch, I could see two black eyes and a large, swollen, but still very crooked, nose.

'Gyric, it's Einvar, he's here.'

'Einvar here? Why would Einvar be here?' replied Gyric, thoughtfully.

'Gyric, if Einvar's here he's not at the inn.'

He jumped to his feet, 'Our weapons! Come on. Let's go.'

We pushed out through the back door, past the startled kitchen staff, who were scouring pans outside, and ran down through the now dark streets. The barking of disturbed dogs followed by the insults of their owners chased us through the night.

'It'll be busy at Hilda's now there are ships coming up the river,' I panted to Gyric.

'Might make it easier to get in, Lodin will let us pass, we keep in with the crowd, then sneak up the ladder when Einvar's men aren't looking,' answered Gyric.

'Not much of a plan,' I said and thought for a moment. 'We won't need Grim. That's good enough for me. Let's give it a go.'

When we arrived the place was rowdy with loud boasts and beer songs. As Gyric had said, Lodin looked the other way. He didn't look happy, not at all.

'Christ Lodin, your face looks like a slapped arse, what's wrong?' I hissed at him.

'I'd forgotten what a bastard that Einvar is,' he answered miserably from behind his table.

'What do you mean?'

'You'll find out soon enough,' he replied.

I wanted to get on, 'Alright Lodin, we owe you. Are our things still in the loft?'

'Ay lad, you'll find Hilda up there too.'

As he said that I realised what was missing. Hilda's laughing backchat with the customers. That's what was missing. Gyric and I slid around the walls crouching a little behind the crowd. As we got close to the loft ladder I spotted one of Einvar's companions of the other night drinking at a table by the barrels. I nudged Gyric and nodded towards the man.

'When he looks the other way, get up the ladder, quick as you can.'

As the man turned back to his mates Gyric climbed the ladder and squeezed through the open trap door. So far so good, I went to follow him. The moment my head rose above the crowd a voice bellowed out.

'It's that fucking red-headed bastard. Stop him!'

I looked over my shoulder. At least two of Einvar's men were pushing through the crowd. I climbed. A hand grabbed my foot. I kicked it off. I felt another hand catch at my calf. I half turned and kicked out at a head. The crowd milled around below me, some trying to stop me, others getting angry as Einvar's men shoved them aside. Fighting erupted. I tried to climb but grasping hands pulled my feet from the rungs. I was clinging on grimly to the side rails when two fighting sailors crashed into the ladder shattering it. The hands on my feet disappeared. I was clinging to the broken rails just below the ceiling. My fingers were slipping and my grip loosened. Any moment now I was going to fall into the maelstrom of men fighting below my flailing legs.

As my too short life flashed before me my hands gave up the struggle. Suddenly my forearms were grasped by two strong hands and I rose into the air passing through the trap. With my legs still dangling out of the hole I found myself face to face with Gyric's grinning mug.

'Pull your legs up, Sar, I can't hold you forever.'

I pulled up my knees and got my feet onto the edge of the hole and kicked backwards as Gyric let go. Now panting and breathless on the loft floor I twisted round to look down into the mass of men below. Through a mixture of brute force, and the loud shouts of men used to working ships in a gale, Einvar's men were calming things down. There must have been more of his crew present because now they were dragging a board and trestles across the room.

'The broken ladder won't hold them back for long,' said Gyric. 'Help me with this.'

He slammed the trap door shut then I helped him drag a chest over it.

'That will slow them down,' he panted. 'Now where are our weapons?'

Faint moonlight glimmered through a railed window hole in the gable end. I started to rummage around the loft when I saw something move. I leaped back, startled, 'Gyric, someone's up here.'

'Boys, boys, is that you Gyric, you and Sar?'

'Christ Sar, its only Hilda like Lodin said,' said Gyric crouching under the pitch of the roof where she lay curled into a ball on a bundle of rags that had once been the curtains she'd been so proud of.

'Our weapons Hilda, where are they?' I demanded.

'Leave off Sar, can't you see she's hurt?'

I couldn't really see her face but could see her point to the shadow under the window. I pulled aside a couple of tanned hides and there they were, my knife, targe and spear and beside them, Gyric's sword in its sheath.

'My throwing axe, where's my axe?'

'It is there. Keep looking,' said Hilda getting to her feet.

The moonlight lit her face to reveal a mass of yellowing bruises around puffy swollen eyes.

'Einvar did that?' I asked.

'Because of us?' cried Gyric.

As she sobbed in agreement we were roughly reminded of our situation when the chest over the trap door started violently banging up and down.

'Because of what she did with us, Gyric. Understand! They'll kill us. We need to get out of here.'

'How?'

My frantically scrabbling hands found the axe and I hacked at the bars sweating. It would take an age to chop through the seasoned, smoked-hard oak.

'This isn't working,' I shouted, casting about my mind for an idea when Gyric smashed his muscly bulk against the heavy battens under the thatch.

They cracked and gave, he piled into them again and they gave some more. A shout came from behind us. I turned to see the chest had moved aside. Two hands and a pair of eyes appeared. We were moments away from assault and inevitable capture.

'Gyric, get your fat arse on that chest. I'll cut us a way out.'

Gyric threw himself over onto the shifting chest. The trap shut with a crash followed by a terrific howl. Gyric started snorting with laughter while I frantically tugged at the broken battens.

'He's left his fingers behind,' chortled Gyric, beside himself at the sight.

It was true. Neatly lined up along the edge of the planking was a row of bleeding fingers. Then the uproar beneath us changed in tone. Heavy axe blows were thudding into the beams of our floor. If we weren't out soon we'd be caught like rats in a hay stack with nowhere to run.

A couple of the roof battens snapped and as they came away I now had room to stamp down on the ones below. Kicking them away I frantically began tearing out bundles of the thick thatch. Hilda rose stiffly and tried to help. A blast of cold night air told me that we'd broken through. The hole was soon big enough for me to escape. I wriggled through and after stamping my feet into the thatch I tore away at the hole to make room for Gyric.

Hilda's face appeared. 'I'm coming with you,' she said, 'I'm not staying here.'

'Oh no you're not,' I said, 'we have enough problems as it is.'

'Yoo,' she answered with that strange Norse word that I'm never sure if it means yes or no. Whatever it means she was going to argue.

'Yoo, I will come and you won't stop me,'

I gave up, knowing I was beaten. Hilda was as stubborn as the rising tide. 'Pass our weapons then, pass them through.'

She passed them out and I carefully laid them on the thatch. Suddenly a great crash startled us as the chest dropped through the floor. Where was Gyric? I breathed a huge sigh of relief as he pushed Hilda through the hole and followed her out. Now we were all kneeling on the slippery thatch, breathing heavily, as we looked over the roofs of Jorvik just slightly blacker than the cloud covered sky. I gave Gyric his sword which he managed to belt around himself as I pushed my knife and axe into my own.

I could hear voices coming from the loft as men climbed up from the room below. A face appeared in the hole then flinched back as I stabbed at it with my spear. I waved at Gyric and Hilda to climb up to the ridge as I poked at heads and hands as they appeared. I was careful not to actually spear anyone. I didn't want to face Siward's justice. After more hacking and tearing sounds, holes started to appear in other parts of the roof. It was time for me to run. I scrambled up the roof after the others and got to the ridge.

'Where to now?' I gasped, looking over the town, 'where now?'

The street was out of the question, so too the back yard of the inn. What followed was a mad scramble over the roofs. Down one slippery thatched slope, then a leap across the narrow gap to the next building, then a frantic upward scrabble. When we got to the ridge, we'd look back to see a band of seamen following. As each roof passed at least one of our pursuers went missing. Soon we were followed by only a couple of men, probably less drunk than the rest.

On the next downslope we dropped off the roof and down into the narrow space under the eaves. There we stayed silent and still. Shortly afterwards two black shapes crossed the gap above our heads. Then we quietly slunk through the streets, to Siward's kitchen.

Chapter Three

The morning sun found me, Gyric and Hilda arguing behind Siward's hall.

'How can we take care of her, Gyric, we don't even have a place ourselves?'

'She can't go back to the inn, can she? Saint's blood Sar, look at her,' shouted Gyric.

I looked at her bruised, tearful face and felt nothing. 'Shouldn't fuck her lodgers then, should she, eh?' I yelled back. 'Why is she our problem?'

'We can't just leave her, Sar.'

'She's got a lot more friends in this town than we have,' I answered.

'None who would cross Einvar over a woman without family and no wealth,' said Hilda, 'but don't worry boys, I'll just go join the other girls down at the mill.'

I saw a puzzled look cross Gyric's face. I could still be shocked by the things he didn't know. Even I, who grew up in a Welsh hamlet, knew that in every English town the working girls plied their trade around the flour mills. 'She means sell her body, Gyric. She'd do well, I guess. She scrubs up lovely as we both know, don't we?'

Hilda slapped my face then Gyric pushed me back into the wall. 'Shut your mouth, Sar, just shut your mouth. She stays with us.'

Looking over his shoulder I realised that a lot of men were coming and going, talking excitedly. 'Here, Gyric, something's going on.'

'I told you to shut up,' said Gyric as he put a protective arm around a much happier Hilda.

'No, I mean it. Look,' I pointed as another group of messengers ran from the hall. 'We need to find Grim.'

'No need for that, lads, 'cause I've found you.' Grim limped towards us, still troubled by last year's wound. 'Hilda,' he nodded once in her direction, then turned to us. 'You two. Got your weapons I see. Good. Your fortunes have changed. We are off to fight Macbethad, the King of Alba.'

'Who for?' asked Gyric, 'We are Harold's men.'

'For your King, Gyric. This venture is at Edward's bequest,' answered Grim. 'You appear to know Burgric. You can serve with him so there is no question as to where your loyalties lie.'

Gyric was happy enough with this but I didn't like Burgric and would far rather have fought for Siward. Most of all I wanted to get back to Harold, pursue my search for Oslaf, and get my revenge.

Two weeks later and we were part of a huge bustling camp south of Jorvik which held Siward's ever growing army. Burgric continued to treat me as Gyric's servant. Gyric was given new clothes, a mail byrnie, a new shield, brightly painted in Burgric's colours and to his great delight, a horse. While he ate at Burgric's table I was given nothing but sour looks and harsh words. In the meantime, Hilda had returned to her old trade of beer-selling due to Lodin's well-timed arrival.

He'd turned up perched on the front of a two wheeled cart drawn by the ugliest mule I'd ever seen. On the cart there was just room for two large barrels of beer and a cask of strong mead. He was grinning from ear to ear as he let himself down to stand, propped on one crutch and a shaft.

'You took a lot of finding, you lot did,' he declared.

I was suspicious, 'You left the inn then?'

'Ay, no one wanted to drink at an inn with the ceiling fallen down and rain coming through the roof. Not exactly a merry place. What with Einvar brooding evil thoughts in the corner and glaring dangerously at anyone who came through the door.'

'Einvar eh? So, where is he? Are you here on his bidding?'

'Nay boy, you needn't worry. When he went I went,' Lodin reassured me.

'He went? Where?'.

'He went back to sea on the Earl's orders. I don't know why and I don't care where. You done with the questions?'

At this Hilda threw her arms around him, kissing and fussing him. Then she asked thoughtfully, 'hmm, one more question. How did you get this cart and its contents?'

'Ah, now. That would be a good question.' Lodin looked nervously at our faces, 'Well Hilda, I knew where you'd hidden your valuables so I traded them in.'

'You traded my things for beer and mead?'

'I did, and this pretty mule and its cart,' confirmed Lodin. He swayed on his crutches so I steadied him down onto one of the tree stumps scattered throughout the camp. As Hilda began to speak, he held up a hand, 'There are hundreds of thirsty men arriving every day.'

'Which means we slake their thirst and fill our purses,' cheered Hilda, embracing Lodin once again.

Lodin directed us to two X-shaped trestles slung under the cart bed. Upon these we set up the first barrel. Almost before Hilda had the barrel tapped men were jostling for a place with a variety of jugs and bowls in hand.

Gyric looked thoughtful. 'Don't unload the other barrel Lodin. Come with me,' he said, helping Lodin back onto the cart. He then took the mule by its bridle and led them away.

I stayed with Hilda while she served, joked and bargained with the growing crowd. Not much later Gyric and Lodin returned, not with barrels, but with the liver and a haunch of a freshly killed deer and a sack of flour with only a few weevils.

'There's money too, if you want it, Burgric's quartermaster will buy as much beer and mead as you can deliver,' said Lodin. 'Gyric, it seems, is well connected.'

The food we'd been given so far had been meagre. Most of the warriors supplemented their rations with funds we did not possess. When Hilda taunted me about my reluctance to bring her along, I could only smile ruefully. After a few weeks of Lodin trundling barrels in and out of Jorvik she was able to buy me good food, some decent clothes and a short cloak. I polished up the guard and the gold and garnet pommel of my knife checking that its blue stone was still safely inset. Then I burnished my targe and the point of my throwing spear and started to look and feel, once again, like the young warrior I was.

'We're even now Sar, alright?' she said, 'You helped me escape and now I've repaid you well.'

'You have,' I replied, 'and taught me a trick or two.'

She caught my meaning and laughing said, 'A favour to the other girls you'll meet.'

I grinned suggestively, 'Any chance….?'

She giggled, 'Not from here to Doomsday, my lad.' Then, after giving a hank of my dark red hair an eye-watering tug, with that well-known flick of her yellow hair, she turned away.

I realised that this was Hilda's way of saying goodbye. Later I said as much to Gyric who had been quartered with Brustan's housecarls.

'That's right, Sar. She told me that she and Lodin have profited enough to set themselves up by the Jorvik docks.'

'What about Einvar?'

'She said she'd deal with that when, or if, he comes back.' He smiled quietly, 'She also said that I'd always be welcome wherever she is. I'm to look her up when we come back from Alba.'

'She didn't say that to me,' I grumbled.

Gyric gave me a long hard stare, then returned to grooming his horse without another word.

With Hilda and Lodin gone I realised that I had no choice but to give in to Burgric's view of me. I became more or less Gyric's servant. I carried his shield, watered his horse and trained alongside him and Burgric's men. Gyric's closeness to Burgric meant he knew more about what was going on.

'There are hundreds of men here now so why aren't we leaving for the North?' I asked him.

'This isn't just a raid like the one we were part of,' he answered. 'We're invading another country so we need a lot of men, an army of men.'

'Why?'

'Burgric says that King Edward sees Macbethad, the present King of Alba as a usurper. He wants to put Maelcolm in his place.'

'So, who's he?'

'He's a younger son of Owain the Bald, King of Strathclyde, he's been fostered at Edwards court.'

I was puzzled. Surely his family had a kingdom already. 'Where's Strathclyde?'

Gyric thought a bit, 'It's sort of on the south-west side of Alba, I think. An old British kingdom, not very big and heavily influenced by Siward. The Archbishop of Jorvik chooses their bishops for them.'

'So what do the people of Alba think about it?'

'Who cares Sar, if our King tells us to fight then we must fight.'

'But I don't see why this Maelcolm needs another kingdom. What's that about?'

'By Saint Oswald's head-bone, I don't know! Ask the King yourself,' snapped Gyric.

'I'd bloody love to. Then I'd be back in the south, with Harold, where I belong. Being in his service, not yours!'

We were moments away from fighting each other when the tension was broken by the arrival of a mud-spattered mare carrying a breathless rider. His horse slid to a halt before us. 'I seek Thegn Burgric, where is he?'

'Who's asking?' says I while Gyric answered, 'He's over there, let me lead you to him.'

The young rider dismounted and handing the reins to me without a glance said, 'Here water this horse and prepare for more. Maelcolm, King of Alba, is on his way.'

'Speak of the Devil,' I took the proffered reins. 'Counting his chickens, aren't you?'

Gyric glared at me then walked off towards Burgric's tents. I stared after them then at the blowing horse beside me. I tethered her in our lines next to Gyric's. Then, grabbing a bucket and a rope, I headed angrily down to the river. Squelching through the gloopy mud I threw the bucket in and drew it out. As I did so my feet slid out from under me and I fell flat on my back. Finding myself staring at the sky I burst out laughing. I couldn't stay angry forever. Maybe my bad temper wasn't paying off. The last thing I needed was to fall out with my one good friend.

Miraculously the bucket still had water in it. Getting back to the horse lines I took off her saddle, let her drink a little at a time and rubbed her down with a bundle of rags kept for the purpose.

By now all the grazing for miles around had been cropped to the bare earth and many of the horses were looking thin. 'There's nothing for you to eat,' I told her, stroking her muzzle gently as she snickered into my palm. I felt more peaceful than I had for weeks.

I walked to Burgric's tents with the drying mud flaking off me to find him bustling about lining his priests and captains up to meet the new arrivals. They, taken by surprise, were running up tightening belts and fastening cloaks. I slid in behind them hanging back in case I was asked to hold more horses.

Then the young prince, Maelcolm, with a few followers, rode in to the camp, travel stained and clearly weary to the bone. He was a tall, fair, slim, young man plainly, though finely, dressed with a neatly trimmed beard unlike the long moustaches of the English warriors. In his prematurely thinning hair was a circlet of fine gold.

As he dismounted Burgric launched into a long speech, praising Maelcolm, King Edward, various bishops and saints and, of course, himself. Maelcolm heard him out for a while then walking up to him, a broad smile on his face, and with his right hand extended he grabbed Burgric's and shaking it vigorously declared, 'May Saint Constantin pluck your stupid head out of your pompous arse and get me a beer.'

I burst out laughing and only when I saw everyone pulling away from me did I realise that he had spoken in Welsh. Burgric, completely unaware of Maelcolm's ridicule, looked around furiously to see me giggling helplessly.

'You, you, what are you laughing at,' he spluttered. He waved at a couple of his men, 'Bring him to me.'

I was dragged in front of him. 'Ugh, you animal, you're covered in stinking mud. What were you laughing at?' he demanded.

I certainly wasn't laughing now. I looked round frantically to see Maelcolm winking and raising his hand to his mouth in a drinking gesture. I also saw a pitcher on a trestle outside a nearby tent.

'He wants a beer, sir,' I explained rushing over to grab the pitcher and a cup.

Maelcolm stepped in and took them from my hands and poured himself a drink. 'The young man speaks true. The ride has been long and hard,' he said, speaking English now.

Thegn Burgric looked searchingly at both of us, his eyes narrowed, 'How was that so funny?'

Maelcolm spoke again, 'I think he was shocked to hear me speaking the language of the Britons. Forgive me, Thegn, for addressing you in my father's tongue. I forgot myself in my excitement at joining your great army.'

'Hmm, Hmm, Welsh you mean, yes, funny language that,' he blustered. He waved towards a large tent, 'Your quarters are there.

Washing water and refreshments await you inside.' With that he stumped off, red faced, his welcoming ceremony ruined.

Maelcolm turned me by the shoulder. 'You are of the Cymri?' he asked me in Welsh.

'I'm not, I'm a Saxon reared in a Welsh village.'

'And I'm a Strathwealas, as you Saxon's call us, fostered in an English court. I'm on my way home, to Cumbraland, home of my ancestors,' he replied.

'I heard you came from Strathclyde,'

'Another name for the same place, in our speech, Ystad Glu. My country straddles the mighty River Clyde, though we are attacked from every side.'

'I heard that you are Siward's puppet and Edward's tool though I never saw you at his court.'

'You know the King's court,' he said, eyeing me searchingly.

'I'm Harold Godwinson's man,' I answered, stretching myself tall.

'Churlish and rude too, are you not? To speak this way to the son of a King'

'Your manners aren't that good either. I grew up hungry and feeding goats, what's your excuse?' I retorted pointedly.

'Yes, you are right. It was unforgivable of me to insult your Thegn,' he answered. 'My foolish tongue, once again.'

I laughed, 'but he is a pompous snob.'

Maelcolm held both my shoulders and looked me straight in the face, 'Burgric's a better man than you think. Despite his ways he's a great leader of men. Not many could begin to organise a force like this.'

He turned to go. Then turned back, 'Your name?'

'Sar,' I answered.

He raised an eyebrow. I knew why. In the Saxon tongue my name is a word for pain. My mother named me, as she named my twin Moira, meaning bitterness.

Sar Nomansson,' I continued before he could ask. 'No one knows who my father is, so Harold named me Nomansson.'

'Well Sar Nomansson, I'd get your clothes washed if I were you,' he said and strolled off towards his waiting men.

I had met the future King of Alba. But first we had to fight MacBethad, and win.

Chapter Four

The army continued to train as it grew. Heavily armed warriors, the bulk of our force, practised the tactics of the front line, the defensive 'Shield Wall' and the aggressive 'Boar's snout.' This was where Gyric would fight, face to face with those who would kill him. Behind them were hundreds of younger men with similar roles to me, would be fighting men, though not armed with swords, byrnies or the great war spears. We were given helmets or boiled leather caps. Some carried hunting bows or slings, some others, like me, had light throwing spears of their own. In training we were issued with bundles of these spears. We had to be able to throw them high and far over our own men into the ranks of the enemy, accuracy did not matter. During lulls in the combat our job would be to ferry spare shields to replace those hacked to pieces in the front line. We had other roles. We might be asked to outflank and harry the foe, or, for the more skilled, to fight in front of our line. I was one of those.

We also learned the banners of our leaders, the formations asked of us and the fighting mettle of our companions. All the King's army were trained soldiers, most of them the King's own thegns and their housecarls. The fyrd had not been called out for this campaign. Few of the younger men had been to war, due to the mainly peaceful nature of King Edward's reign. More of Earl Siward's men were battle hardened after raids and counter raids between the Northumbrians and the Scots. As the senior Thegn, Burgric led the King's men.

The Northumbrians were led by Siward's first born son, Osbeorn Poleaxe. Waltheof, Siward's younger son, being only ten, was left behind, noisily protesting. Our overall commander was, of course, the great, fierce old warrior, Earl Siward himself.

Finally, after the last ox-drawn wain slowly joined the vast heaving supply train, we set off.

We were now a huge army, somewhere between two or three thousand strong, I guessed, though some, including Siward, had gone north by sea. We, the unlucky ones to my mind, trudged our way on and alongside the remains of an ancient road. Stretching into the distance in a dead straight line it took us up over bleak and treeless moors. Startled skylarks chirruped their way into the sky while small flocks of sheep bounded away protected by Siward's rough justice from meat hungry men. Their shepherds leant stoically upon their crooks and watched us pass while their boys and dogs ran excitedly alongside us. When we made camp in the long summer evenings the endless torment of midges turned the army into a bad-tempered grumbling horde. As the nights fell, wolves howled.

Gyric gentled his spooked horse, 'Easy girl, easy.' He looked at me as I rubbed her down with twists of dried grass, 'Wolves, you heard them before?'

'Yes, there are many in Wales but they never troubled us.'

'There's not many left down south. There are wolf pelts in my father's hall but I've never seen a live one. Eerie aren't they.'

'I'm more worried about my sore feet than wolves,' I said ruefully, showing him the holes in my shoes.

'See Burgric's quartermaster.'

'Could try I suppose,' I answered without much hope.

'Burgric's not so bad, Sar. Look I told him that you can speak with Dolfin's men and mostly understand Siward's Northumbrians. Not only that, you can swap jokes with Maelcolm and his Strathwealas escort.'

Dolfin Finntor's men were warriors from the mountains and lakes of west Northumbria. They spoke a tangled mixture of Norse and Irish familiar to me from the traders who roamed the Safearn Sea. Their ships plied the Irish Sea while they defended their small territory with obstinate ferocity owing as much, if not more, allegiance to the Kings of Dyflin than to those of the English.

'Dolfin's men are hard to understand but the Northumbrians speak English, only with a lot of Danish mixed in. What's the problem?'

Gyric laughed, 'For Burgric the Godwinsons are foreigners because their mother is Danish.'

'Haven't most the country a Danish grandfather?'

'Like me,' said Gyric, 'the armies of Cnut and his father made sure of that, but mainly in the North and East. Burgric's family are Mercians. They only get invaded by the Welsh who don't stay long.'

'Just take what they want and leave,' I sniggered. I don't know why but sometimes I liked the idea of the Welsh having a go at the English. Although I was born in Wales my mother always insisted that we were not of the Cymri. 'You're a Saxon, my son, and don't you forget it,' she would insist. When our village was sacked speaking English saved my life.

'Anyway Sar, he wants you around to interpret.'

'Does that mean I get a horse?'

'I don't suppose it does, but you'll get better food, and shoes.'

Truth was I had no choice, so I ended up running from leader to leader carrying messages, much as I had for Harold and Godwin's much smaller force the summer before last. I ate better and got new shoes. I learnt what the army was doing. We would march north pillaging until we came to the Firth of Forth, a big sea inlet, where ships would meet us with more men and supplies. Meanwhile the men of Strathclyde and their allies would raid Alba from the west. Then we would join to destroy MacBethad and his army.

After more days of trudging north, we came to a great wall. I was told it went from coast to coast and had been built by the Romans.

It was a marvellous thing that showed the greatness of the world had passed. We marched through it at Corebricg, a miserable town much ravaged by raiding Scots. Saint Wilfred had a church there, built of stones stolen from the wall by his holiness or so I was told. Many of us filed in to pray for our souls and the souls of the men we hoped to kill. Everywhere north of this all dwellings we found were hovels made of turf. More dispiriting days passed, wearily reaching the crest of a hill only to find another valley and yet another hill, we passed into Alba, the land of the Scots, though you could not tell. All the houses here too were miserable abandoned turf hovels. We torched them but there were no merry crackling flames. They just smouldered, miserably.

At dawn the next day we attacked Geddwerde, a proper town with a market place, large church and abandoned walls. This was more like it. We stormed into the mostly empty streets. The few men who resisted were gleefully hacked down and the town pillaged. The looted goods and valuables disappeared into our vast throng like raindrops into sand but we all felt much better. Before long the fires began and we watched the town burn. The war had begun.

Nothing changed though. We continued to trudge north dragging the cursed ox-wains behind us with their concealed loads. Those that had carried supplies had long gone, their timbers burned on cooking fires upon which the oxen that had pulled them boiled in huge cauldrons. We came to the shores of the Firth where the fleet awaited us. We turned west, the fleet rowing alongside as once again we marched past huge hills and empty settlements. The men grew sour. Patrols would go out and disappear. Occasionally survivors returned to speak of shadows rising from the mist in heather or woods to drag men off their horses. Nowhere could men meet face to face and fight these elusive Scots.

The river narrowed to a ford of sunken hurdles, crossed by a footbridge of logs which prevented ships going further inland. There was a small town here, proper houses built of wood though all eerily deserted, empty of both men and beasts. The leading ships of Siward's fleet came to a halt, just about floating at the height of the tide, stranded in mud for the rest.

Siward and Osbeorn came ashore to meet with Burgric and Maelcolm. As a messenger I felt I should be there in case I was needed so I pushed through to hear Siward's powerful voice rise above the complaints of the crowd.

'You will get your chance to fight!' he roared, 'soon our allies, the Strathwaelas, and Finntor's friends from Ireland will join us and then we will fight,'

Those who could hear cheered and roared and those who couldn't joined in just for the hell of it. Siward had casks of ale and bread brought ashore and soon the cheering redoubled as Siward climbed a small mound from where he could be seen by all.

'We had hoped,' he shouted, 'your leaders and I, that the Scots would have faced us sooner. With your force coming from the South and ours to the North of them we'd have grasped them in our fist.' He shook his right fist in the air, as the crowd roared back, 'And, killed them all.' He paused, 'I've no doubt you would have, you fine warriors, no doubt at all.' Then, gesturing to one of his men, he bellowed, 'and to that we will drink.'

One of his thegns handed him a magnificently decorated long, curved and twisted drinking horn. Grasping it in his huge hand he raised it with one arm, 'Skal!' he cried, 'skal' and so saying he brought it to his lips and drank, and drank, and drank as the tip of the horn rose higher and higher into the sky. The crowd hushed, enthralled by this mighty feat. Finally, Siward pulled the horn from his lips, turning it upside down to show it was empty. He belched loud and long, then looking fiercely into the eyes of the nearest men he yelled; 'Drink you bastards, drink.' We obliged willingly, toasting and cheering. The tensions of the march draining out of us as Joy and purpose, ale and food, flooded in.

Siward waited as the cheering stilled, 'Our allies,' he said, 'are not far away. The men of Cumbraland gather their forces. Until they arrive, rest, eat and prepare for war.'

Osbeorn climbed up beside him, taller even than his father, and raising the massive pole-axe he carried, cried out, 'Raise your weapons for your Earl, your King and Saint Clement and shout for me. Death to the Scots, Death to the Scots!'

The cry rippled out amongst the huge mass of men until it became a great roar, 'Death to the Scots', over and over again. The men on the boats disembarked and soon we were showing them our blistered feet and laughing as they wobbled about on their cramped sea legs complaining of their blistered arses. I had no desire to see those.

I began to see Maelcolm's point, even as the ruckus continued Burgric and his housecarls organised the army into their lines. Ordering latrines and horse lines to be set downriver and water to be collected above the bridge with the grudging compliance of weary men. Scouts and pickets were set out as they had been every night and the ox-wains drawn into the centre of the camp. The already huge army had grown by half again and still it remained a disciplined force. My duties done I went to find Grim. I had some questions to ask.

I found him ashore close to Siward's standard eating and drinking with the other housecarls. He turned as I came up.

'Hello Sar,' he said, 'Had a good walk since we last met, did you?'

I grimaced ruefully. 'Everyone lives in turf dung heaps from the Wall to here. Why is that? Don't they know what trees are for?' I asked

'Never one for the pleasantries were you boy?' he grinned, 'How are you, Grim? Did you have an easy voyage, Grim? 'Offer you a drink, Grim?'

'So, don't they?'

Grim answered through a full mouth, 'Not worth bothering just to watch them burn?'

'Eh?'

He put down his knife and took a swig from his cup. 'Look we raid the Scots and the Scots raid us. When you raid somewhere what do you do?'

'You pillage the houses, burn them down and steal the livestock,' I answered.

'If you were getting raided a lot…' he continued.

'You wouldn't bother building a house!' I finished for him.

'You got it boy. Up here the main wealth is cattle. Mostly you know when a raid is coming.' Smiling at me he guessed my next question, 'Spies, gossip or a careful lookout, sometimes just the smell of the last place burning. Whatever way the warning comes, you round up your wealth, cattle, and herd it and your people into hiding.' He patiently returned to his food.

'Grim', I asked thoughtfully, 'Why weren't our allies waiting for us. They come from up here don't they.' Sitting down on an upturned barrel abandoned by another diner I pestered him further, 'So why weren't they here? Can we trust them to come?'

Grim sucked his teeth and looked at me shrewdly, 'Any of this your business?'

"Tis if I get killed up here.'

'Well, you won't be worrying at all then, will you? You'll be singing with the angels,' he chortled, clearly amused at his own wit.

This was a new Grim to me, I'd never seen him so happy, let alone making jokes. I looked around at the sea of sweaty, dirty men slipping around in the wet dust of a passing summer shower or the sticky mud of the riverbank and couldn't for the life of me think why.

Shaking this thought from my head I persisted, 'So they weren't here, why not?'

I knew Grim liked me, he liked me because his brother had cared for me and we had avenged him together. We'd raided together and he'd seen me fight. He shoved his platter towards me and I helped myself to some bannock and ale as he explained.

'Think about it like this. Alba, where the Scots live,' he held a finger up, stopping me before I asked the obvious question, 'is a powerful country led by a shrewd and ruthless king. Cumbraland is a small country squabbled over by the sons and nephews of Owain the Bald, who lived too long but died too soon.'

'Eh? What do you mean?'

'Forty years ago, Owain's Stratwealas and the Scots gave us a thrashing and his kingdom regained some of its lost power.'

'Ah, so, our allies were once our enemies. See I told you we couldn't trust them.'

'You asked me if we could, not quite the same thing, is it?' Grim furrowed his brows at me. 'As I was saying the sons and nephews of Owain.'

'Like Maelcolm?' I said, excited now.

Grim gave me a look, 'what do you know of Maelcolm?'

'I met him.'

'The sons and nephews squabble, so we interfere. Siward wants influence, and the Scots interfere because they too want influence,' he paused, 'You met him?'

'Yes, he speaks Welsh.'

'He's not forgotten the tongue of his people then. What did you make of him?'

I sat back and stopped shovelling food into my face, 'Hmm well, he's funny.'

'Funny?' Grim wasn't amused.

'And friendly.'

'Friendly?'

'Yes, to me anyway.'

'As a man I mean, what was he like as a man?'

'His hairs thinning on top though he seems quite young.'

'Like his father. He's Owain's son then, sired by an old dog on a young bitch no doubt.'

I thought some more, 'He told me to respect Burgric.'

Grim's eyebrows shot up, 'Really, how did that come about?'

I told him. Grim was even less amused now, 'Mocks a man to his face then praises him behind his back?'

'I suppose so, though it didn't feel quite like that.'

Grim took a swig from his cup, 'He's right about Burgric though.'

'Which bit,' I asked, 'the organiser or the ass?'

Grim suddenly burst out laughing, ale snorting from his nostrils, 'Both, boy, both.'

I looked at him sideways, not sure what to make of this new side of Grim who then looked askance back at me, suddenly serious again.

'As a man, Sar, as a man. What do you make of him?' he said again.

'You know Grim, he's a good bloke, easy going, but maybe, well, maybe not so very tough.'

'You mean weak?' the ultimate insult in Grim's hard world.

'Not exactly, no, I think he could be strong, fearless even, just not ruthless maybe.' I couldn't think what it was about him. 'Something wavering about him? He's not like the King or the Earls, Harold, Tostig or Siward. Different as they are, they all have something. He's not tough like them.'

'They all lust for power and grasp it hard.' Grim looked down at the table, quiet now and pensive. 'Thanks Sar, for your thoughts. Think no more of this my lad and get along.'

I rose, bowed my head, and got along before realising that I still didn't know why our allies weren't here.

Chapter Five

Finally, our allies arrived and with them a new surprise. I was stood by Maelcolm trying to translate the jokes with which he greeted his fellow countrymen to Burgric when a great cheering arose from Dolfinn's cohort. Distracted I looked over to see among the waving standards a tubular banner of a snapping snake with a long red forked tongue. Thord, I thought to myself, from Dyflin. I stammered out something as I returned to my task. One thing was clear though, the Strathwaelas were far more excited about fighting the Scots than they were about their new and untried leader.

I also learned why they'd held back. They needed to be sure of Siward's intentions. For the Strathwaelas to form their army too soon would have alerted MacBethad and risk slaughter. Too late and they'd miss the plunder. To mine and Gyric's delight among the Norsemen from Dyflin we found Jokul, our blood-brother who, as before, had come with his father Thord, seeking wealth and excitement.

Not that we got much time to talk. We embraced, marvelled at the changes in each other, and then were called back to our posts for now the hunt was well and truly on. A myriad of tracks, those of men, horses and cattle led us northwards over more hill ranges and alongside a huge lake until eventually we closed on Scone. The home of the royal palaces and monasteries near the crowning place of the Kings of Alba. As our army approached scouts came in with reports of a huge army to the north-west of us. Our own, now massive army, ground to a halt on the banks of a large but fordable river between us and Scone. There was no sign of the enemy bar their tracks.

Siward ordered his personal housecarls across the river on horseback. After it was clear that they would not be attacked they rode forward and formed a screen between Scone and the rest of us. We marched, wet to the waist and grumbling, past the wealthiest settlement we'd yet seen in the whole of Alba. It was clear why. If allowed, half our army would be lost in amongst the monastery, farms and palace buildings in an orgy of drinking and looting. We marched on. As the sun lowered in the sky behind us it lit up a massive hill, black with a swarming, heaving mass of men and banners. The setting sun glittered redly upon a myriad of spear points and helmets. One of the Strathwaelas told us its name in the tongue of the Scots. 'Dunsinnan. The hill of the ants it means,' he said staring fearfully towards it 'and they're there, thousands of them, waiting for us.' And that was just how it looked, like an ant's nest teeming with innumerable ants; their pincers ready to pierce our flesh.

'By Saint Botwulf's webbed feet there's a lot of them,' I gasped out to Gyric whose saddle I'd been clinging to trying to ease the pain in my feet. Botwulf had become a favoured saint of mine since we'd cleared the Fenlands of the Wash.

He let out his breath in a long, long sigh, 'There are, aren't there.' He turned in his saddle to look back at our army slowly broadening out as it came to a halt, 'I thought our force was huge but it looks like the Scots have twice the warriors we have.'

'Too many for them all to be trained fighters, I hope. But many more than I thought MacBethad could muster to his cause' said Burgric, making me jump, unaware that he and Osbeorn had ridden up behind us.

'Hmm, can't send out scouts now but I'm guessing his enemies hate us more than they hate him,' Osbeorn replied.

'And they have the ground. That old hill fort is easily defended and formidable to attack.' It was Siward's voice, unusually quiet. 'We have to fight them here. If we try to move away, or try to outflank them, we open our rear or flanks to attack. By abandoning their royal palace they've outsmarted us.'

I turned to look at them as Osbeorn spoke, 'Fear not father, I shall beat them without you crying in the background.' He raised his weapon. A pole-axe, the kind they use to stun cattle. It is a much heavier thing than the two-handed bearded axe that itself took a strong warrior to wield. I'd not seen Osbeorn Pole-axe close to before but now I could see how he got the name. He was a huge man in his prime, bigger even than his father, thirty, thirty-five maybe.

Siward cuffed him across the head, 'Cheeky young pup,' he growled, 'not too old for a beating.' He was obviously deeply proud of his warrior son.

'Ah' said Burgric, as he noticed me, 'Aah, it's that Welsh boy. I've got work for you.'

This was followed by a whole series of messages I was to take to each of the leaders as to where to put their men, night pickets and so on. Gyric had to ride alongside me as Burgric demanded, 'so they know you're not some heathen Scot out to deceive.' I cursed under my breath resentfully for by now most of them knew me well enough. I'd carried orders, translated dialects from one cohort to another, and reported back to Burgric for weeks now but he still treated me like a surly churl. To be fair I was surly to him but I was treated well by the receivers of my missives. Sometimes I was rewarded with gifts of now scarce food and even the odd worn penny.

Burgric had us all in our battle positions as we were so near to the enemy. I had to sleep in front of what would be the shield wall with one companion. He was to carry a very large roughly made shield while I had bundles of odd-looking throwing spears called angons. The shield carrier, Sibyhrt was his name, was a short thickset man from Mercia. He wore no byrnie or mail, just a rawhide jerkin and a leather cap similar to the one I'd been issued. We'd been paired up for one particular task. There were other pairs like us at intervals all along our front. When we'd had it explained in practice it felt fine. Now with only a picket line between us and that vast hoard I felt rather differently.

The days were still long, longer than I'd ever known, more than a month past midsummer so once night fell the dawn was not far away. The smell of roasting meat blew over us from the hill while we shared flat bread and tallow.

'I use this stuff to grease the axles on my wain', he grumbled but steadily ate his way through all his share. 'Do you know what day it is tomorrow?' he asked me.

'Nah'

'It's the day of the Seven Sleepers, you heard of them?'

'Oh yes, they fell asleep for hundreds of years and escaped death or something,' I answered, vaguely remembering a tale my Step-Da told me.

Sibyhrt sighed, 'I'd just like to sleep until tomorrow is over, and wake up alive in my home with my oxen and my woman.'

I sighed too, remembering the warm snug of my mother, siblings and our goats in the half-hut half-cave dug out from the old, brick fortress walls of our home in Caerdydd. My mother dead, and my siblings, God knows where. I keened silently to myself and fell into a fitful sleep.

I'm in a dark hall, or maybe a cave. The walls are streaming with blood. The faces of the dead loom over me. The faces of those I have killed, those I have seen die. Osric the last man I killed, slowly bleeding to death from dozens of cuts as his weary eyes stare out at me, reproachfully, from under the rim of his helmet. He turns away and behind him stands his father, Eardwulf, the first man I killed. I cannot see his face, concealed behind the face plate of his boar crested helmet. Black holes stare at me, chillingly. I fight to move. I'm held. Held by invisible bonds pinning me down. The faces of the other dead come one after another. They turn to look at me, and with their own sad, lost, accusing eyes they stare into mine.

I'm pleading with I don't know who, 'I didn't mean to do this, I didn't want any of this. I was just a hungry boy who herded goats, by the Saints, forgive me.'

My mother's face blocks all else out bloody and smashed as it was when she was killed, 'Forgive you nothing! You are not done yet my child, my weapon. There are more murders to avenge. Oslaf still lives and you let his brat survive. You are not done yet.'

'I showed mercy to a child,' I sobbed.

Always angry and fierce my mother in life, she had lost none of this in death. 'Mercy, mercy is for fools,' she said scornfully. As I recoiled her eyes softened. Her hand reached out and caressed my face. Drawing a finger along the scar Oslaf had carved into my jawbone she declared weirdly, 'The day tomorrow will be long, long and bloody. Danger comes from behind. Your enemy is your friend. You are but a twig on a limb of a great tree. The branch will hold the twig.'

'But mother, will I live, will I live?' I cried out, 'will I live.'

'That Sar, is down to fate.'

I spread out my arms, now free, to plead or to hug, to be hugged. I wanted some warmth from her. I'd always wanted some warmth from her. She drew back and all the faces tumbled away into a whirling gyre of blood and the sad, reproachful eyes of the dead. I startled awake feeling sick, covered in sweat and shaken. My teeth were chattering though the sweet July morning was already warm.

'You might live if you get some of this down your gullet,' said Sibyhrt pushing a loaded wooden platter in my face.

Embarrassed I grabbed the platter, 'You heard me? I was talking?'

'Don't worry yourself lad, plenty of men dreamt hard last night,' he said and laid a steadying hand on my shoulder. I nearly cried.

'Come', he said, 'eat up, they're in no hurry to start over there.'

I remembered where I was. The hill in the grey light of the fore-dawn still lay moss-covered by a vast crowd of fighting men. They weren't swarming about, indeed there was little movement of any kind. Small pillars of smoke rose into the still air.

Dumbly I looked at my platter, it smelt good. I breathed in the aroma, meat, meat boiled in whole barley. I took a taste. It was even salted.

I began to bolt it down, swallowing gristle and the tough chunks of beef unchewed, when I heard Sibyhrt snuffling beside me. I turned to see tears streaming down his face as he tried to push the food into his mouth.

'This meat is the last of our ox teams. This could be my own darlings I've reared since they were calved. They've served me and my family well. I've pushed them hard for weeks and now they are dead.' Sibyhrt began to wail louder and louder.

I didn't have a clue what to do. His oxen for fuck's sake! We were sat opposite a vast army of warriors whose only desire was to kill us all and he was crying over cattle. He must have read my mind.

'You think I'm stupid, crying over my darlings? You woke up crying over pictures in your dreams,' he spluttered out at me, snot dribbling from his nose.

'I did my friend, I did,' I replied and cautiously tried his tactic. I put my hand on his shoulders and began to rub them. 'There, there, things will feel differently later.' A sure bet, I thought, as before long we'll be fighting for our lives.

It seemed to work, his sobs subsided and he began again to shovel his food into his mouth. I, strangely, felt a sudden warmth towards this humble man. A simple cow-herd who was now in the fore-front of a huge battle. Smiling to myself I remembered that I had been a mere goat-boy who'd never even seen an armed warrior until that fateful morning not so long ago.

We ate, then prepared for the ordeal to come. I was struggling to pull my leather cap down over my thick, dark red, hair but each time I pulled it down it would pop up before I could tie the thong under my chin. After finding ourselves giggling uselessly, Sibyhrt grabbed my hair.

'Come'ere, look, I'll plait your hair. A thick strong plait can take a blow, even a blade strike. I've heard that some Welshmen do this before a fight.'

He began muttering to himself as he worked, 'Strange hair, thick and coarse like a horse's and such a strange red, dark red, darker than I've ever seen.'

'How come your hairs so dark boy?' he asked aloud as he separated it into thick strands. 'I've seen more red hairs up here than I seen in a life time before but they're shiny bright like copper, not like yours.'

'My real father I suppose, my twin has hair like this but my mother didn't.' Tears ran slowly down my cheeks. Sibhyrt said nothing but paused and put his palm on my shoulder then worked on.

I stayed sat as he stood behind me. It was a strange tender moment. Just before we'd been giggling like young girls and now, he was doing my hair while I wept like a child.

'There', he said when he was done, 'don't you look pretty.' He'd tied my hair into three long plaits tied at the end with thin strips of leather. I grabbed a plait in my fist. Thick and strong as a mainsail rope it was. Maybe he had a point.

Suddenly the whole line erupted in shouted orders, the beating of drums and the wailing of bullroarers. It was time to get into place. Seized with a sudden urgency I pulled my cock out to piss. I was not the only one, a pungent steam rose up from the ranks. The tension mounted as the host in front of us surged into motion. Their drums answered ours accompanied by a weird wailing sound like the strangling of cats.

Sibhyrt grimaced at me, 'Think they're throttling their women folk before we can get at them?'

I laughed, nervously, unable to answer as my mouth dried up. I hitched my targe up behind my back then I checked my bundle of angons and my own throwing spear. Then made sure my knife was ready in my belly sheath, a thin string holding it in place. Then I checked my little axe was loose in my belt but not too loose. All were sharp enough to shave with.

Sibyrht thumped me. I jumped. 'Check your shoes lad, check them.'

Speechlessly I nodded, tightened them, then checked all my gear again. The drums stopped. I turned to look at our line. The mass of men had turned into a row of shields, helmets and spear points. I thought I could see Gyric but I wasn't sure. Behind them sat small groups of our leading men on horses and beside them our banners clearly lit by the morning sun. I squinted into that self-same sun and prayed to the saint of my childhood. Saint Diw, who with Gyric's help, had saved me once before. I looked again at Sibyrht and hoped my face wasn't as white as his. Then the drums began again.

Chapter Six

Thump, thump, thump, each thump a pace. The first twelve were for Sibyhrt and me, and the other forlorn pairs strung along our line. Despite the noise of the drums, the bellowing horns and the eerie wails of the bullroarers it seemed strangely quiet as we stepped forward, nine, ten, eleven, twelve. Then with a great shout the whole mass of men behind us began to move. I swear the earth shook. Our cry was followed by an enormous clamour from the hill before us. I kept pacing forward. Long unhurried paces. I felt oddly detached from the world around me, crickets sprang up around my feet and swallows whirled in the sky above. I saw a leveret quivering in its form, unsure whether to run or flatten itself into the ground. The ground began to rise and grow rockier. An arrow thudded into a nearby patch of turf, another skittered off from an outcrop of stone.

Suddenly everything speeded up. A man in mail, helmeted and with a shield had little to fear from arrows but one strike could kill or maim me. I ducked in sharply behind Sibyhrt's great shield, kept my head down and paced on to the beat.

Each side of me, twenty paces away were other pairs like Sibyhrt and I, and beyond them more pairs. In each pair was a man like myself. A man who could throw a spear further and more accurately than most. We moved forward.

Arrows still snickered by, not many, then one or two spears hit the ground ahead of us. 'Throw them now,' I thought, 'throw as many as you like.'

Then crunch, one, almost spent, hit our shield and fell out. I stopped, raised my arm and waved it in the air. I heard shouts and horns blowing. The drums stopped. The roar from in front crashed over like a giant wave. All the pairs marched forward five more paces and stopped. Now we were within their spear throwing range. I puked, spat, swallowed and dropped my bundle of spears. Now was the time to do the job I'd trained for.

I crouched behind Sibyhrt and spread out my strange spears, angons they were called. An angon has a short, sharp, barbed head followed by a thin length of iron before it joins the shaft. There's a reason for this. I hefted the first in my hand just as a spear juddered into our shield. I could feel Sibhyrt brace as I quickly sought a target and threw.

Suddenly I became truly aware of the army in front of us. Until now they'd been a mass of confusion and noise beyond the fearful squirming of my guts. Now I could see individual warriors, banners, a howling mass of ferocious savagery all aimed at me. To one side I could see a mass of huge skin clad men leaping and ululating shrilly while from somewhere behind them came the strange wailing sound. A shiver ran through me and I began to sweat as my mouth filled with a sallow liquid. Directly in front of us were men armed more like those behind me. Helmeted, with long spears, standing firm behind their wall of shields.

'Aim for their shields', I'd been told, 'Not the man, the shield.' Truth is if you aim for the man, he tends to put his shield in the way. Whatever. I threw and ducked. My mind reeling with what I had seen. As I stood and threw again, I saw some of those strange long shields we had seen in the fight at the Lundunburh gate. Normans here too, I guessed.

On the third throw I caught a glimpse of a man wrestling with his shield, vainly trying to extract an angon. Just as I ducked a spear glanced off the top of our shield, caught the side of my cap. Wickedly sharp it severed my chin strap. My ungainly cap flew away. 'Diawl, that was close', I gasped gulping, 'I could fucking die here.' I crouched sucking in air, trying to regain my courage. It was working, Burgric's plan. A well thrown angon's barbed head pierces a shield then the thin iron shank bends rendering the spear unusable and the shield a useless burden.

I puked again, this time my breakfast came up. I looked at the half-digested lumps of ox regretfully as my drool strung me to the ground. 'Diw Sant preserve me', I cried to the saint of my childhood. Then I stood again and threw.

By now Sibhyrt was in a half crouch, visibly shaking and praying, 'Mother Mary help me, Mother Mary help me!' over and over to himself. Spears kept thumping into the crude shield and kicking up the grass around us. We had no need to pull them out. We would not be fighting with this shield but the extra weight was dragging on Sibhyrt. We couldn't stay much longer. I jumped up threw, dropped, jumped, threw, dropped. By now I wasn't aiming, I didn't care. Burgric's plan might be a good one but I realised we were pieces to be sacrificed in some hellish game. I cursed him as I looked back at our lines. Men were cheering us on. I looked to our sides. One man lay under his shield while the spear-thrower choked as bloody froth bubbled from his mouth, a spear jutting from his chest. On my other side the thrower was scrabbling on the ground, blood sheeting down his face from a gaping wound across his forehead. I had three angons left and my own spear.

I leapt up and threw again vaguely aware that Sibhyrt's chant had changed to 'Mother Mary save my soul, save my soul.' He wasn't expecting to live. I crouched down behind him unable to believe that the sun had hardly moved. I felt that we'd been here forever. I swung my small shield down from my back, threw away it's rope and clasped the hand bar firmly behind the boss. Kneeling I looked around the side of the shield. I could see more men throwing away now useless shields. Something parted in their line and two huge grey dogs coursed out thundering in our direction, divots flying from their racing paws.

I felt around in the grass for another spear, found one and stood to face the furious snarl and the bared fangs flying towards me. I threw hastily and scored the rearmost dog down his flank. It screamed and circled on himself biting furiously at his own hindquarter. The foremost was on the shield, biting over the rim at Sibyhrt's head, mauling his leather cap. Sibhyrt pulled back, dropping the shield with its small forest of impaled spears. The huge dog leapt for his face. It tore at Sibhyrt's arms as he tried to protect himself, blood and drool spraying all around. There seemed no time to draw my seax so I clouted the dog hard in the head with my right fist. It seemed not to notice. I swapped arms and pounded it again with my small shield, pounding and pounding while Sibhyrt subsided into a ball on the ground. The dog collapsed; its ribs were heaving but its lolling tongue stilled as its eyes rolled back in its head.

'Run Sibhyrt, run!' I cried trying to drag him along. Spears started slicing through the air around me then with a great roar the enemy charged down the hill.

I let him go and ran for my life. Coming to our own shield wall I fought for a gap. All helmeted men look much the same but I sought Gyric's eyes. Maybe him, maybe another man let me through as I leapt up and over the shields. In the second row I turned to see Sibhyrt's face on the wrong side of our shield wall, eyes wide and torn face bloodied. He was too near the enemy charge and no-one would let him through. Between the now lowered spear points of our shield wall and the frenzied hacking of the enemy assault he was torn down and lost.

Aghast, I turned for the rear pushing tearfully through the thick ranks until they opened out. I fell, sobbing, face down to the ground, completely spent. Then I lost it. I found myself chewing the grass, and clutching handfuls of soil, screaming and pounding the earth. Something poked me hard in the side. I flailed around to find a spear butt in my hand. I turned over into the shadow of a fully armed man.

'Get off me you fucker, get away from me!' I screamed pushing the shaft away from me. It sharply returned and clouted me on the side of my head. I reeled stunned. I'd escaped from the enemy, now I'm being beaten by my own side.

Whoever it was knelt beside me. He was wearing one of those helmets that only has a nose guard, no eye guards or cheek pieces. As my eyes unblurred I realised it was Grim. 'Come son,' he said, almost kindly, 'come son, pull yourself together. It's a battle, what did you expect?' He squatted down beside me one hand on my shoulder.

'I was out there Grim, out between two huge armies. Thrown to the fucking wolves', I said, still sobbing but more quietly now.

'Well, hmmm, fucking dogs anyway', said Grim smiling wryly.

'Why Sibhyrt? He was just a carter. No soldier. Why Sibhyrt?' Then I caught Grim's comment. 'Yes dogs.' I almost smiled. 'You saw then?'

'I saw.'

My breath still shuddered in and out. 'I've never been so scared Grim, not even when I fought Oslaf.'

'Hmmm I know son. Now get up and do what you're meant to do.'

'I think I'm meant to be dead aren't I,' I spat back at him.

He slapped me, 'Do as you are fucking told. We are fighting men. Now go fight.'

As he walked off, I picked myself up, searched for my targe and made sure my seax was still firmly in its sheath. I knew what I was meant to do. Seeking out Burgric's banner I headed towards it. I saw Burgric riding his horse back and forth behind our section and was tempted to attack him. I swallowed my bile, that was a fight that could wait.

I had two tasks now, to ferry spare shields from our baggage to the front and to find fallen throwing spears to cast far and long over the fighting men into their ranks behind. At first there were few spears to find and the call for shields was great as in the bitter fighting they were hacked to pieces. We were moving slowly backwards being pushed down the hill. This meant they were finding more spears and we less. Every so often one would drop from the sky and slice into the ground, a shield or flesh. It was ugly, men would reel out of the fight bearing shattered or impaled shields which I and others like me would replace. Some were cut about horribly, unrecognisable in their terror. They were left. They would have to wait. Every man was needed.

All around me men were dying or catching their breath, staunching lighter wounds to return to the fight. I picked up spears and threw them. Ran back and forth with shields. We were still being pushed back. I could see Siward on his horse directing more men into the fray. It felt good to know the old warrior was still there, in command.

All of our leaders were shouting, 'Hold fast, hold fast, drive them off', and then slowly it became clear that we were retreating no more. All along the line the exhausted armies pulled apart. The first charge of the Scots and their allies had failed. It was not even noon.

I was now ordered to carry water skins and never have I seen men so grateful. I made my way to the front. It was ghastly, corpses lay everywhere. Many of the front rank were gone and their places had been taken by men from the second or even the third line. I feared for Gyric but could not find him.

The drums rolled again. The lines firmed up. The messengers rode back and forth. The commanders clustered then dispersed. They gave us new orders. Our army formed into three massive wedges. I moved into position behind Burgric's banner, armed with a couple of throwing spears.

We marched forward steadily, implacably. The Scots gave ground sidling uphill, unsure where to make a stand. I got the odd glimpse of their front line over our front ranks. There were shield-less men in their wall. I began to recognise Burgric's skill as a commander. All the spare shields we had lugged or shipped so far, the cartloads of angons. They were making a difference.

Passing over the ground upon which we had fought was chilling. We were constantly stepping round or on the bodies of the wounded, dead and dying. Strewn guts steaming and blood, quickly jellying under the remorseless sun, made for slippery footing. I salvaged three more throwing spears and kept a place about five ranks back from the front as we staggered uphill. I was fretting about Gyric. By the grace of God, I'd not seen his corpse but I'd not seen him either. By rights he would be somewhere in front of Burgric's banner. The drums stopped. We stopped. We were now further up the hill than before the Scots had made their charge. As the hill steepened our ranks curved more around it pushing them in on themselves. This meant more of their ranks could throw down on us while we had the harder task of throwing up. I dropped my bundle, took a spear, trotted back a few paces then ran forward and threw. Now, I'm good at this but to run uphill, then throw far is hard. My spear did drop into their ranks but not far in. Their spears, rocks and arrows were falling on us like the Devil's hail.

We faltered as men began to drop. Our commanders roared and beat at our backs to push us up and on. We charged up the now steep slope. For the men in their padded byrnies and mail while carrying heavy war spears this was gruelling. We didn't have far to go. They didn't wait for us. They charged down as we charged up. The clash was horrendous, the noise cracked the sky. Their vast horde engulfed our wedges until they became bulges then back to one continuous shield wall.

Tactics became redundant all that was left was to fight wall to wall, face to face. Hundreds, maybe thousands of men, screaming, hacking, bellowing war cries and still above it all rose the wailing of instruments and the clamour of the drums. They gave you courage those drums, lost in the noise you had no time to feel fear. My spears thrown I pushed my arm through my shield strap and with both hands, wielded a war spear I found abandoned by a man who, face slashed to the bone, reeled blindly from the slaughter. I was now the third rank and could push the spear point at the faces of their foremost warriors. I stabbed and shoved, more a distraction than a deadly threat as only the point could reach but that could take an eye or give time for a deadly thrust from one of ours. Our trained discipline held as this bloody assault went on. Their army was much more mixed than ours, clusters of well-armed warriors were supported by what looked like armed farmers. Many of them were clutching broken shields or none at all. They were falling like leaves in a storm but as we tried to climb over their dead and dying, they were replaced as quickly as they died. There were so many of them. They just kept coming, and coming, and coming, in endless waves, fearsome in their wild bravery.

There were no pauses now, just a constant churning as exhausted and wounded men fell out and others pushed their way into the front. I was hoarse but knew not what I shouted. The icy calm I'd experienced in fights before never came. I fought frenziedly on and on from behind the heavily armed front rows. Jabbing and thrusting over the shoulders of our shield wall. Alongside me now were men carrying the long war axes. Using them to hook shields, helmets, mail and clothing to help the front line. We were so packed together that wielding them as axes was impossible. A rock hit me in the face and I fell backwards into our men. For a moment I passed out and woke to find I was being trampled. I rolled into a ball with my targe over my head until I could find a space to stand. Staggering to my feet I was met by a boy carrying a water skin.

Now I was the grateful one. Taking the skin from him I drank and drank then I thrust him back down the hill. 'Get away boy, get away from all this,' I yelled into his startled little face. He burst into tears and ran. I headed back to our banner and passed the skin to a mailed man who was crawling around in circles in the floor.

'You alright?' I asked, passing him the skin.

He retched and sat up, 'Ugh, bit dizzy I suppose.'

I peered into his face, 'Gyric, it's you, thank God, it's you.'

'Sar' he nodded, 'I need to get back,' He drank and retched again. 'It's terrifying in there Sar. Once they got past the spears, we were crammed so close you could only stab with knives. For a while I could not move my arms, held face to face with some Scot trying to bite my nose off. I nutted him with my helmet rim again and again until he passed out and slid down into the throng to be trampled to death.'

His eyes were crazed, pupils so wide the whole iris looked black. I helped him to his feet. He was shield-less but no-one was bringing any more. I cast around until I found one under a dead man. I saw his sword was still unsheathed but he was clutching a long blood soaked seax. He leant on the shield, stood himself up, put the strap over his shoulder and his hand inside the boss. Grabbing a broken war spear with about an arms-length of shaft behind the head I loped after him as he walked back into the fight.

The sun was behind us now. The battle had already lasted most of a long summers day but still it raged on.

Chapter Seven

As we pushed our way back into the fight, I could see that the banners of the nearest commanders had grown much closer. This meant that we were losing so many men we could not keep our lines extended. During the early part of the battle the banners had moved further apart as we'd stretched to avoid being outflanked. Looking over the warring soldiers I could see that the enemy's banners were also closing together around the top of the hill.

Our commanders were now grouped behind us riding back and forth with little to do but encourage us on. There seemed to be no more men in reserve yet our shield wall held and so did that of the Scots. The men in the first wall to collapse faced savage slaughter as they chose encirclement or rout. The Scots, perhaps, could retreat and rally in the great vastness of their hinterland but not us. Here, in a foreign land and hated by the natives, we would all be cut down somewhere between here and the border. Killed or enslaved, not a man would make it home.

To our left Osbeorn's cohort was fighting under Siward's raven. The spooky flapping wings of his standard leant, like a predator, stooped over the fight, evoking the presence of ancient gods of death and war. Under it somewhere, Grim would be hacking away if he still lived. To our right was a cluster of banners belonging to the Irish Norsemen among which flew the tubular snapping serpent of Thord's bussecarls.

The clamour of clashing arms and the screams of men fighting under the raven grew even more fierce. In the corner of my eye, I saw the banner stagger and fall. The groan that followed was so loud it could be heard over the surrounding clamour. Our flank units began to hesitate. If those next to us gave we would be exposed and faced being attacked from the sides. Then, with a great roar the raven rose again, and our line surged forward and pushed the enemy back.

Our confidence restored we fought on desperately. I stood behind Gyric's left shoulder stabbing savagely at any threat to him or his shield mate. As before the throng became so tight that we could barely wield our weapons. I could only manage short, sharp down-thrusts with my spear. The front rank stabbed and chopped with hand axes or short seax's under and over their shields. The foe did the same to us. Then something gave. The sun began to set into our enemy's eyes and they faltered. They began to give ground and started clustering around the banners of their lords. Our line started to shift and heave as resistance in some areas weakened and men started to push forward. Although their wall had breached, they were not yet beaten. They started forming armed islands, slowly fighting their way back along the ridge.

Suddenly, shockingly, we were no longer fighting crushed together and our line burst forward with the pressure of men from behind. To our front was a cohort of men fighting under a snarling wolf's head flag, flying above a wolf's pelt suspended from a crossbar. They formed into a circle with spears and swords facing out, some of us ran to encircle them. As I moved past Gyric he crashed face down to the ground. I turned to see where the blow had come from when something thumped hard into the left side of my neck. My spear fell to the floor and I stumbled sideways reaching to my belt in small of my back to pull out my little axe. I had no sense of who had attacked me when I saw a hand raised, silhouetted black, against the sun. A hand missing its fingers.

My mind flashed back to the inn in Jorvik and the row of fingers on the loft floor. I wasn't being attacked by the Scots. I quickly gauged the distance and threw the axe. My friend travelled true and hard. Its blade struck the fingerless man full in his face. Knowing he was finished I scrabbled to pull my seax from my belly sheath to deal with whoever had struck me. A foot smashed into my right arm and the seax fell from my numb fingers. I was now half kneeling on the ground next to Gyric's fallen body as the battle swirled on around us. I twisted about to see a helmeted man raising his long-bearded axe aiming to cleave my skull. Even as I braced to receive my death-wound I could see the end of a nose poking clearly to one side of its guard.

'Einvar!' I thought, 'The bastard has got his revenge.' He only had one object in mind, my death. He snarled something, then, even as his axe curved through the air, a blade ripped through his windpipe and with a surprised gurgle he toppled sideways, blood spurting in gouts as he fell. I found myself being dragged to my feet by a tall red-haired man dressed in fine mail though helmetless and without a shield. He pushed me behind him and scooped up my seax. Somehow now I was in amongst the Scots below the banner of the wolf.

I stared at the man who had saved me. His hair was dark red, as dark as mine. He stepped back as his men moved in front of him and he turned to stare back at me. Einvar's blood still dripping from his blade. His eyes were amber, flecked with gold. The eyes of Moira, my twin. He looked at my seax in his hand, staring at its ornate hilt and the distinctive blue stone, then back at me. He yelled something at me in a language I didn't know.

'I don't know what you're saying.' I yelled back at him in Danish.

His eyes flickered and he held the hilt in my face, 'Where did you get this?' he asked changing his tongue to that lilting Danish of the Norse.

Still trying to take in his likeness to my sister I spluttered, 'That's mine. From my mother. Give it back to me!'

The battle rages on around us as we seemed becalmed in its midst. 'It was mine once. There's not two of these on God's earth', he said to me, his amber eyes staring straight into mine.

I felt so confused, he had saved my life but now he had my seax, the only thing that joined me to my lost family and my childhood home.

'My name is Sar Nomansson so who the fuck are you?' I retorted, trying to grab it back but he was too quick.

'Erland' he replied, Erland, son of Thorfinn, Lord of the Isles of Orkney.'

'Well, Erland Thorfinnson that knife is mine.'

He looked down at the fine hilt with the deeply worn blade and gave me a shrewd look. 'Nomansson eh? Odd name', he said in a strangely gentle voice, 'we're all somebodies son. It's been used hard this knife, and sharpened carelessly but once this shining blade was longer, deeper and rusting when I found it but mine it was and mine it is now, again.'

For a moment my mind flew back to my earliest memories, those of my mother's incessant sharpening of this blade on our hearth stone. Then I remembered my dream and her warning. She'd been right, danger had come from behind.

Then the calm broke, the roar of battle surged in. A warrior grabbed his arm, yelling into his face. He turned to see his soldiers stepping rapidly backwards. His encircled force was attempting a fighting retreat. My mind whorled as I saw a long-shafted axe hacking down upon his line. I was in danger of being killed by my own side. Maybe I should retreat and run with my saviours? I made one last effort to grab my seax from the now distracted stranger but once again I failed. He tore it out of my reach and turned back to the fight. As he did so their line broke and I threw myself onto the ground as a mass of English warriors surged over us led by a wild man wielding a huge bearded axe.

From my low vantage point, I could see the enemy soldiers turn on their heels and run. Our men followed, cutting down the slowest before panting to a stop to reform. I tentatively began to get up. I did not want to die now, mistaken for a Scot. The axe bearing wild man, ghastly red with fresh blood, streaked over old blood dried black, bore down on me. In one hand he held effortlessly held the axe while tugging at the straps of his helmet with the other.

Holding out my empty arms I yelled, 'I'm an Englishman, a Saxon, don't kill me.'

'I know who you are you twat, don't you know me? He replied as he finally got his helmet off. 'Why do you think I went charging in there?'

It was Gyric.

I threw my arms around him instead, so pleased was I to see that lopsided grin. As I did cheers broke out all along our line. I looked around to see we were on the long broad ridge of Dunsinane hill and ahead of us what remained of our enemies were broken and running. We had won.

'Did you see him Gyric, the man who saved me?' What was left of the setting sun cast long shadows as we walked down the hill picking our way through the broken bodies of so many men. Eagles, kites, buzzards and ravens were already glutting themselves upon the fallen. Gaping wounds and staring eyes gave them easy inroads upon which to feast.

'I didn't see you saved', answered Gyric, 'I wasn't conscious. I awoke to see you dragged into the ranks of the enemy.'

'It was all confusion. I think they thought I was one of theirs.'
'Eh?'

'Einvar and his friends were attacking me.'

'And you looked like them.'

Now it was me who said, 'Eh?'

'Yeah, you looked just like the man you were arguing with when their line broke', said Gyric.

'He looked like Moira.'

'Your twin, who looks like you.'

'He had her eyes.' I stopped walking and squatted staring at the ground to collect my thoughts. 'My mother came to me in a dream. She warned me. She spoke of danger from behind and something about branches of a tree.'

'The danger from behind certainly happened.' Gyric grinned. ruefully rubbing the back of his head.

'I don't know what you're smiling about I thought you were dead.' I said. 'He knew the hilt of my knife, Gyric, he'd known it when it was still a proper seax. He said something about it having been rusty when he found it.'

'Really, so come on Sar, it was you who told me. Where did your mother get the seax?'

'She took it from my father before throwing herself in the sea.'

'And your father was rumoured to have dug in the mounds of the kings.'

'So I was told.'

'And the hilt was very old, ancient even.'

'He was my father?' I couldn't believe it, 'That's just crazy, you're saying he knew it because he'd dug it up. That he was the man my mother ran away with and then from?'

'Think it through, Sar, think it through.'

This was way too much, way too much to take in. 'What I do know Gyric is that he took it with him. He took from me the only thing that joined me to the world Oslaf and his father took me from.'

Gyric looked at me and suddenly started laughing, 'Your hair. What's happened there?'

'What's so funny?' My head did feel a bit unsteady but I'd taken a couple of really hard knocks. My left plait was hanging on by just a few hairs. The rest of it was cut clean through.

'That plait may have saved your life,' said Gyric, now serious. 'Your shoulder and neck are bruised bloody.'

'Sibhyrt made those plaits' I gulped, 'And now he's dead, another man who befriended me has died Gyric. You should stay away from me.'

Gyric held me in his arms, 'Don't start that nonsense again Sar, it's just that their fate and mine are different.'

I sobbed for Sibhyrt, that humble man and for Muirchu who'd taught me to fight. They were dead, so why was I still alive?

Chapter Eight

Nobody had ever known a battle to last as long as this one. We had fought from the early morning until the setting of the sun on a long summer's day. Battles usually end with the chasing down of enemy survivors as discipline breaks down and enraged men are released. Then the looting of corpses, torture and slaying of the wounded and the enslaving of any surrendered fit enough to be sold.

This battle ended in near darkness with exhausted, thirst crazed warriors stumbling down the hill seeking water and rest. Too tired to eat or to find our banners in the dark, men grouped together and fell into fitful sleep. Sleep disturbed by fearful dreams from which many awoke screaming, to a waking nightmare of wolves and dogs snarling and fighting over the remains of their dead friends.

Judging by the stars I had not slept long when I first awoke. I felt like I had floated up from some deep abyss. I sat up, here and there small fires flickered. A choir of priests and monks could be heard droning mournfully as they processed through the camp blessing the dead and our victory alike. The cries of the wounded carried far across the clear night air, a choir of unaided misery. My body was pulled back to the ground by sheer weight of unconquerable weariness and then back into the abyss. In there now was the image of a mighty tree its branches and twigs dripping with blood. In the tree, the faces of Erland and many others unknown to me. His arms became the branches and, somehow, I was a twig with my twin, a twig beside me. These weird images faded and my seax filled my vision and again I floated into wakefulness.

My seax was gone. I had found my mother's family because of that weapon and now had my father found me? Did I even want that? I'd never known him and my mother had risked her life to escape him. He meant nothing to me but ugliness and death, until now, when, if he was my father, he'd saved my life. His coming had ruined my mother's family and now he had the one thing that joined me to my roots.

Suddenly furious I got up into the grey light of the false dawn. Only a few men were stirring as I made my way up the hill following the course if yesterday's fight. I found poor Sibhyrt's corpse. The crows had already taken his eyes. They had brown bodies the crows up here, not all black like ours, but they ate carrion just the same. After muttering a prayer and covering his face I picked up a throwing spear in case of wolves and went on. I found the big crude shield we had fought behind and one dead dog. I could hear a whimpering somewhere nearby and there was the other great hound.

He was trapped beneath the body of a fallen enemy, possibly one of the Normans judging by his long mail coat. He growled softly at me. His head was badly misshapen from where I'd hit him, one eye a slit in his face. Between growls he panted, his muzzle coated with dried saliva. I held a hand out to him. He snapped at it. I snatched it back. I sat on my haunches and chatted softly to him. I figured I probably looked as big a mess as he did. I was stiff where I'd received blows and my face felt twisted, swollen out of shape from when the rock had hit me. I looked around. Not far away lay a body opened up by weapons or wolves. I pulled out a piece of his liver and held it out to the dog. He took it feebly but didn't eat it.

'I think you are too thirsty but I'm in no hurry to set you free,' I said to him remembering the ferocity of his attack. This reminded me of my own thirst and pulling the lining out of a no longer needed helmet I set off back down the hill. Being some distance from the river we'd been reliant on water carriers bringing barrels and skins.

I found a half empty skin and after quenching my thirst I filled the helmet and trotted stiffly back up the hill.

'By the saints I don't know why I'm doing this,' I said to the dog, holding the helmet up to his jaws. He lapped the water up sideways, spooning it in with his tongue. The effort seemed to fade him then, after a pause, he lapped again. I fed him the man's liver until without thought my fingers were in his jaws. Realising, I was about to pull away when his tongue came out and licked them. I let him lick my bloodstained hand clean then slowly moved it over his head. He snarled, made to snap but held back. I stroked the side of his big head making noises like I would with a horse. Propping the helmet up to one side I stood. He growled again. I began to lift the body off of him. He yelped in pain snapping, but not at me.

'Are you hurt?' I said pulling at the dead weight. After much painful effort I lifted the corpse away. My stiffened muscles protested and I knew I would be blackened by bruises as the day wore on. The sun was making its way up as the dog tried to rise. He pushed up on his front legs but his hindquarters stayed flat on the floor.

'Aaah, have you broken your back, little fellow,' I crooned. I decided to let him drink some more. Still in the same position he drank some more. I reached behind me to where I'd left the spear. Sliding my hand up to just behind the spearhead I prepared to stab him in the throat. I felt sick and hesitated and as I paused, he lurched forward and his back legs followed. I fell back and the great hound was standing over me.

My hand tensed around the spear shaft but then he lowered his head and snuffled around my face. 'No teeth,' I thought. Tense, but not afraid I lay there. His hind legs were trembling and I guessed they'd gone numb, pinned down so long by the dead man's corpse. He turned back to the helmet and licked out the last drops. I slowly sat up and fed him some more human offal.

I don't know why I did this. This dog and I had tried to kill each other less than a day ago. I got up and walked on up the hill. The dog followed me staggering a little. The carnage was terrible. Here and there were banks of bodies where one side or the other had made a stand. Then clearer ground and another bank of bodies. Then as I walked towards the summit the bodies got thicker and thicker. Here and there I saw faces I knew and felt glad I'd made no friends along the way but, by them, I knew I was following the course of my fight as well as theirs. Behind me the dog started a high-pitched weird howling. I turned to find him licking the blooded face of a fallen warrior. Then he laid across the body and lifting his head made the most mournful howl I had ever heard.

I left him keening over what I guessed was the corpse of his owner and walked on up the hill. I found Einvar's body, already torn by wolves and his split skull emptied of its brains, the last specks of which were being picked out by a bold little robin as I stood there. I looked around and found what I was seeking. Buried in a man's face was my little axe. It wrenched free with a gruesome sound somewhere between a slurp and a crunch. Now at least I had one of my weapons.

At the top of the hill, I tried to work out the way by which Erland and his men had fled. I followed it for a while and found the odd man cut down from behind but no red-haired man and no golden hilted seax. I gave up and took a decent seax from a fallen man. I thought of taking a sword but knew I'd not get to keep it. I picked up a couple more throwing spears and headed back. As I turned, I realised I was being tracked by the great hound, still wobbly on his legs but determined not to be left behind.

'Let him come,' I thought as I slowly walked back down the hill. By the time I got back to our camp he was only a few feet behind me his big, shaggy grey head swaying from side to side as he loped along. I realised he was carrying something in his mouth. He dropped it and stood back, his tail waving slowly from side to side. I picked it up, still wary of this powerful beast. It was a piece of leather. Broad and soft and one end with a ringleted hole it then tapered into an arm's length of ornately plaited work with a tubular silver finial. I'd seen similar things held by Harold's huntsmen. It was a slip lead, and a very fine one at that. The dog was trying to tell me something but did I want to know? I poked the lead into my belt and seeing Burgric's banner I made for that.

Burgric was there too. With his right arm in a sling, he was being shoved into the saddle of his horse. When settled he looked us over. There were a lot less of us now and not a man was unscathed. 'Food and drink are on the way,' he began. We cheered feebly. I'll say one thing for Burgric, he knew soldiers.

He went on, 'You are to eat and then we begin the pursuit. You are not to loot the dead.' We groaned dutifully as expected. 'We have people to do that for you, you will be recompensed splendidly for your victory.' We stirred, pleased at this. 'There are many wounded, they too are being cared for.' Another feeble cheer. 'I know you need to rest but today we need to seal our victory and I need you to hunt down as many Scots and their allies as you can. They must not be allowed to reform.'

We grumbled, men began to sit down or shout out, 'What about the reserves?'

'There are no reserves,' answered Burgric, 'Every armed man went into the fight yesterday, Every one.'

'Even those guarding Scone,' another voice yelled out.

'Yes, even those, but before you disappear to loot the palaces and monasteries you should know that Siward's surviving thegns and their men will be stationed there.'

Discontented voices rose, 'Why them? We fought as hard as any. Lost more than most and they get the spoils.'

Burgric grew red and visibly angry, 'Men, you are not wrong but you will not be wronged. You should know that the Earl has suffered greatly too. His cohort was savaged terribly. He has lost his eldest son and all he asked was whether his wounds were on his chest or his back. He was not grasping for wealth or grumbling at his fate. Osbeorn is dead, so too is one of Siward's nephew's, his namesake.'

This caused a stir, Osbeorn was greatly admired as too was the younger Siward. While Burgric sat waiting we talked among ourselves concluding that his death was what led to the great groan during the battle and the wavering before our final and victorious attack. Osbeorn's death had to be avenged. His father's stoicism impressed us and we shifted from a formless mob more or less into ranks.

Burgric spoke again, 'Eat, arm your selves, I'll be back soon.' He rode off to join the other commanders.

We sat to eat with our backs to the battleground. Behind us the vast hill was alive with squabbling birds of all kinds. Their racket overlay the steady buzzing of millions of flies while occasional breezes wafted the stench of rotting flesh in our direction. Our victory breakfast was not a happy one.

When our horses were brought up there were so few of us that we all got a mount. We headed off following the spore of our defeated foe. Burgric lead the way, I fell in beside Gyric, grateful that my companion had survived as many of our comrades grieved lost friends. The dog, unasked, loped along beside me clearly used to following mounted men. We found numerous herds of cattle grazing in the valleys which were ignored for now. Our quarry was men. Numerous tracks led away in diverse directions through this land of hills, scrub and woodland. Our force wended its way along a long valley heading north-east. I hoped in my heart we were pursuing the men who had fought under the banner of the wolf. We quickly came across wounded men vainly hiding in thickets or the banks of streams. They were quickly cut down and stripped of anything of value. Then we started to come across groups of followers. Women, monks, some children or older men, they too were stripped and when enough were grouped together they were roped and herded back towards our camp. I avoided this duty. I knew the fate that awaited many of them and I didn't want to see it.

After this we began finding groups of men, only lightly armed but who had run themselves into the ground. They were soon subdued, stripped bare and tied, wrists and necks, into rows of defeated, beaten survivors. Any leaders were singled out. Their arms were taken but otherwise they were unmolested and kept separate from their men. I rode up and down seeking a red-haired man with a richly hilted seax. There were quite a few red-heads among the Scots, but a bright red, as Sibhyrt said, like polished copper, not the dark red I shared with my quarry.

We rode on through small fields of ripening oats and barley yellowing against the green. The occasional blown horse or mule grazed forlornly on the deserted crops that surrounded the burning and devastated homesteads we destroyed as we passed.

Later we came across units still prepared to fight. After short, bitter conflicts that led to more casualties, we would cut them down vengefully. They should know when to give up. As the day wore to an end, I'd still not seen a wolf's head banner nor any man that might be Erland. Tired, dispirited and hungry we wearily turned our mounts and traced our way back to the camp at Scone.

Chapter Nine

For the next few days we continued hunting fugitives. I would go out with my own cohort fruitlessly seeking Erland until we returned to camp. Then I would search through the prisoners other cohorts had captured, again to no avail. Then, red-eyed with weariness, I would eat the now plentiful beef and mutton then sleep.

Gyric was getting tired of my obsession, 'Sar, he's gone. His men left the battle in good order. They probably ran the whole first night.'

'Could you have run? After that fight?'

'Maybe not, but well led and being hunted, maybe I could.' Gyric wasn't giving an inch.

I knew he was right, MacBethad himself had not been captured and he was the main prize. His defeat and execution were the reasons we were here. We'd beaten his army but not the man. By now we'd come to understand the vastness of the wilderness that led in almost every possible direction but south.

I laid back using the great hound as a pillow. He lifted his head, gave me a lick and settled back down contentedly.

'He's certainly taken to you that dog', Gyric said, stating the obvious.

It was true, so much so that he would growl fiercely at anyone who came near me. Some of the men complained but enough liked having him around for things to even out. Then one day when we'd been hunting fugitives, he'd put up a deer, coursed it and pulled it to the ground by its neck. By the time we'd caught up with him the deer was dead, choked. This is quite feat for a lone dog of any kind. After that no one complained. As for me I knew Earl Harold would give much for a dog like this to hunt and to breed from and I started to look forward to getting back into his household. It had been a long time.

We were now camped in and around Scone itself. The royal buildings were more like a cluster of houses, halls, sheds and stables with chapels and a monastery attached. It was more like one of King Edward's palaces than Siward's great long house.

Everything of value not belonging to the church had been stripped away. Maelcolm may be getting a kingdom but he wasn't getting much of a treasury. I saw him here and there dressed in fine clothes followed by clerics and nobles all vying for his attention. He did not look happy.

He was crowned soon after in a double ceremony. Firstly, an endless service of chanting monks where he had to sit on a stone in his robes while a bishop did various rites. He should have had an Archbishop really but Aeldred of Jorvik was travelling to see the German Emperor, or so we were told. If the Scots had one, he wasn't around.

Then, led by a choir, they processed out and made their way to the Hill of Belief, a flat-topped mound not far away. Here Maelcolm was raised aloft on a platform of shields and all the Scottish leaders had to swear fealty. There weren't many of them and most of those were prisoners. They sullenly raised their swords in the air then quickly had them removed. Even the Strathwaelas didn't raise much of a cheer. As all the nobility walked back to attend the feast, I saw Siward stagger slightly. He seemed to have shrunk since the battle, since the loss of his son.

For us this cheerless affair was an excuse for a shindig. We drank and feasted and made the most of it. For Gyric and I it was a chance to mooch around the palace buildings. We found the Kingmaking stone in the chapel. A young monk timidly explained that it had fallen out of the sky in ancient times. Other monks were chanting at each other, either the end of the coronation service or one of the regular prayers. I was drunk enough to not know the time of day.

'It's Abraham's Pillow,' said the monk reverently, 'sent to us by God from the heavens.'

I looked at it, just a rounded black stone. 'Pillow, psst, Abraham must have had a hard life', I scoffed. I looked at it more carefully, it seemed to have strange spiral whorls in it and definitely looked old, but then rocks do.

'If it's hit with a hammer it rings, like a bell but softer', continued the monk.

I wobbled a bit and went to sit on it when I was surrounded by three burly monks.

'Make it ring,' I said, 'let me tap it with my axe.'

Warily they got between me and the stone. They'd had to deal with a lot of drunk and offensive soldiers and some of them had got hurt. The dog didn't help, he started growling menacingly at the monks and the tension rose. I started to get angry and pulled the little axe from my belt when Gyric pulled me away.

'Sar, this is a house of God, these are holy men, behave yourself,' he said, pulling me away to the grateful smiles of the shaking monks.

Now Gyric's an amiable man but there's lines you can't cross with him. Offending churchmen is one of them, making jokes about his sisters is another. My Step-Da was a drinker and for a moment I saw him in myself. This could go one of two ways. I get mad and everyone would hate me tomorrow or I find something else to do.

I guess I wasn't too drunk, I put the axe back in my belt and said 'Let's go find Jokul, haven't seen him since the battle.'

This was true, we'd been worked so hard that we'd seen his father's banner but had not caught up with him at all. After stealing a small barrel from a comatose quartermaster, we made our way to Thord's camp.

We got there to find his men surrounded a blazing pyre, the mood was sombre, many of them were kneeling in prayer. At one end of the pyre was a raised platform and, on that platform, sat a man in his full war-gear. Above his head flapped the writhing serpent banner we'd known from long ago. Its actions mimicking the twisting flames below.

I sobered up fast, 'Saints above, Gyric, that's Jokul sat up there', I whispered hoarsely.

'If that's Jokul this can only mean one thing', said Gyric.

'Thord's on the pyre, Duw, that's not Christian.' I meant the fire. We buried people when they died.

'Maybe it's different for them. Thord was a great warrior. I don't know,' said Gyric thoughtfully. 'It's too many days after the battle for him to have died in it. Too many, maybe he died of wounds.'

The men lined up and, one by one, saluted Jokul as he sat watching the fire, some stopped to say a few words. He nodded grimly. We joined them to pay our respects. Jokul greeted us briefly his father's helmet under his arm. 'Strange,' he said. 'My father's helmet is too small for me. He always seemed so big.' His lips trembled and he visibly pulled himself together. He said, 'I can't talk now, come find me tomorrow brothers, we'll talk then.'

I left the barrel with him. It was hard to believe Thord was dead. He'd terrified me that time on the beach after I bested his son and nearly dropped a rock on his head and now, he was gone. I felt sad and lonely as Gyric, the dog and I made our way back to the camp.

It was well into August by now and we had plundered the country of everything worth taking. We fattened their cattle on the nearly ripened barley and oats in their fields ready to be herded southwards. A pestilence among the English cattle had raged so fiercely that these beasts would command a high price in the south. With no grain and no cattle, the people of these parts faced a harsh winter. Our camp was surrounded by lowing herds, pens of miserable slaves and piles of goods of every description from furs and skins to gold platters, rich vestments and fine arms.

We'd been told that we'd buried fifteen hundred of our own men and that the abandoned bodies of our enemies amounted to twice that. Many of our leaders had died in the fight or from wounds in the days that followed. Limbs blackened and stank as fevered men died horribly. Then for a while we had time to grieve and recover and even to enjoy our victory and the pay we had received. Things were looking up which was why we'd been so surprised to find Thord dead.

It was late in the day before Burgric let us leave. We had to walk some distance through the camps to Jokul's area. As we did, we could hear men groaning and the camp smelt even more rank than usual. We found Jokul staring miserably at the ashes of the pyre.

He nodded in greeting, 'I tried to give him the ending he would have wanted. He liked to tell tales of his forebears and their ends were always fiery, not a damp, muddy hole.'

I retrieved the barrel from where I'd left it. It turned out to hold a strong ale with a fine flavour to toast the death of a great warrior. One of his men found us some wooden cups and I poured.

'I'm the leader of these men now,' said Jokul, 'my father is a hard act to follow.'

My curiosity overcame my discretion, 'So, how did he die, Jokul? This long after the fight.'

Jokul looked sadly at me, 'You knew my father, he would have wanted to die with his weapons in hand fighting some great foe after stealing all his riches. He dreamt of a death that they'd make songs about.'

'Really', I said, 'he was so hard and ruthless I'd not have seen him as a dreamer at all.'

'We'd grown close after we got back from Lundenburh. I'd never expected that. I'd been so afraid of him yet this last year he's been more like a brother to me.'

I felt awkward around Jokul's grief and didn't know what to do. I drank and stared at the ground while Gyric sat beside Jokul putting an arm round his shoulders.

Jokul started sobbing, 'He died shitting liquid shit and blood. He'd been lightly wounded and had been a bit feverish when suddenly he was ill.'

'Christ, the bloody flux.' Gyric was horrified. 'My father, Skalpi, has told me about this. It can destroy an army. It's happened before.'

Jokul pulled himself together, 'It has, really? I lead these men. I should get them out of here.'

'You lead them now, Jokul?' I asked.

'Who else?' My father owns most of the ships we came in,' he answered. 'It's his banner we fight under.'

I felt a bit humbled, here I was a nobody with an Earl's house-carl on one side of me and the leader of a notorious warband on the other.

Gyric said, 'Where are your ships then? You arrived with the Strathwealas and joined Dolfinn's men.'

'He died too, did you know?' said Jokul, 'in the battle. He had the death my father would have wanted.'

We all drank again as the shadows grew longer. The talk went back and forth as we caught up with each other's stories.

Then, getting to his feet, Gyric said, 'Come, let's take a walk, go somewhere quiet.'

Jokul agreed, stood up and ordered one of his men to go get him another small barrel. 'It's strange telling people what to do. Keep expecting my old man to shout at me.' The man returned carrying a barrel. Taking it from him Jokul said, 'This is beer made by the monks from fermented fruits. Strong stuff my friends.'

'I have an idea,' I said, 'follow me.'

I led them to a small physic garden behind the cloisters of the monastery. Since all the vegetables had been stolen from the gardens as well as all the wealth inside no-one wanted to come here except a few frightened forlorn monks.

Settling on a bench Gyric declared nodding towards the church, 'I'm not sure we should have taken all their wealth. Might be bad luck.'

Jokul spat, 'They take enough from us, anyway all the nobles keep their wealth in the church, everyone knows that. If we didn't, there wouldn't be much to loot at all. Then what would be the point of raiding them? How would men get paid?'

I could see Gyric thinking about this and then, about to come up with an argument he shrugged, giggled and gave up. 'Aaah fuck it, not sure it's right though.'

I told Jokul about what happened in the battle. He looked at me incredulous. 'This man saved you. Why? You were his enemy?'

'I think when he saw Einvar attack me he thought I was one of theirs,' I said.

'Yeah, can be hard to tell when things get messy,' he acknowledged.

'I think he was my father Jokul.'

'I lose mine and you find yours,' Jokul mused emptying his cup once again. 'Not very likely though is it? Really? You meet your father in the middle of a battle at the other end of a country you've never been in before. I don't believe it.'

I wasn't sure myself. It was weird but then was it my weird, my fate? Who can say what's likely or not? Strange things happen, look how I'd found my aunt. Now that too was an odd tale. 'You remember how my aunt knew me by the hilt of my knife, that old worn seax I had?'

'No, what you on about?'

'Myn uffern,' I cursed. We had a lot of catching up to do. Then Gyric spoke up and told him the tale.

Jokul said, 'You were with Toki then? What happened to him?'

We told him of Toki's death and of all the events at Wincestre and at Belestede and the revenge we took with Harold's aid.

He looked at me impressed, 'You've come a long way since we fought on the beach.'

'And so have you,' I answered, 'look at you, Here, a toast to us all.'

We drank heavily, the beer was delicious, fruity and strong.

Gyric got off the bench, staggered to the wall to piss and mused, 'I could be a monk you know.'

Jokul scoffed, 'You, a monk, ha ha. I've just been hearing how you charged after Sar wielding a battle-axe like you were born carrying it.'

Gyric smiled amiably, 'Yes, I've found my weapon.' He leant up on an elbow, 'but you know. I could go for a monk. Live a peaceful life.'

Jokul belly laughed, 'There'd be no-one to rescue Sar then would there? Seems he needs it, you and his father in one battle. Oh, and a beautiful witch of the Cornwaelas.'

I sulked, I still pined after Morwed, 'She's not a witch, and anyway she was returning a favour.'

Jokul drank again, 'Still needed rescuing, didn't you? Always did, first time I saw you Harold had rescued you from that bastard that put that scar on your face.'

I rubbed the scar Oslaf had traced from my ear to my chin. I was getting angry now, 'Fuck off Jokul, before I have to put you down again.'

'Oh yea, well you can try, you skinny shit,' said Jokul throwing his cup on the ground.

'Come on friends, let it go, we've had enough fighting, be peaceful now. Fill your cups, let's drink to our good fortune. Many have died but we're still here to drink under the stars,' said Gyric putting an arm around my shoulders. The dog, who'd leaped up growling, settled back down making little puffing sounds.

Jokul simmered down too, 'Aye, you're right. Many dead. Though as my father would have said, "more loot for the rest of us".'

We drank on for a while, lost in our thoughts. I'd not thought about Morwed for a while and now I missed her with a sharp pang of loss. Don't know why. She won't have anything to do with me.

Jokul broke the silence, 'You know, that Oslaf, he's in Dyflin right now. Or he was when we left.'

Gyric and I both sat up sharply, 'He's where?' we said as one.

'Dyflin, didn't I just say?'

Instantly I was consumed with rage. I got up and paced around, the dog watched me intently. 'He's still alive, I knew it. I've got to kill him, nothing is over until I do, nothing.'

Gyric too seemed to have sobered up fast, 'Of course, it makes sense. He would have to go somewhere and he knew people from when his father and Harold went there.'

'Doing much the same as well', said Jokul, 'Aims to get a fleet together and raid England.'

'He doesn't have that much clout', said Gyric. 'His family might be wealthy but they never had that much influence.'

'He approached my father. We have three raiding ships and full crews. Well, we did until the other week.' For a moment Jokul saddened and tears sprung into his eyes. 'He claimed he was working on an Earl's behalf.'

Gyric and I exchanged looks. 'Did he say which Earl', I asked.

'No, but he said something about a Welshman called Gruffudd', answered Jokul. 'Reckoned he could pay for as many ships and their crews as could be found.'

'Gruffudd's not an uncommon name for the Welsh,' I said, but there's only two that matter, 'Gruffud ap Rhydderch who ruled where I used to live and Gruffud ap Llywelyn, who calls himself king and rules in the north.

'Wasn't it Gruffud ap Rhydderch's brother's head that was brought to Edward at Christmas,' said Gyric.

I thought back to that terrible day when I'd eavesdropped on Godwin's family though the head business was common knowledge. 'Yeah, Rhys that would have been. I guess that would give him a good reason to attack England.'

Gyric said, 'But why would Aelfgar do that? His father is an Earl and so is he.'

'Truth is', I said, 'I don't give a shit, I need to get to Ireland as quickly as I can and kill that fucking bastard as painfully as I can.'

The dog joined me in a long sing-song howl that made us all laugh.

'Tell you what though Sar, our Earl needs to know about this. I have to get south fast and tell him what we know.'

Jokul looked bemused at our intensity, 'What's the hurry friends? Not sure I should have told you all this. Don't want to arrive and find you waiting for me with an army.'

'Will you be joining him?' asked Gyric.

'I might, don't know. I've got to get back to my ships at Cathures and then back to Ireland with skeleton crews and a lot of loot and then be ready to sail again next spring.' Jokul started to think this through. 'I'm not sure. I've got to convince them all to stay with me now my father's dead. Tell you what though', he looked up grinning now, 'no-one's going anywhere tonight and I'm too drunk to work out a thing right now.'

'But not drunk enough to forget,' I yelled picking up our empty cups and with that we got to finishing off the barrel before slipping into blessed unconsciousness.

Chapter Ten

I woke up with a painfully full bladder in a chilly grey drizzle. Shivering I pissed against the wall and tried to wrestle my mind back to the night before. Saint Diw, did I feel bad? A smith was pounding an anvil behind my left eye. I retched up a little drool and stumbled to the stone bench. As I did the dog pushed his way through the unlatched garden gate looking pleased with himself. I guessed he'd breakfasted somehow. Good, not my problem.

Oslaf, in Dyflin, that was the thought I was chasing. I have to get to him but how? My head hurt so much I couldn't think. I saw the barrel and gave it a shake. There was still a little left. With shaking hands, I felt around in the bushes for a cup. The herby smells, usually a delight, made me want to puke. I found a cup, filled it and drank, pleased I'd woken up before the others as there wasn't much left. What there was, I drank.

I started to feel a bit better. I could hear singing from the church so it must be Lauds as the sun was barely up. The monks would be about soon. I kicked the other two awake. As they grumpily rose, I suggested we find a well as I was now dying with thirst. Jokul shook the barrel unhappily while I looked on with wide-eyed innocence. Gyric just clamped his hands to the side of his head and groaned.

Jokul stomped off and we followed. We came to the well and, pushing aside the novices who were waiting, we helped ourselves, drinking straight from the bucket. Then after washing our heads in the cold refreshing water we sat in the cloisters. These were wooden buildings, roofed, but open fronted around a square attached to the church.

Up to this point we'd barely said a word but my need was great so I started. 'Jokul, you remember what you told us about Oslaf?' I asked, leaning forward. He nodded so I carried on, 'You, nor your father, have sworn any oaths to him?'

Jokul shook his head. Relieved I sat back and leant against the wall, one problem was out of the way. 'Would you take me with you to Ireland, to Dyflin when you sail?'

Jokul thought for a moment, 'Let me get this right, you want me to take you to Dyflin to kill the man who might be my next paymaster. Is that it?'

'Who would know Jokul, who would know?' I countered.

'I could use another man at the oars, a few men really,' he said as he thought things through. 'We're wealthy now. My bussecarls and I. Though there's a lot less of us. It's quite likely that none will want to raid next year. I'm not sure I'll want to myself.'

'So, you'll take me?'

'Course I'll take you Sar, we're blood brothers, you, I and that would be monk here,' said Jokul pushing at Gyric's shoulder. With that he got up and hugged us both.

Gyric was smiling broadly, friends mattered more to him than just about anything. 'We were boys then really. Weren't we? Just boys,' and then his mood changed to sadness, 'just children, not so long ago and we've seen so much.'

Suddenly he was crying, sobbing his heart out, 'I want to go home Sar, I've had enough. Ever since that battle I've had to hold myself together. I just want to go home.'

'But you can now Gyric, don't you see? You can go back with Burgric. Siward's orders won't matter anymore. And anyway, you have to go back. You have to tell Earl Harold. You need to get going as soon as possible. Maybe you can get on one of the boats and sail to Jorvik,' I said, 'You have to get back.'

Gyric wiped snot off his face with his sleeve. Our clothes were all newish, taken from the dead mostly and washed in the river.

He nodded, his chest was heaving and his shoulders still shuddered but he sat up and grinned feebly, 'I still have the headache from hell, Sar, but you need to think about a few things.'

'Hmmm, well before I waste my time while you try to put sense into his head I must go to my men,' said Jokul. He stood up, straightened his long cloak and left, 'Come find me soon Sar, we leave in two days.'

'So, what did you want to say Gyric?' I asked after we'd watched him go.

'You need to do something about that hair, it's still chopped away on one side and long on the other. Makes you look stupid.'

I'd forgotten about that, 'Not a problem, can cut the lot off. Too hot and sweaty anyway.'

'Saved your life though didn't it.'

'Thanks to Sibhyrt.'

'And look when you get to Dyflin you mustn't be recognised. Oslaf knows who you are,' Gyric pointed out.

'Don't care if he fucking does. Soon as I see him, I'm going to kill him.'

'No Sar, you are not. You've fought him before and he bested you. He will be among friends. You will be in a foreign land.'

'And somehow I have to get back,' I answered starting to see things more clearly. 'I have to stay in Ireland and be part of the fleet that returns. Then I have to kill him.'

'Or escape and warn the English.'

'Or both.'

This wasn't going to be easy. I had to overwinter in Dyflin somewhere near my enemy. Not be recognised as English, that wouldn't be too hard. Just speak Welsh and a little Norse-Irish. 'I need to cover my hair Gyric. He'd recognise me from a distance.'

'Or dye it. You can't get close. You've that scar on your face as well. He'll know that scar. He put it there.'

I rubbed it, something I often did when I thought of Oslaf. 'You need to stop doing that as well. Draws attention to it,' said Gyric. He added, 'That dog stands out a bit too.'

'I'm taking the dog. Maybe people will notice him and not me.'

'If you're lucky. It's just as well you've lost your seax. That is a talking point you could never explain away.'

'Not lost, stolen, but I suppose you're right,' I said ruefully.

We started to make our way back to the camp back through the physic garden. There was a monk there tut-tutting as he straightened up the bushes we had crushed during our drinking session. Just as we passed, I saw him clipping twigs from a sage bush.

'Luck is smiling on us Gyric,' I said and went up to the monk. I was only asking him for the shears when he collapsed to his knees.

Gyric laughed softly, 'Come Sar, we've frightened him.'

I'd forgotten how we look to most people used as I was to walking about as part of an army. Gyric and I, two young warriors. Me with a throwing spear, a seax and my targe which I carried everywhere and Gyric with his huge axe as well as a sword. Even though he wasn't wearing mail we were nightmarish to this poor monk.

I gently took the shears from him. They were a lovely piece of work, like sheep shears with a springy back and crossing blades but much smaller. The monk didn't understand a word I said but eventually I got him to stand up and do what I wanted. With shaky hands he cut my hair quite short all round. Not short enough to look like a slave but short enough that I shivered as the air hit the back of my neck.

I gave him a penny which made this the most expensive haircut the world had ever known but I felt bad about frightening him. I was about to keep the shears but Gyric gave me a look so I returned them. The monk made me think.

'Gyric, you remember Aethelric, he was a monk and he did a lot of writing.'

'Ink, of course, your hair, make it black.'

Turning to the monk he asked about ink. The monk didn't understand us. I tried all the languages I knew and Gyric tried talking very loudly in English. Nothing worked and the monk began shaking again.

'Gyric, he'll speak Latin.'

'Yes, but I don't.'

'But you know they copy out scriptures, right?'

'Ah yes, in the scriptorium, got it.'

The monk began to nod, then clearly wished he hadn't as Gyric slowly and loudly mouthed, 'Scriptorium. You know, scriptorium.'

'He won't want to take us there,' Gyric said turning to me. 'It's special to them.'

'I'll give them fucking special. Christ Gyric, everything worth having has been stolen already. You know they probably hate us.' I looked at all my hair on the ground and picked it all up. 'I'm not leaving any of this for them to make curses on me,' I said, all of a sudden fearful.

I don't know if seeing me do this made the monk change his mind but he started nodding, 'Scriptorium,' he said pulling on Gyric's snotty sleeve.

He led us around the buildings to a shuttered room. There were a couple of monks in the gloom but as a shutter was raised you could see the place had been thoroughly ransacked. Books were valuable. The desks they stood at had been stood back up but all the cupboards had their fronts torn away. Only dirty sheets of crumpled parchment remained but sure enough amongst the debris we found a few stoppered pots of ink.

'Yes!' I crowed triumphantly, 'this will do.' I stashed them in my bag very satisfied with myself when I looked up to see Gyric and the monks looking at me reproachfully. Sucking my teeth, I picked out the most worn cut penny I could find and handed it over. 'Why Gyric, we robbed them of everything and now I have to pay them. It makes no sense.'

'Good luck Sar, don't want to tempt the elves to mischief by stealing from these humble monks. You are about to embark on a perilous journey.'

I nodded. It was a good point.

Before I could leave, I needed to go and find Grim. As usual he wasn't far from Siward's banner. We'd not spoken since the battle, as I served with Burgric. He and Siward had been hunting in different directions.

Grim greeted me with his usual grunt.

I responded cheerfully asking after his health and that of his lord.

'Siward's not good, Sar, but keep that to yourself. Grief for Osbeorn is eating him away and he has the flux. I'll be glad to get home away from this shithole. We'll not catch MacBethad now anyway.'

I told him what I had heard and what I planned to do.

'And Gyric is to go south to tell your lord?

'Yes,' I said, 'I thought he could return with Burgric and the other King's thegns.'

I paused, 'Look you Grim, I've earned my pay and my share of the spoils but I won't be here to get them. Thord's, I mean Jokul's, crews will get theirs but I fought under Burgric's banner. I'm not saying I don't trust him but I don't think he'll pay if he can't see my face.'

Grim nodded, 'I'll speak up for you boy. You fought well in that battle. I saw you reeling around with your face bloody and swelling. You went back in as good as blind in one eye.'

My heart swelled, 'Thanks, Grim, means a lot.'

'I knew you had courage. Remember I saw you fight Osric, but a battle is a different thing from a raid or a skirmish.'

I thought back and shuddered. I told him how I usually get these cold, calm moments when I fight but that during the battle it never came. Just hours of frantic fear and reaction.

'That's how it is for most men Sar, you are lucky that you get that clarity when you do. Something similar happens to me. Not cold, but somehow everything can seem to slow and I have more time than my opponent.'

I was surprised, I'd not heard that before. 'And in a battle?'

'You've no real control. Blows can come from anywhere. Are the men each side of you holding? And you can't see your feet, or theirs, or even their eyes if they're coming from the side. The shield wall is a different thing Sar, nothing readies you for that.'

'We won though, didn't we?' I thought for a moment, 'I didn't understand Burgric, his endless preparations, carts full of spears, the trudging for hundreds of miles carrying and dragging spare shields, and food and carts. And no women or followers, but it worked. Even putting us out in front of the wall throwing those angons.' I remembered Sibhyrt's death and shuddered, 'I hated him for that, but it worked.'

'It did, Sar, it's not just courage and brawn or Harold's charm and cleverness that deserve respect. Burgric plans and thinks ahead.'

He took my arm and turned me toward him, his eyes looked directly into mine from under his thick eyebrows. I took in his craggy scarred face, usually so dour but in this moment, he looked at me with affection. 'Sar,' he said, 'you were a good friend to my brother and without you I'd still not have avenged his death. You've proved yourself a warrior, a loyal follower and a trustworthy friend.'

He coughed looking sheepish, 'I tested you hard and at times thought badly of you. There's little I can do for you now but make sure you leave as prepared as possible, come walk with me.'

With that he took me to meet Siward's armourer who completely re-equipped me. I left with new belts and straps, whetstones, both rough and fine, a newly burnished seax, a stocky short knife useful for eating or close quarter nastiness and two very fine throwing spears. I was offered a war spear, mail, a fine shield and a sword but I turned them down. I still believed I was better off fighting light and relying on my speed to stay alive. I kept my little axe and my targe both of which had served me well and I kept the blackjack I'd found so handy when working in the tavern. It was a fine thing. Its handle was the toe and foot of a small deer with the hide of the shin filled with sand after the bone was taken out. Whack someone over the head and they fell down like a stone, stunned but not dead.

I was also given a fine woollen cloak, bit smelly, but with so much oil in the wool it would take a lot for mud or rain to soak through and best of all, boots. Boots soaked in a mixture of pitch and mutton fat. Dry feet, how I love to have dry feet in the cold months of the year.

My heart was bursting, I couldn't thank them enough and then to top it all Grim pushed a bulging purse into my hand. 'Don't thank me, son, I'll take it back out of your pay. Your friend Gyric. I'll get him as far south as I can. Oslaf in Ireland can only mean Aelfgar is up to something. Like your Earl Harold was, eh? Myself, I don't trust either of them but I'd rather Harold to that brooding Earl Aelfgar.'

There was only one more goodbye to make before I joined Jokul, that to Gyric. The following day I carried on doing various tasks to get Burgric's command ready to leave. Then as the twilight fell, I found him in the horse lines close to their tents. I showed him my finery and my new weapons and boots. Nothing fancy but of good quality all of which pleased me hugely. Gyric made all the right noises but was clearly not that interested. Then I noticed that he looked plainer than usual, hanging from his neck on a leather thong was a simple wooden cross and when I looked down, he was barefoot.

'By the Saints, Gyric, what's going on?'

He looked down at his feet sinking into the mud and chuckled, 'I think I'm learning to dance keeping my feet out of the way of these horse's hooves,'

'Seriously?'

He took a deep breath, 'Sar, after we left the monastery, I talked to one of our own priests about the battle and its aftermath, about the killings we've seen and done these last two years. I attended a mass and made confession.'

'You did?' I answered surprised, I went to mass when we had to, said the Paternoster and amened at all the right times but that was it.

'I did Sar, you should try it. I feel so much better now. The priest said that as we'd been blessed before going into battle that those killings weren't really sins.'

'I bet the other side had priests too,' I answered unthinkingly.

Gyric thought, looked sad and carried on, 'the priest said that it was harder for men to do good deeds as we were approaching the end of times.'

'Oh, Doomsday and that you mean?'

'Yes, you can tell it's coming because there is so much sin in the world, and warfare, and also nothing new is great compared with the ancients. Even those who were pagan.'

I thought back to the massive ruined fort I'd grown up in. Our home a cave burrowed out from its thick brick walls, the huge foundations the wooden walls of Lundenburh had been built upon and the great wall we'd crossed on the way here that they say goes from sea to sea. Beautiful though our wooden houses and halls were, they were not mighty like those ruins the Romans had left.

I conceded the point but why no shoes, no fine metal worked buckles and cloak pins, his sword in a plain wooden and leather sheath and the cross around his neck?

'The priest says that even though good deeds are hard for a soldier I can do penance. I am to refuse vanity and to go barefoot until I have reached the city of Jorvik and attended a mass.'

Remembering the walk up I shuddered, 'That's madness Gyric, unless you go by ship.'

Me, I preferred not to wear my shoes on the deck, wet feet or not, as long as the planks are well worn beyond splintering you have a surer footing than any leather sole.

'I am to ride Sar, I'm good with horses and we have less riders and more mounts than when we marched here.'

'It'll be freezing by the time you get to Jorvik, and you'll ride through gorse and dismount on any kind on ground.' I thought of my own calloused feet now getting softer as I spent more and more of my time shod, 'and you've never gone barefoot Gyric, not even as a child.'

He shrugged, 'It wouldn't be much of a penance if it didn't cause some pain.'

My mind was racing, I knew Gyric was as stubborn as an old nanny goat when he chose. 'Tell you what though Gyric, go find Hilda when you get to Jorvik. She should know that Einvar is dead and she'll warm your feet up for you.'

Gyric grimaced ruefully, 'I shall not be warming my feet in any woman's bed until I am truly married Sar. I will though carry that message. She should know that she is free.'

'By Cuthbert's saintly onions Gyric, you're a fucking crazy man,' I was thinking that Hilda's bed would be the best cure for his ills. She was wise in her way and understood the hurts of men better than any priest, but I bit my tongue. What was the use?

Gyric changed the subject, 'That dog, you named it yet?'

Relieved I said, 'Yes.' I hadn't, but I suddenly knew what his name would be, 'I'm calling him Sibhyrt'

'After the carter?'

'He was more than a carter, he was my friend,' I said, tearing up.

'It's a good name,' Gyric answered fondling Sib's head. The great dog seemed to understand who I cared for, he was very aloof with most people, but he pushed his head into Gyric's side his feathered tail whipping from side to side.

'I've got to go Gyric. Don't forget your task. There's treachery afoot, who knows where Aelfgar's ambition will lead.'

'Take care Sar, don't try for Oslaf's death unless you can get away. I want to see my friend again.'

I felt awkward, not knowing what to say. We put our arms around each other for a long time. 'I'll see you next year, Gyric, I'll see you next year.'

We pulled apart. 'Next year,' he answered and turned back to grooming his horse.

I walked away, feeling sad and suddenly very, very alone. The dog walked close by me his big head swinging from side to side. I looked at him, glad for his company. 'You know dog, you needed a new name. Sibhyrt, I'm going to call you, Sib for short.' For the first time I put the collar round his neck and slipped the leash through its hole and we ambled our way towards Jokul's camp. Man and dog together, ready to take on the world.

Part Two

Chapter Eleven

Jokul's camp seemed untidy after Burgric's. Men and fires all over the place instead of in lines. Away from the sea they slept like any other warriors, wrapped in their cloaks, feet towards the fires, weapons near their hands.

I passed the pickets with a hail, they all knew who I was and I soon found Jokul's fire close to his banner, and with the help of a growl or two from Sib I pushed us in and wrapped in my new cloak, with my dog's warm back to mine, I fell into the deep hole of sleep.

I dreamt I was in a dark wood armed with a seax and my targe. A voice would call from ahead, I would turn, and then the voice would call from another direction, I would turn again. The voices would change and though I knew not the words I knew that some were English, some Welsh, Danish, Irish and all the mixed-up argot in between. I turned and turned again, each time to see another path that was strange to me. I heard the voices of men, of women and the plaintive cries of children. All was strange, all was eerie, then all of a sudden something dark roared out at me from the shadows and I awoke in a cold sweat.

As I awoke, I was thinking of Moira, my twin. I'd been told she lived in the north, in a land of snow where the wolverine hunts. I was journeying westwards from the most northerly place I'd ever been. I maybe had a child in the distant southeast with its mother, Ymma, who I'd deserted. I had a half-brother and sister, Adaf and Elena, in the distant southwest, if they still survived. I was journeying to the west, to seek revenge, not south to my lord, Earl Harold to whom I was sworn. I could dress this up as a quest on his behalf, but it wasn't. I wanted Oslaf's head on a pole for my sake not anyone else's. I thought of Candalo at Harold's court, and his daughter Morwed, who'd taken my heart but didn't want it. For a moment I faltered in my resolve. It would be so easy, to get up, go find Gyric and set off south with the only real friend I'd ever known.

I thought of the dream, all those different directions but the force that overwhelmed me was my hate, my fierce anger and the dark, hard stone in the heart of me. My hatred won. I stood up, brushed myself down, rubbed my teeth with my finger, spat and faced the day.

I soon found myself useful, a group of the Strathwealas were arguing fiercely with Jokul. They were haggling over the price of the horses they had delivered for our journey to Jokul's ships.

They were claiming Jokul had misunderstood them because he could not speak their language. They were claiming their price reflected the sale of the horses while Jokul only desired to use them to ride to Cathures. Which, being in the Kingdom of the Strathwealas meant they'd get them back whatever.

The Strathwealas affected not to understand, to insist on the full price of purchase. I jumped in, speaking the language of my childhood which all of the Cymri understood full well. They were taken aback, there was now no way they could play their game. We still ended up paying well over the odds but far less than they had asked. Truth was we had to travel through their kingdom and we needed to get to our ships.

Jokul was furious, darkly muttering in that sing-song form of Danish the Norsemen speak mixed with the Irish of his homeland about their ingratitude. After all we'd come to fight their fight, not ours, and how he'd a good mind to raid their kingdom himself next year with all the bussecarls in Ireland. I hushed him, if there was one thing I'd learned, it was that you never knew who spoke what language up here. There were Britons speaking English, Gaels speaking Norse and Norsemen whose first language was Gaelic let alone the Irish and the Danish speakers. It would be a fine thing to have fought so hard for so much wealth to lose it in a fight over some run-down ponies. Eventually the price was settled, the pack-horses, such as they were, loaded, the riding mounts, mounted and then we headed west.

We set off with our faces into a rain so cold it cut. With our hoods over our heads and our hands busy trying to urge on these miserable beasts I had no chance to get to know my companions. While making camp as darkness fell, I noticed a man, just another shapeless mass in cloak and hood, who seemed to be riding a finer horse than most, keeping a little distant from the crew. As the men bedded down, he'd sidled in among the packhorses and laid himself down between them and the pickets. I was tired, I did not know these men well so feared to look a fool if I were to raise the alarm for nothing. I bedded down too. No-one even bothered to try and light a fire. These were men who could sleep at sea, awake and raid, fight and row away, to sleep at sea again. Soon they were all snoring apart from the pickets.

I was restless, Sib could sense it so he was restless too. He fidgeted, I fidgeted, it was no good, I had to know who that man was. Moving in a low crouch I slunk around the camp followed by Sib who moved as silently as a ghost. He was a fine dog, whoever had trained him knew what he was doing. Even as we moved around the horses, they barely snickered, aware of us but not startled, they turned a little with wary eyes but saw us as no threat. I'd left my targe and spears where I'd been trying to sleep. I pulled my knife from my belt and almost crawled to where I'd last seen him. As I got close, I could see that he too, was struggling to sleep, or didn't want to. He was shifting about, peering around, clearly nervous.

I stopped, crouched low and watched him for a while, glad for the lack of a fire to reveal our eyes by their glow in the dark. I slunk forward. He might be nervous but he had no craft. I pounced and was upon him before he had time to react. With my knife to his throat and a large dog, teeth bared in a snarl standing over him, he gave up without a fight.

'Who are you?' I hissed in Welsh, by now I'd come to believe he was a Strathwealas here to infiltrate our camp.

In a way I wasn't so far from the truth. 'Don't hurt me, I'm not an enemy,' he answered clearly frightened and shaking like a leaf.

I knew the voice, 'Maelcolm,' I said, 'is it you?'

In a strangled voice he whispered that it was, 'Please don't give me away. Give me a chance to explain.'

'I think you'd better had,' I snarled at him.

'C-c-c-could you take your knife from my windpipe please, and that dog's breath is making me faint.'

I moved the knife away a tad and gestured to Sib to lie down. He did, but did not take his eyes off the young prince.

'I thought you were the Lord of Alba, King of the Scots, why in God's name are you here?'

We continued to speak in Welsh. 'They are all crazy men up here. How in hell am I to rule the Scots? They don't want me and I can't even understand what they're saying. As soon as Siward's troops leave I'm dead meat.'

'But what about the Strathwealas?'

'For the most part they don't give a shit, they just wanted MacBethad off their backs. As he's escaped, they're terrified he'll be back with an army to exact revenge. They'd hand me over quick as a fucking weasel.'

'But you've relatives here.'

'That's a mixed blessing, Sar.' Even as he spoke his eyes were darting fearfully in every direction. 'Under our system any of a man's male relatives can contest the throne. My cousins who rule Strathclyde,' he used the English word, 'fear that I might claim their throne.' 'And I'd be right to do that' he added fiercely, 'in my father's name. He then seemed to droop back into misery, 'Besides none of us can rule without Siward's backing and he is ill and grieving his son.'

I remembered Grim's words. Siward was not a young man.

Maelcolm went on, 'Osbeorn's death means his Earldom will change hands if Siward dies. Waltheof is too young to inherit.'

'But King Edward will back you.'

'I've just been sent up here to stir the pot,' he answered sadly, 'I'm a piece to be sacrificed to justify his next move.'

'So, why would he do that?'

'I don't really know Sar. You know there's another Maelcolm at his court. There's always another Maelcolm to throw into the mix of English intrigues in the north.'

'You make no sense.' I said impatiently, while trying to decide what I was to do about him.

'No, I do, I do. There's another Maelcolm, a real prince of Alba, son of the man MacBethad usurped.'

I was dumfounded now, so what had we been fighting for?

I said it out loud, 'So what were we fighting for?'

Maelcolm looked at me, 'You don't really understand much, do you?'

'I know enough to know that Kings and Earls are always up to some trickery.' I thought for a bit, 'Bishops too maybe, and thegns perhaps, even merchants and tavern owners. Yeah, everyone is out to get someone or trying to stop someone getting to them.'

'Not so simple then. King Edward and the northern Earls can't take and keep Alba and the other Scottish kingdoms like Strathclyde but they can keep them weak enough to keep them off of England's back.'

I began to understand, 'By keeping them fighting each other they won't be fighting the English.'

'You have it, but MacBethad, maybe, could have united the north of Britain so he had to be stopped.'

'And by making you Lord of Alba he made sure the squabbling would continue.'

Maelcolm nodded, 'If MacBethad had died then brother would have fought brother and cousin, cousin. All the royal families are mixed up through marriage, alliances and blood-feuds. It's like a boiling pot and I was thrown in to make it bubble over.' He looked up, 'MacBethad is weakened but not beaten, so now Edward will need a puppet king to unite enough Scots against MacBethad.'

'And then what?'

'Who knows, either way a lot of warriors up here will have died and a lot of wealth been wasted. Edward is shrewd and with your Earl Harold and his brother Tostig he is well advised. Me. I think the Lady Gytha works behind the scenes.'

'Gytha, what do you mean,'

'Well, Sar, who do you think is the brains behind the Godwinsons?'

I'd never thought about it but now he said it I could see the truth in that. I'd met Gytha, By Saint Botwulf she frightened me more than any man. I knew her power, she knew where my sister was and she used it to use me.

'She certainly keeps the peace in that family since Godwin died.' As I spoke, I felt disloyal and almost looked over my shoulder to see if anyone was listening.

'I think she was the mind behind his return. I spent years at King Edwards court. I can only speak Welsh because my servants came with me as a child. I was a hostage really. You learn to look and listen when your life depends on the whims of scheming Kings.' He paused, 'And I can see a threat coming from a mile away which is why I am here.'

'So, let me get this right. You are escaping from the Scots who don't want you through the country, Strathclyde, where half your relatives would rather see you dead?'

He looked miserable and blinked back tears, 'I had to try something. I have to get away.'

'I'll talk to Jokul in the morning,' I said, 'and we must get you out of those fine clothes and swap your horse for a nag. Or maybe you could join the slaves. We could shave your head and drag you along behind with the others.'

Jokul had about twenty young male slaves tied together to give him men to row and to sell in Ireland. I hated to see them, once proud warriors reduced to nothing. I supposed it was better than being dead but every time I saw them, I was reminded of my sister's fate and my failure to free her.

Maelcolm looked horrified.

'You'll need to hide yourself. You take after your father, don't you?'

'I've been told so. The baldness anyway, I don't remember ever seeing him.'

'The best way to hide a bald head is to shave it. That is if Jokul wouldn't just prefer to hand you over.'

Maelcolm started shaking again and weeping like a little child.

'Fucking hell, man, pull yourself together, you're not dead yet.'

He looked at me, still snivelling, 'I've got money, I can pay. Look,' he pulled out a large purse and tugged open the drawstring.

I looked in. It was full of coins, some of them gold. I'd never seen a gold coin but knew as soon as I did what they were. Now I did look over my shoulders, 'For Christ's sake put that away.'

I was pleased though. I knew Jokul and his kind. Wealth and reputation were what they cared about. To spirit away a Scottish prince and a bag of gold would make a fine story at a feast and his grudge against the Strathwealas wouldn't hurt.

Turned out I was right. Jokul took a lot of the money and did Maelcolm the favour of making him his personal slave. He also rode his horse. The rest of his money was given to me to look after. That I didn't mind. The poor bastard was stripped almost naked and had his head roughly shaved. Soon he was covered in mud and scratches and looked just like any of the other beaten men running along behind our trotting horses. He was so grateful to Jokul and me that I could barely look him in the eye.

It was on this journey that I began to try the ink on my hair. I learned that I had to make sure it was really dry before I could risk the rain or else I'd find black streaks running down to my chin. It stung if it got into any cuts but slowly my hair began to darken. I was teased a bit by some of the other men and realised I'd have to dye my eyebrows too. They didn't ask many questions though. I guessed more than a few of them were fugitives or outlaws themselves. As Jokul's friend they soon accepted me as one of them, and that also went for the dog.

On the last night of the trail Jokul made us travel through the night as fast as the slaves could run. We kept going through the next day leaving the Strathwealan horse dealers far behind us. We got to Cathures to find Jokul's three warships and two fat bellied knarrs, large cargo carrying ships, safely tied under guard at the quayside. Our goods and Maelcolm's horse went on the knarrs and the bussecarls onto the warships while Jokul sold all the other horses to a local dealer with no mention of his previous arrangement. As we were rowing away, we could see an almighty row breaking out between the men on the quay and the foam-streaked horsemen who had galloped in, just in time to see us leave.

Laughing heartily, we rowed steadily away, carried westward by the flow of the great river of the Clyde.

Chapter Twelve

It was a great river, but not great like the Temese, and it soon broadened out into the salt sea. On our right, as we were leaving, we passed a huge double-peaked rock hill with sheer sides topped with ruins and with a cluster of buildings huddled around its base.

'Dùn Breatainn, the Gaels call that, the fort of the British,' Jokul said from behind my shoulder as I gazed up at its massive bulk. 'It was once the capital of Strathclyde, the centre of the kingdom, now it marks the edge.'

'Tell me more,' I said, feeling that Jokul was wanting to be asked.

'My ancestors took that fortress and enslaved their ruling family including King Arthgal ap Dyfnwa. We left with two hundred ships full of English, Pictish and Strathwealan slaves. Since then, the rock has never been fortified again. They say it was a great fight following a siege.'

I looked at the rock, how could anyone fight their way up that? I was impressed and said so, then I thought. 'Pictish, what's that?' I said.

'Don't really know Sar, some forgotten tribe or people I suppose, that's just how the story's told.' He paused, thought for a while, 'They didn't eat fish.'

'What! Not eat fish, they're everywhere. Why would they not eat fish?'

Jokul shrugged, 'Don't know, that's what they say.'

A whole people gone, and all we know about them is that they didn't eat fish. I puzzled over that for a while. Then I asked, 'So, when did all this happen?'

'Oh, my grandfather's, grandfather's, grandfather's time. Now my father Thord, his father was Imar, named after one of the kings who took the rock. Imar's father was Ubba, I think who was the son of another Thord who left Ireland when we were forced out, or was he the one who went back when we fought our way back in. Now, his father was....' Jokul's voice faded away as I drifted off into the sounds of the sea birds and the rising swell as we moved further out from the land and into the fresh salt air of the ocean.

We didn't go far that first day. Jokul wanted to cross to Ireland with one long pull, even if the wind was against us. Which, he said, it usually was on the return journey. Our little fleet rested between the lee of a large wooded island next to a small one. Some of the men swung themselves over the side swearing that the sea water cured all ills while others stood back and cursed them for fools. I stripped and jumped into the chilly waters while Sib whined plaintively from the ship. I laughed and dived and felt free from all cares until the cold began to bite and I hurriedly scrambled back out, laughing and joking with the other wet souls.

I liked being at sea, I'd seen the fierce ship eating rocks of Pentwithstart, a boast that few could make, and I'd sailed the whole south coast of England with my Earl. Only a couple of years ago. It felt so much longer. A year already since the murder of my aunt, my little cousins and my friend. Murdered because of me. As the island's shadow crept across us with the setting sun the joy left me. I wrapped myself up in my cloak and slept uneasily, rocked by the swell.

I was shaken awake just before dawn. Jokul was in a hurry to leave so we broke our fast on scraps and set to the oars. It only took a few strokes and my back started to protest. To all our benefits they'd pillaged plenty of sheepskins which saved the inevitable sore arses for the unaccustomed oarsmen. Thankfully we did not have to row far. As we came past the end of the island Jokul called for the sail to be raised and unfurled. We had a favourable wind.

The sail billowed out. By some mastery of seamanship, I did not understand, we could sail half into the wind and still move forward with the great sails angled across our decks. We headed out into the open sea. As soon as we did the ship started lurching in all directions. Banging sounds came from beneath the hull. Sib was instantly sick and I soon followed. I found Maelcolm, now clean and well-dressed again, puking beside me over the gunwale.

'Saint's bones!' he said, 'if I'd known sailing would be like this I would have stayed on land.'

'It wasn't like this when I sailed before,' I spluttered back as my breakfast flew out of me.

I could hear Jokul laughing at our misery, 'This is the Irish sea boys, choppy waters for proper seamen.'

Trembling I sat up, I could see what he meant. Instead of the waves coming in swells all from one direction those around us seemed to be coming from all over.

'It's all the different ways the sea comes in and out. Tides from the south and the north-west. Winds messed about by the bits of land all around. Beats a boat up really hard, beats up people too,' Jokul continued grinning from ear to ear through his black beard.

I looked across at the spiralling masts of the other ships and puked again not at all comforted by Jokul's words. I took in Jokul's ship for the first time. A skeide, close to the water and cramped, a fast raiding ship that needed skilled management, but it was beautifully built out of oak. I stroked the close grain and saw how well it was caulked. Not a leak anywhere, heads on all the rivets I could see and each strake as close to its neighbour as any strake could be. I forgot my seasickness and looked up to find Jokul looking down at me.

'You see my fine ship? A real beauty she is. Heavy but "strong and fast and built to last" as my father would say. He launched her for this raid, *Irish Maiden*, he called her.' Jokul smiled sadly,

'I think he was dreaming of his younger days, maybe when my mother was still young,'

'Your ma's Irish.'

'Aye, and fierce with it, if she'd thought it was named after any other maiden, we'd have never left harbour. I'm dreading my homecoming and having to tell her of her husband's death,'

I didn't know what to say. I braced myself and stood up beside him. I put my hand on his shoulder and we travelled that way for a short while. I could see tears in his eyes. Then he coughed and went to man the steering oar.

I squatted back down, feeling better while Maelcolm retched miserably by my side. Sib seemed to be feeling better too. I put my arm over his shoulder and we looked out over the waves together. Suddenly seagulls were diving into the water just off to larboard, then all around us. Excited mayhem broke out on board. A few of the men were opening their chests and pulling out bundles of line. It was hard to move around in the ship with all the oars, shields, war spears, loot and the odd bow on board but in no time, men were throwing lines out as far as they could. I could see equal uproar on the other ships.

'Is it herring?'

'No, mackerel, I think.'

'You've caught me fucking ear, you bastard.'

'Never mind, you'll live.'

The bussecarls excited chatter mystified me until suddenly men were drawing their lines back out from the water along with gleaming mackerel, wildly thrashing, as they brought them on board.

With no room to move we had to grab them fast.

'Put your thumb in their mouths and bend them back, kills them quick,' someone yelled at me as two fish started jumping around in my lap. It did kill them, snapped their spines, but they still flapped around.

'Unhook them, you dimwit,' yelled a man further down the crowded ship, which was now rocking wildly.

Ah, I could see now that they had bone hooks in their mouths. I drew them out and saw that a feather had been tied with horse hair to each one. Astonished and delighted I passed the line carefully back down the ship. Then my fish started flapping again, slipping out of my hands as I tried to hold them down. All along the deck, fish were flapping among our tangled feet as the whole crew turned into a bunch of gleeful boys. The lines went out again and before long there were at least two fish to every man on board. Quickly they were gutted and their guts thrown leeward, caught in the air by the clamouring gulls.

After noon the wind dropped and the great sail was brought down. Now we had to earn our keep. I took an oar with one of Jokul's men. Sadb Hosvir. His first name means sweet, an Irish girl's name. His face is burned all down one side, one eye peers out from a twisted socket while the other side of his face is flawless. On the scarred side twisted ropes of skin draw his face into an eerie smile. Stand on his left and you see a handsome young Viking with flowing golden hair, from the right, a scarred horror. Hence the name.

'It won't be for long,' he grunted, 'we've made good time and are not far from Ireland.'

'Dyflin,' I asked surprised.

'Oh no, we'll have to row down the coast for a day or three.' He spat on the deck, 'Depends on the wind and the whims of Echmarach mac Ragnaill.'

'Who?'

'The Lord of the Isle of Mann.'

'Tell me more,' I grunted, breathing in hard as I pulled on the oar, something in me was still collecting knowledge to take back to Harold.

'You heard of the King of Leinster, Diarmait?'

I nodded, 'Yeah.' I had, I knew he'd helped Harold before his return to England and my humble life fell apart.

'Echmarach ruled Dyflin before King Diarmait fought him out, but he still rules Mann.'

'So?'

'So, Mann is an Island in the Irish Sea and he sends out ships to demand tribute from passing vessels.'

'Do we pay it?'

'Be better for all of us if they do not get to see what is in our ships. They don't risk losing warriors over a few bales of wool or strings of dried cod, but what we have is worth fighting for.'

'Let's hope they don't find us. The ocean is large and I've seen too many fine lives cut short at Dunsinnan.'

Sahb Hosvir, 'Me too, besides I have a child I've yet to meet waiting for me in Dyflin. If he and his mother survived the birth.'

'You've a wife?'

'I have,' he smiled tenderly. 'Aideen, she took the rage out of me and put the sweet back in Sahb Hosvir.'

I smiled back and, companions now, we leant into the oar.

We soon came close to land, a large wooded inlet where a river curled in around a large, long bar of sand. We drew the ships close to the bar, anchored in the shallow water. A number of us waded ashore carrying baskets of mackerel. A couple of our ships had been towing small rowing boats and these, with a couple of bussecarls in each, crossed the river mouth to the small settlement on the other side. They soon came back loaded with firewood and a small clay pot of glowing embers. Before long we were warming ourselves by a large fire. Then, to my surprise, the fire was demolished and the burning cinders drawn out into a long hollow in the sands. The mackerel were laid upon them by swift able hands. After a short while they were turned over and we queued up to scoop the now fragile fish onto the blades of our knives or seaxes. Some blowing and the cool evening air and we could pick off the delicious flesh with our fingers. Ale, poured generously into wooden cups, followed.

We exchanged stories, some tried riddles. I never got riddles, just couldn't get my head around them though more foolish men than I could get them straight away. Sod it, I thought, and, after scooping out a hollow in the sand for my hip, fell into a deep sleep, oblivious to the men carousing all around me.

I was woken by a man shaking my shoulder. Whispering he passed me a small horn and a long war spear. It was my turn on the picket. I sat looking over a quiet sea merely riffled by a light breeze which rocked our ships like cradles. A bright moon, nearly full, silvered the dark waters and a myriad of stars cloaked the cloudless sky. Wrapping my cloak tight around me I sat taking in all this beauty until the first grey light of dawn started to pinken in the east.

We set off when the tide reached about the same height it was when we arrived. Coming out of the river mouth we turned south. Jokul had the knarrs hugging the coastline with one of the warships on the seaward side. Our skeide and another like it sailed further out to sea keeping the rest of our ships' mastheads just in sight on the horizon.

As we weren't rowing, I joined Jokul at the prow, where Sib had taken to standing like a second head to the finely carved dragon post. He'd recovered from his sickness and, apart from stealing fish, which he ate whole, had endeared himself to the whole crew.

'Why're we hanging back like this,' I asked Jokul. 'Shouldn't we be protecting the cargoes?'

'Hmmm maybe, if Echmarach has patrols out they'll be one or two ships. If they see one fighting ship and two laden knarrs low in the water they'll be tempted to attack them,' he replied.

'But surely that's what we don't want?' I questioned, mystified.

'No, what we don't want is them signalling to other ships to come and join them. If they do, they will outnumber us.'

'They might signal anyway,' I objected. I didn't want to lose my money or fight on a ship where there's nowhere to run to.

'They might, but if I'm any judge of men they'll be ruled by greed and glory and they'll not want to share it,' Jokul grinned slyly and stroked his beard.

'Maybe they won't come at all,' I said, squatting down beside Sib, suddenly starting to feel queasy again.

They did. It was just before noon when we saw two sails to the south east of us. We saw them turn to bear down on our ships.

'They've chosen their spot well. There're no inlets for ships to hide in along this stretch of coast. There's no choice but to beach ships on the sand, fight or surrender,' Jokul shouted as he headed up to the stern to direct the steersman. I returned to my place, made sure my throwing spears and my targe were at hand and helped Sahb Hosvir ready the oar should we need it.

By now the sail was already belly full of wind and we were skating across the waves. Excited men checked their gear, loosening swords and knives in their sheaths. Three men strung bows then covered them to keep the spray off their strings. You could feel the urgency in the air. We had to catch up with our boats before the enemy ships could do much damage.

'If we're lucky they'll be too busy to see us coming,' said Hosvir.

'Why aren't we rowing?' I asked.

'We're sailing too fast, wouldn't help, but we might need them when we close.'

As it turned out, we didn't. We arrived in time to find our fighting ship being attacked on both sides. Arrows and spears were flying between the three ships. There was no sign that we'd been seen. One of their ships was fully alongside ours. The other had lined up its prow with the stern. I could see men lifting oars ready to throw them across to make a bridge and attack while most of the crew were occupied fighting on the other side. Their ships were designed for fighting at sea, busses, with higher sides and a deeper draught. They also carried larger crews.

'What has Jokul got us into,' I thought, but I could see the true meaning of bussecarls now. These men were well prepared to fight at sea, every man had a throwing spear and short sturdy swords, seaxes or short-handled axes for close fighting

'As soon as we get near, lose your shield Sar,' said Hosvir. 'Remember, everything is moving. You need a spare hand. Keep your knees bent and loose, they'll keep you balanced.'

We were barely a bowshot away when the first of the enemy saw us. They could be seen frantically trying to get their mates to see the threat as we bore down on them. Our companion slid between our ship and one of theirs while we also drew up along their outer side. Our sail was coming down as our bowmen let off a few arrows into the rearmost of their crew. The rest of us stood and, as we passed by, threw a volley of spears into the packed bodies on the enemy ship.

What next? I thought, as now they were behind us.

'Oars!' yelled Jokul, 'Oars.'

Next moment we're all sat down with our oars out heaving upon them with all our might. We turned, our ship bucking and protesting as we lay across the wind. I looked up to see their other ship breaking away from the fight and heading straight for our side.

It was a strange fight, everyone was cursing and yelling but the wind took the sounds away and all I could see were the gaping mouths of fierce, frightened, angry men. Then, somehow, we turned, shipped our oars and threw another volley of spears into their second ship. By good fortune, or an archer's skill, one of our arrows struck their steersman and they lost control. The ship veered wildly to starboard and their sail smacked into the mast bringing them up short in a chaos of struggling men and rigging. We again took to rowing. Our two other fighting ships, now each side of their remaining ship slid by us, carried on by the wind we were now rowing against. We wrenched our ship around again, every muscle screaming with the effort, to find them some distance away. The first of our ships to be attacked now peeled away, their exhausted crew, chests heaving, slumped to the deck. For now, they were out of the fight.

Once again, we rowed furiously to get back to the fight. My chest hurt with the effort and my arms felt ready to drop off. Then, again, we shipped our oars. We had reached the stern of their ship and grapnels flew out and we hauled our ship up to their gunwales. Now it was their turn to be attacked from both sides. Once we were tied, we queued up to board. My heart pounded and my mouth went dry, all the weariness left my body as I prepared to fight. Our men went over, climbing and fighting for a foothold on their ship. Somehow, we got one and then it was my turn to board. I took a deep breath and that icy calm I'd thought I'd lost came upon me. There seemed to be plenty of time for everything. I put my left hand out and grabbed the rail of their ship, a foot and a half higher than ours and pulled myself over. The boat beneath my feet fell away and I was dangling in the air. Then the sea moved again and the planks were pushing my knees to my chin. I pushed off hard and found that I was on the enemy ship. I rolled as an axe thudded into the deck not far from my head. I rolled again to see Hosvir's fist crushing into a man's skull. The axe had stayed in the deck so I tugged it out with my left hand and swung it into the man's face. He fell dead on the spot. Hosvir was laughing, stabbing with his seax while punching out with his other fist.

I got up beside him, half crouched to cope with the rise and fall of the deck. I too fought two handed. Fielding blows with the axe and hacking out with my seax. Then the ship gave a mighty lurch and I had to drop the axe and grab the nearest solid object. Then I was fighting on my knees, stabbing upwards until I could drag myself to my feet on a thwart. I realised the ship was constructed differently to ours. Only needing to sail for a day they had no chests for the crew to row from but benches that ran from side to side across the ship. As we broke from the stern, I managed to climb up on one and hack down on oncoming heads and arms as they tried to force us back off their ship. I sliced deeply into a man's forearm seeing his look of dismay as his hand refused to obey him and dropped his weapon. I kicked him in the face then almost fell. I'd forgotten about the moving sea beneath us. Hosvir pushed me back up. Then in one of those strange moments of calm I could see Maelcolm screaming wordlessly as he furiously stabbed and hacked liked a berserker with no will to live. Then at that moment, our men from our other two ships joined the fight. Once the Manxmen realised they were being attacked from all directions they gave up the fight, dropping their weapons. A couple more were killed before we understood that they'd surrendered. Then the fighting stopped.

We looked towards their other ship but it was sailing away. They knew they were beaten and had clearly decided to cut their losses. Jokul did not give chase. He was only a few years older than I but you could see the respect his men had for him. Now he stood tall, blood dripping from an axe in his hand, every inch the man his father had been. He'd led his men and managed his ships in a difficult fight and they had won. Not only had they won but they had captives and the greatest prize of all, a fine ship Echmarach didn't control any more.

We stripped the captives, taking anything that could be used. The badly wounded were cast overboard. I saw the man, whose forearm I had cut to the bone, thrown over. Somehow, he kept afloat, paddling in a circle. I had visions of him floundering in the sea as our sails dwindled into the distance. I took an oar and pushed him under.

The rest we tied to the thwarts and their hands to the oars. They looked resigned to their defeat. I asked Jokul about this and he said that, due to all the complicated family ties around the Irish Sea, these captives would be well treated and swapped or ransomed. They'd not be sent to the slave pens that made Dyflin so famous.

Chapter Thirteen

We reached Dyflin before sunset, the wind had favoured us which meant we could take care of our wounded and lay out the dead. As we approached ships came out to meet us from a couple of small quays on the coast. I could see a wooden wall behind them but not the large town I'd expected though it gave out a lot of smoke. Once we'd been given the once over to make certain that we were friendly, sails now down, we rowed past the quays to a river mouth. A large ship, mast-less but heavily manned was moored across it. We paused as huge tarred ropes hauled it to one side allowing us passage. We rowed in and, to my amazement, the river broadened out into a great lake.

'We call that 'The Pool', said Hosvir, his pride in his home town clearly written on the unscarred side of his face.

'Look at all those quays!' I said, excitedly, 'and all the shipping.' I'd not seen anything like this since I'd left Lundenburh. This was a wonderful natural harbour, easily defendable from the sea. The town was walled and the walls looked in good repair. It stank, of course, like all towns, but I knew after a few days I wouldn't notice it. We anchored in 'The Pool' and settled down for our last night under the stars.

Just as well too. We woke up to a hard, sleety rain borne on a chilling east wind. Winter had begun. We were given access to a quay and we began to unload, one ship at a time. Jokul's family had the use of a small barn near the dock into which we ferried all the loot to be divided. The slaves were penned into one end, they too had been tied to oars in the knarrs but for the whole journey, and like many of us, sported huge raw patches where blisters had burst. This took all day. Most of us were chatting happily as friends, wives and children turned up to greet them and they faced the prospect of going to their own homes. There were tears, laments and bouts of fierce keening as people turned up to find their husbands, sons or fathers had died or returned maimed and would fight no more.

As we had no homes to go to, Maelcolm and I slept in the barn alongside a few other men left as guards. We could have no fire because of the hay stored alongside our goods, besides we had no food to cook. Jokul couldn't think of everything and had been keen to get home. I persuaded Maelcolm that it would be a good idea to treat everyone so he gave me a silver penny, barely worn, from the money I had returned to him. One of the guards came with me and I ventured out into the town. It was crowded with narrow streets and like Jorvik, had houses built end on to them. The houses, though well built, were walled with wattled and daub. I guessed large trees were not so easy to get here. Everywhere there were busy workshops, with whole families doing what work they could by light of fires and the dying sun. Taverns on every corner and bothies selling food blocked the road wherever they could find a space. We soon found one, managed by a limping man, a young boy and a bright young woman who we could persuade to earn our penny. We moved them, their cauldron and all their goods to a tight space outside our barn. It wasn't long before they were cooking up a stew of roots, leeks, dried peas, a pig's head and trotters all flavoured with sage. It was a good time of year for food. We emptied our bowls like gluttons, then another man went out and came back with cheese, bread and to my delight, a barrel of beor, a drink made from fermented hedge fruits, my absolute favourite. Our cooks joined us and we made merry. I felt sorry for the newly created slaves at the back of the barn, and for a small trinket persuaded the boy to get me two buckets of water, which arrived back surprisingly full considering the crowds.

Despite the scoffing of my companions, I held each captive up, their hands were tied and their feet clamped at the ankles between the two bottom rungs of the pen, gave them each a cup of water and fed them a small bowl each of all the breadcrumbs and cheese crusts stirred into the dregs of the stew. I was still uncomfortable around slaves because of my guilt about my sister's fate.

Our cooks left, dragging their belongings on a small sledge that cut through the muddy streets and the slimy planked walkways better than any wheeled cart. They were happy, so were we, and we all slept well that night.

On the next day there was the division of the spoils. So much wealth had been taken from the Scots that all of Jokul's men were made rich that day. I sat there hoping that someone had reserved my share of the spoils back home. I knew though, that they would not be shared nearly so equally as those here. Even so, Jokul, as the main leader and having the largest share of the ships came away a truly wealthy man. For my part in the sea fight I gained a sword, with belt and scabbard, and a set of clothes slightly less bloodstained than those I was wearing and a good strong leather sack to carry them in.

Maelcolm and I spent the evening at Jokul's home. I don't know what I'd expected but this town, apart from the King's compound, had no great halls or longhouses. Jokul's home was just a very fine house of a regular size, thought it stretched a fair way back from its street frontage. Inside it was lined with wall hangings and trophy weapons but otherwise was just a comfortable well-stocked home. When I walked out the back to use the privy, I passed a milch cow in a shed, a grain store and a pit filled with sealed crocks. In the roof of their house hung sides of bacon, dried fish and salted cheeses. From the abundance of foodstuffs and the stores in their barn I guessed that somewhere they owned, or had arrangements with, farms outside of the town.

We sat down to eat. As soon the food appeared Sib and Jokul's two dogs started growling and squabbling. I put Sib's leash on and held him by my side. I could see that Jokul's mother, whose head was buried under a shawl of mourning, was not happy. Maelcolm, I and especially my dog, had interrupted the mixed joy and grief of her son returning and learning of the death of her husband. By the behaviour of the other adults and children in the house it was clear she ruled with a firm hand. The food was plentiful but the meal was polite, joyless and it became clear to me that, if I was looking for somewhere to stay in Dyflin, Jokul's home was not it.

We asked Jokul's permission to stay in the barn until we could find lodgings. He agreed and Maelcolm and I walked silently back with the reality of our rushed decisions sinking in. The next morning we took stock.

'What are we going to do Sar?,' asked Maelcolm timidly, who seemed lower and more miserable than ever.

'What do you mean, we?' I retorted, irritated because I had no idea.

'You and me, I mean, here we are in the same boat so speak,' for some reason he'd answered me in Welsh.

'We're not in the same boat,' I answered, also in Welsh. I guessed he was using it to show we had things in common. 'You have a pouch full of coins, your fine clothes and shoes while I have my weapons, a sword I don't need and two sets of overworn clothes. How the fuck are we the same?

He flushed, bright red, right up to his bald head. 'Oh, I'm so sorry, I hadn't even thought. Here you have half of what I've got.' With that he pulls out his pouch and starts pouring coins into the trampled straw of the barn floor.

'Saint Diw, put that away, don't ever let anyone see how much money you have. Do you want to get your throat slit and your body slid into a cess pool? By Botwulf you're a liability not a companion,' I was angry and almost missed the point that he was giving me more money than I'd ever seen.

His eyes filled with tears and with shaking hands he covered his face.

'What's with you Maelcolm, only a couple of days ago you were fighting like a demon.'

'Only 'cos I didn't care. Sar, I've messed things up, I've run away from the only challenge of my life. I've never even had to really think for myself, I've been a hostage since childhood. I was a boy in Queen Emma's court before Edward even came to the throne.'

I sat back on my heels and thought. We probably were better trying to stay together and he could fight. I'd seen him, he'd clearly been trained.

'Alright, look, you've got to sort yourself out a bit. Like you giving so much money, your horse and your weapons to Jokul.'

'I needed him to take me.'

'But you didn't even try to bargain. You can't just do that.'

Maelcolm nodded miserably.

I tried again, 'So, what would you give me for this sword. I clearly value it highly and don't need to sell it.'

'I'll give you half my money like I said,' he replied.

I felt defeated, 'Look you know I don't really care about this sword. I'm fully armed and don't have anywhere to keep it. It's just the stuff you say to get more money.'

'Oh, you want more?' he said, pushing his pouch towards me.

'Oh, I give up. I want you to bargain me down to something near what it's worth. Or the least I will take to sell it. Same thing really. My job is knowing that you don't have one is to get you to pay the most you'll pay for it, see?'

Maelcolm was looking so confused that I burst out laughing. I helped myself to a few of his coins, more than the sword was worth and said, 'Right, we'll stay together but you make no bargains and when I do you watch my back and when it counts, I'll watch yours.'

With so much plunder in the town, food and lodgings got expensive while clothes and weapons fell in price. I bought myself a couple more fine throwing spears and some humble clothes for Maelcolm to wear. We hid our spare belongings deep in the hay of the barn but with the nights getting cold we needed a home with a fire and a safe place for our belongings. We hung around the town all day occasionally getting fed at the homes of Jokul's men who we knew. Sabh Hosvir offered us a place by his hearth but it was clear that his young family didn't really have the room for us. I was facing other problems too. I was running out of the ink I was dying my hair and more and more beard with. In the coping with the day-to-day life, I was beginning to forget why I was here. Then one day we were hanging around, drinking, outside a tavern when Sib started tugging on his leash and growling.

'This dog for sale? I could pay you well.'

It was a voice I knew all too well. The voice of my greatest enemy, Oslaf.

Luckily it had been drizzling so I had my head covered by my hood. I muttered that it was not for sale with a strong Irish accent. I looked at his feet, there were other well shod feet around him. He wasn't alone. I couldn't kill him here anyway. Not and survive.

'You don't look like a rich man that you could turn down a good offer,' he said, trying to stroke Sib's head. Sib was growling menacingly and I knew from experience what might happen next.

'Leave him be,' I said, 'else he'll bite you.'

He stepped back and I risked looking up hoping that my beard was black enough and my face shadowed. I found myself looking into his eerily pale, cold blue eyes. He had that humourless smirk on his face that I loathed. I quickly shifted my gaze as I saw a flicker of recognition in his.

'Have we met before?' he asked.

'Huh, can't be,' I growled, turning back to my drink, 'Dog's not for sale, alright.'

'Hmmm, well maybe not, but I'll know that dog if I see him again. If you change your mind…'

'Come away man,' said one of his companions in English, 'he's just an Irish savage. The dog looks vicious to me anyway.'

They turned and walked away.

I let go my breath and spat out the bile in my mouth. I turned to my drink to see Maelcolm staring at me. I'd forgotten he was there.

'What was that about?' he asked me.

I looked at him thoughtfully, at least he'd had the sense to keep his mouth shut. Then I swallowed the last of my ale for the little warmth it gave.

'Let's see if there's room inside.'

We went in, the place had emptied out as dusk fell, only the lodgers and the hardened drinkers still huddled round a fire. I used a cut half penny for another jug, some bread, a platter of cold mutton, cheese and a few good apples and walked to a table in the corner. I wasn't in the mood to argue.

'I need to tell you something, Maelcolm, but you have to keep it to yourself,' I said in Welsh.

He nodded, his eyes wide. I decided to take that risk so as we shared our meal, him, the dog and I, I told him my story. I told him about how I had killed Oslaf's father. How Osalf had almost killed me. How Morwed saved my life and why. I told him how I became Earl Harold's man and why he also wanted Oslaf's head. And, after a long pause I told him how Oslaf's mother, Katla, had taken revenge, killing my aunt Ealhild, her children and retainers and my mentor, Toki. Holding back my tears I told him how, Grim, Gyric and I had sought vengeance, and with the help of mercenaries, had killed Katla, burned down her hall and how I had killed Osric. The only thing I didn't tell him was how, or why, I'd let Oslaf's young son, Eardmund live. I was still puzzling over that myself.

Maelcolm listened silently, letting me speak, with neither sobs or silly jokes. I was so full of feelings that all I could do was stare at the table while Sib whimpered and thrust his great head into my lap.

'We need to get out of town, Sar. No-one is going anywhere until the winter passes, you can get on his track before the spring.'

He was right. We ducked out of the tavern to find it was now pitch-black outside. The town gates would all be shut by now so for tonight our only choice was to go back to our draughty barn.

The next morning we made the decision that we were not going back to the barn. I knew the most sensible thing I could do was get rid of the dog. I wasn't willing to do that. We gathered all our belongings and at first light headed towards Jokul's home. I trusted Jokul more than any other man other than Gyric. I was sure that our boyish blood brothering meant as much to him as it did to me.

The only thing that worried me was his mother.

I knocked on his door, the days being short I knew people would be stirring. A young slave girl opened it. I was reminded of Ymma, it was clear she'd been up re-kindling the fire and preparing food. We told her who we were and she disappeared back inside to return a moment later and beckon us in. We sat by the central hearth warming our chilled selves while the girl put a pot of broth over the flames.

Once it had boiled, she broke crusts into two bowls and gesturing at some spoons handed them over to us. She then took two more bowls, filled them and left the room. As she left Jokul's mother came in. Her embroidered shawl was over her head but not her face and a vivid green silk cap covered her hairline.

I was better prepared for her this time and in my limited Irish I bid her good morning in her own tongue.

She nodded. 'Jokul's not here,' she said, seating herself across the hearth from us. 'What do you want from him?'

'Advice, mainly,' I answered, putting my bowl aside.

'Mainly?'

'Somewhere to leave some belongings, money even,' Maelcolm put in.

Her eyes swivelled to his and back to mine.

'Your friend, if that is what he is, is too quick to trust,' she answered exactly echoing my own thoughts, 'and what advice?'

I hesitated; it was Jokul I wanted to talk to.

'You're wondering whether you can trust me, Sar, is that not the case? Why would you? Why should I trust you? My husband had to stop you dropping a rock on my son's head.

You think that recommends you to me?' she continued.

'Lady Etromma, I,' I tried to speak.

'You do actually know my name then? You never used it the other night when you dined at my table.'

'Lady..'

'We have no ladies here,' she interrupted me again.

I was confused and became tongue tied.

Suddenly she laughed, 'You're easy you are, still not much more than a boy. Had you right on the spot,' she chuckled some more. 'Don't worry yourself Sar, I was shocked the other night and did not make you welcome. I know my son, my only son, rates you highly, though you are clearly a bit shifty. What is it that you need?'

'We need to get out of Dyflin, we need somewhere to stay, he,' I said, nodding at Maelcolm, 'does need to hide some money. I had decided to trust her. 'Horses would be good too,' I added as an afterthought.

'Horses you can forget. The rest I could help with,' Etromma answered. 'My family has land a day's ride from here. We will let you hide there.'

'Thank you,' I answered humbly, grateful for the chance of shelter for the winter.

'I carry much coin, and fear to take it on the road,' said Maelcolm.

Etromma smiled, 'I will always take your coins Maelcolm.'

Maelcolm was taken aback, 'I m..mm…mean just to look after.'

'She knows what you mean, Maelcolm,' I said, 'now give me your purse.'

I opened the purse, still shocked by its weight and size. 'I will trust you Etromma, because you are Jokul's mother.'

'And you have no choice.'

I looked her straight in the eye, 'We have no choice, but remember we know where you live.'

She hissed and drew back sharply, 'are you threatening me?'

'No,' I said, 'it's just that we'll need to know where to find you when we return.'

She chuckled again, her humour was a little dark.

'But,' I said loudly, 'we would not dream of asking you to do this for nothing.'

I drew out two of the gold coins from Maelcolm's purse and passed one to her. 'This is for our winter's keep and this one is for when we collect our belongings,' I said putting it inside a small pouch I carried on a thong around my neck.

With that she went off and came back with a quill, a small piece of parchment and a pot of ink.

'Come to the table and count your money out,' she said, and I will give you a parchment to show I have it,'

'You can write,' I said surprised. I was expecting a tally stick.

'Many of the Irish can do our letters Sar, we are a learned people.'

'And you can read?' I said to Maelcolm.

'I grew up in a royal court, of course I can read,' he answered

'And write?'

'No, a noble man has people to do that for him.'

I turned to Etromma, 'You can see why we need your silence because it's so hard for him to keep his.'

They did an accounting, wrote it down and then signed their names. Now it was my turn to surprise them and I scratched my shaky signature, Sar Nomansson.

Then Etromma took a knife and cut the paper jaggedly in half, right through the signatures. She kept one and handed the other to Maelcolm.

'I'll have that,' I said and grabbed it from him and stuffed that into my little pouch too.

Chapter Fourteen

We left Etromma's with a net full of bread and cheese, a pot of ink and directions to a small settlement around the church of Saint Mo-Lua to the east of the town. It wasn't far. We'd need to stay the night then a boy would find us at the church in the morning and take us to a place from which we could get good directions.

As we passed out through the east gate beyond the market Maelcolm who'd been obviously brooding spoke out. 'Talking about bad bargains, you just gave that woman gold for doing practically nothing.'

'No, we were asking a lot.'

'You don't even know if we can trust her.'

'She's Jokul's mother and I trust him.'

'Jokul doesn't even know what we've given her.'

Truth was, this fact had been dawning on me. Somehow, she had allayed my normal suspiciousness of everyone. I decided to keep this thought to myself.

'So, he'll know when we get back won't he?' I snapped back.

'If we get back.'

'So what. If we don't get back it won't matter anyway.'

We trudged on through a chilly wind and rain so fine it soaked you through before you noticed you were getting wet. Our felted cloaks got heavier with every step.

When we got to the church, we found a foul-smelling bunch of houses clustered around a shambles. Bellowing cattle, bleating sheep and squealing pigs told us it probably supplied the whole of Dyflin.

'This place feels dangerous,' I said to Maelcolm, 'be on your guard.'

Slaughtering places breed rough, brutal men but when trouble came it came in the form of a thieving boy. We'd slopped our way through the central street to behind the church seeking the priest's house when I felt a slight tug on the small satchel I had hanging off my belt. I whirled round to see a stripling boy with ragged black hair running away from me. I shouted, Maelcolm spread his arms out to block the thief. He quickly drew back yelling. The thief had cut him. I pushed my cloak back took one of my spears and threw it after the dodging and weaving boy. It grazed off his ribs and stuck into the mud, quivering. Then another boy threw himself in the path of the fleeing thief and brought him to the ground. I rushed up, dropped my other spear, grabbed his curly black hair, put my knife to his throat. I had him, or so I thought. He squirmed round, leaving some of his hair in my clenched fist, and swiped his knife across my face. I pulled my head back. The blade missed my nose by a hair's breadth. He was up on his feet. I lashed out with my right leg, falling over. He was back on the ground. I scrabbled towards him. For a moment we were face to face. Christ, he was young, not even fluff on his beardless chin. I saw his dark eyes flicker and without thinking threw up my arm grabbing his knife hand at the wrist. He did a sideways jump, skip and twisted out from my grip. I thought I was fast but this lad was like lightning. Back on his feet again he turned to run. I lurched forward and seized his ankle. He fell. We were both now, faces down in the muddy street. Then Sib leapt upon the boy, his jaws closing around the back of the thief's neck. He dropped his knife. All fight was gone.

'Give me one good reason I shouldn't kill you now,' I shouted.

'I can give you your little bag back,' he answered in halting Norse.

Which reminded me, I'd dropped my bag up the road but Maelcolm was learning fast and had already picked it up along with my other spear.

'Don't kill him,' came a new voice.

I looked up to see the young lad whose family had fed us on the first night.

'So, it was you who stopped him?'

He nodded shyly.

'You don't want me to kill him?'

'No.'

'His knife for his life,' I said, giving him the thief's knife.

He grinned and thanked me.

'Can you get me some rope?' I asked,

He nodded and ran away to come back with a couple of lengths of rope made of twisted rawhide. A perk of the butchering trade I guessed. He gave it me and I tied the thief's hands behind his back then made a loop around his neck. As I did so I saw the scars of a slave ring on his collar bones and under his chin. Now I had him on a lead.

I turned to the second boy, who had straight raggedly blond hair and the gap-toothed smile of a child who was still waiting for all his second teeth, and asked him about places to stay and where you would take a thief.

'Back to Dyflin,' he answered, the thief visibly flinched. He was definitely an escaped slave.

'As for somewhere to stay, I could take you to our house.' The boy continued.

'Your name, lad?' asked Maelcolm in Norse of sorts.

'Lochlainn,' he answered, proudly, the name means Viking to the Irish.

'Fair enough mighty warrior,' I said, 'lead on.'

I'm not sure his parents were that pleased to see us, certainly not at first. Two armed men with a large dog and a boy on a lead. Inside their very small house were six children going down in size from Lochlainn to a baby.

My satchel, covered in mud with its straps severed, still held my purse. I fished out a half penny and held it in the firelight.

'Food and shelter for the night?' I asked. 'And a salve for my friends wound.'

The woman's face lit up cheerfully nodding. I could see their poverty meant a hard winter ahead.

'Double it. Firewood is scarce,' came a surly growl from the father who had hung back in the shadows.

'Keep it burning all night and I will.' I was covered in mud, wet through and too grateful to be indoors to haggle so I gave him a penny. I saw Maelcolm's sharp glance, what with my deal with Etromma and now this, his doubts must be growing. I couldn't care less right now.

Their pot was back on the hearth. The man stooped out the door and shortly came back with some washed cow guts and a chunk of tripe. The woman threw in barley, carrots, water and a bunch of herbs on top of whatever was already in the pot. The umbles were chopped up, the tripe diced and soon a fine thick stew was bubbling.

Maelcolm looked askance at this humble meal as it was dolloped onto his platter without salt or bread but the rest of us wolfed it down. He soon came around to finding this peasant food was not so bad. Hunger, is the best sauce. Before long the pot was on its side with the children scooping out the last remnants.

After I fed him, I put the runaway between me and the dog for the night. With all the bodies and the steaming wet clothes, the night was spent in a thick warm fug that reminded me of winter nights when I was a boy. All it missed was the smell of goats to make it complete.

We awoke to the sound of a screaming baby and Sib growling at the more adventurous children. He seemed alright around them, just pushing them away with his big head or mouthing them in gentle threat. They giggled and drew back but by the time three of them were plaguing him I could see he was getting uneasy. Fearing he would bite one, I decided to get up. Maelcolm was still snoring but the runaway slave boy's eyes were wide open gazing attentively around.

I wondered if I should just let him go but I knew his life would be bleak, and probably short, if he was to go on as he was. He seemed bright, quick but could I ever trust him? I needed to piss. I shooed the kids away from the dog, pulled on the boy's lead and taking a spear headed out to the edge of the small settlement. I pissed, then untied the boy's hands and turned my back so he could do the needful. After I smelt his shit, I turned to find him hurriedly pulling up his britches.

I tied his hands in front of him this time and, seeing the deep marks on his wrists, not so hard.

'I'm not going to hurt you, and I'm not going to take you back to Dyflin,' I said, 'but I'm not sure what use you are to me.'

He grunted, his eyes not meeting mine. I sensed he was warily relieved. I'd have been wary too. I might just be disarming him before I slit his throat.

By now Maelcolm was up and about. Sib had slipped away and returned with some offal hanging from his jaws which he threw into the air, caught, and quickly swallowed. Even if he was found stealing few men would risk taking food from his mouth. I told Maelcolm that I'd decided to take the boy with us. There was a mist rising from the wet ground as we left with Lochlainn guiding us to the priest's house, or I should say, hovel. He was a miserable bastard but he agreed to us staying in his little church until Etromma's messenger came to find us.

We shared a meagre breakfast from the supplies Etromma gave us, keeping some back for the road ahead and waited. And waited. Maelcolm and the boy chatted quietly while I tried to rest getting increasingly worried that Etromma had let us down and possibly intended to steal our money. Or at least, hope we never came back to collect it. On the other hand, I believed her about a farm or farms outside of town because of how well set up they were. When the priest next came in to chant to his empty church, I questioned him.

Etromma did have farms to the East of here. He'd seen her passing by and knew her men sold stock to the butchers here. I asked him where the farm was.

'To the East of here, only one road goes that way, well used, can't miss it.' He put his hand out, 'Support a poor priest to care for his flock?'

I pretended not to see the outstretched palm. I saw no sign that he cared for his flock, and the empty, barren, look of his church told me his flock did not care for him.

I thanked him and turning to the others told them we were leaving. I found that Maelcolm had taken the rope from around the boy's neck and untied his hands. 'He says he's called Bruni and he won't run. He'd like to stay with us. He'll do anything you want.'

I looked closely at the boy for the first time. Bruni, he was brown, his skin was brown. I rubbed his face with the wet corner of my cloth. It stayed brown. Strange.

'Where you from then Bruni?'

He said, in what clearly was a language I'd never heard before, 'Al Qayrawan.'

'Huh? Where's that?'

'Hot place, south, by the sea.'

I remembered how Harold had dealt with me and earned my loyalty.

'You on your own?' I asked.

He nodded.

'You serve me well and I'll teach you how to fight. Would that work for you? You're quick but slight, there's ways you can learn.'

'Like you,' he answered, with a strange smile that seemed to hide something I could not fathom.

He said it as a statement, not a question. I nodded, 'So, you'll serve me then.'

I shrugged and we walked outside to find that the mist had thickened. The only road went either to Dyflin or the other way, that must be East. We gave the boy some spare clothes from our pack and headed away from this miserable little village. We walked for a long time as the mist thickened into a thick fog, chilling us to the bone. We stayed on the widest track but by now none of us knew the direction we were heading. We crossed a bridge and waded a ford. It felt better to move than to stop so we kept on walking. If Etromma's farm was on this road we had probably passed it unseen and unseeing.

Darkness came early and we were stumbling along each clinging with one hand to the rope we'd used to tie Bruni for fear of losing each other. We blundered on in the hope that there would be some building by the road itself. The ground began to rise and we realised we were among trees. What we'd thought was the road was now a thin track pocked with the hoofprints of pack ponies and small cattle. Everything was dripping, we were soaked through and large drops plummeting off the boughs overhead added to our misery. There was no chance of making a fire. We were all wearily dragging our feet when the fog whitened. We guessed that a big moon was rising above the mist. We decided to head uphill.

The trees began to thin, get shorter, until after passing through a fringe of birch and hawthorn we came out of the woods and above the fog. For a moment our weariness left us. From above the fog looked like a vast silver sea, lit up by the great, full, moon from which the hilltops arose like islands. A huge belt of shining stars swept across the crystal-clear sky. We gazed upwards, awestruck, then we found a hollow in a bank above a small stream and, shivering, we huddled together. I felt confused, unsure, my heart seemed to be beating slower and slower. As tiredness overwhelmed me my last thoughts were would we freeze to death tonight? Had I lead my small company to die in the hills, to be eaten as carrion?

Chapter Fifteen

Shooting pains scorching through my hands and feet brought me suddenly awake from a dream where I was being swept along in the air. I knew instantly that I was not still on the mountain side. I felt for my weapons, not only did I not have them, I was also naked. I was well wrapped in beaver pelts with a heavy cow hide draped over the top so no one wanted me dead. I took a slow breath and drifted back into darkness.

When I next awoke a young woman, who looked vaguely familiar, was putting a cup of herb smelling tea to my lips. I tried to grasp the cup myself but my hands wouldn't grip.

She smiled at me, 'Don't try, you're lucky to have only lost a fingertip.'

My left hand was sore and she was right, my little finger tip was gone. From the top joint there was nothing there but a twist of skin with a thread tied round it.

I drank the liquid, what else was there to do? The young woman moved away. I could see Maelcolm sitting up not far from me but when I tried to call out no sound came. Then the space was filled by another woman, older, small but wiry but with brown skin and blue eyes. Her face was kindly but stern. She spoke to me in Irish but strangely accented and slowly, like when you have to translate in your head as you go. I was fine with that. My Irish wasn't too clever either.

'You are in a home of the first people. We found you on the mountain. We took your weapons. Moved your bodies. You were lying on top, your arm around your friend with the girl buried beneath you both. We saw her dark skin and thought she was one of ours. Her eyes shut. Needed to know if she was your captive. We brought you all here. Understand?'

'Where's my dog?'

'No dogs, three people. No dog. Understand'

I nodded, my head swimming and speaking hoarsely, 'Girl? What girl?'

'Argh, you are as stupid as your friend,' she said, spitting onto the earthen floor.

My eyes widened as I understood.

She nodded.

As she did so, no longer a boy, Bruni, returned with a mischievous smile and a bowl of rich meat broth. She spooned it into me with a bronze spoon as fine as any you would see in an Earl's home but well worn.

'You're a girl,' I croaked.

She smiled and raised an eyebrow, 'seems I saved your life this time. If it wasn't for me, they'd have never have taken you in. Now stop talking and drink.'

I did as I was told and slept some more.

When I next woke up, I felt more like my usual self and I could sit and look around. I was in an oddly shaped hall. It had one huge beam rising from one corner to the centre of the roof. I realised that the beam was a whole tree trunk with its bark still on. I looked around some more and saw that the whole tree was the house. Wherever a branch held weight, or was useful for the people here, it had been left. Some were part of the walls, or beams supporting the main trunk, others had clothes and utensils hanging from them. Otherwise, the walls were of wattle woven upon a low turf wall. There was a small fire flickering in a stone hearth its scant smoke trickling out somewhere in the roof. Here and there skins were drying or curing and many bunches of dried herbs swung gently from the roof. I couldn't see a way out.

'Old man tree. Fall storm many years. Make home for first people.'

I turned to find a man with the same appearance as the woman was sat behind me. He showed me a long bronze blade in his hand, its edge was keen. I got the message.

'Where is everybody?'

'Why? You don't like me,' the dark man scowled at me fiercely, pointing his blade at me.

I held my hands up, palms towards him, 'No, no, I like you fine, please.'

'Ha, ha, haha, your face, hee hee,' he was beside himself, laughing, at me.

'Oh, yea, you got me,' I said, laughing too, with some relief.

'Pretty good, I make joke in tongue not mine.'

'Yes, good joke, very funny.' I suppose it was really. I smiled. 'I do like your home.'

'Good home. Hard find. Why you red hair black?'

How would I explain this? 'Hide from enemy. Don't want him to see me.'

'Hide from enemy? Go enemy not find you. How he find you, if not where he is?'

I thought about that and my hatred burned again. 'Revenge, I want revenge.'

He rocked back on his heels, as he did it came to me why this small hall seemed so empty. No benches or tables.

'Revenge,' he nodded then looked straight into my eyes, 'careful it not eat you.'

'It eats me all the time.' I answered, 'all the time.'

Shortly after this people started to return. They came in through a hole in the roof and climbed down one of the branches which had notches cut in for the purpose. Even the toddlers, of which there were few. I was relieved to see Maelcolm back clumsily down the branch followed by Bruni's much more graceful descent. I decided that she made a very lovely girl.

* * *

I learnt a lot in the next few days. I learnt that these people had been here when the land was young, had once herded cattle but now lived on wild things, that they used to make bronze with copper dug from where the waters meet and tin from a river that also gave gold. It was true that many of them wore gold rings or torques. That before men came with iron, they ruled the land. That women rule here and ancestry is measured through the mothers. Now they lived hidden and owned no more than they could carry. They worshipped the moon and stars. One reason we were cared for was being found on the full moon.

I also learnt that Bruni had been captured by raiding desert men who sold her to slavers on a long white beach where the sea lay to the north. That her slave collars had grown with her until it was decided she was tame enough to go without. Around the time her breasts began to grow her value changed. While waiting to be resold she escaped the slave pens in Dyflin, and found the village where we found her. Herds of animals, traders passing through, made it easy to pass as another dirty boy scratching a living. Hiding in the fields by day and coming out at dusk she'd managed, helped by the lengthening nights, until the cold weather came 'in this miserable wet dung-heap of a country where the sun never shone' as she put it.

I soon went outside and saw that the whole hall was turfed from the ground to the apex. Many of the great tree's roots were exposed to the weather but enough lay in the earth for a part of it to live. Just above the entrance a branch still held the dying leaves of this year's growth. It looked exactly like a small tree growing in the top of a mound. In daylight, and only if you looked hard, the only sign of the dwellers inside was a faint haze above the hole.

I wasn't sure how free we were. We had our clothes but not our bags or weapons. Very few of them spoke with us and only in a limited way. We seemed to be in a small heavily wooded valley through which a stream ran over ledges of rock to disappear into a narrow gorge at the bottom. Like their home there seemed to be no obvious ways in or out. If any of us ventured any distance from the home, someone was there holding a spear or a bow. No gestures were made, no words spoken but we turned back every time.

We were not mistreated in any way and for now it suited my purposes that we stay hidden and cared for but I'd begun to worry. The nights were long and the days shortening fast and we were stuck here with these strange people who had no priests or churches and seemingly no lords or slaves and where was Sib?

Not only that but Maelcolm was brooding again. Why had he given up his crown? Should he have stayed? Is he a coward? Why is he going bald so young? He should have gone with Jokul, back to England, run away to France? Had Etromma sent us to our deaths? He should never have trusted me? And on and on.

Bruni was just happy to be alive, eating well and no one was threatening her. She lived in the present and, at that moment, the present was good.

But I worried, why were we being kept? These were people living on the edge. Very good at it no doubt but they didn't need extra mouths.

It wasn't long before I found out.

They came for me in the night. I came up from a deep sleep, groggy and befuddled and being grabbed by many hands. It was black as soot, even the hearth held no glowing embers. I thrashed about wildly but my limbs felt leaden and I was quickly subdued, stripped naked, tied, gagged and blindfolded. I was vaguely aware that I was being half dragged, half pushed through the hole in the roof. The sudden blow of cold air brought me momentarily to my senses as I was slid down through new snow. I tried to get to my feet but was dragged, stumbling and sliding painfully for some distance then the air changed. No wind and the cries of my captors echoed strangely then they all went quiet. I was stood up, bleeding from many cuts and scratches and I felt a rope, a noose, pass over my head and tighten on my throat.

Something pointed prodded me in the back and the rope dragged me forward. Barefoot I stumbled over a wet rock floor, surprisingly smooth. I was in a cave. I knew it now. Then I heard the thin high-pitched tune of a bone flute coming from some distant place. There was a murmuring of voices and I realised that many people were around me. Then a drum began to sound, boom, boom, boom. As each boom echoed, I was dragged another step. More flutes joined the first. I could feel the crowd sway around me. The flutes rose to a great crescendo as the drums beat faster and faster. On some signal, everything went silent and the crowd stopped moving. I was thrown to my knees.

My hands were untied but strong arms held my arms outstretched on either side. Whoever held the noose moved to behind me, it was neither tight nor loose. In the darkness and the silence my fear grew. Then the drums began again and the blindfold was removed. I found myself surrounded by figures with animal heads, or masks. There were wolves, antlered stags, badgers, beavers, otters even eagles, wings outstretched above the others. They were all lit by the flickering of a small fire, their shadows danced on the stone walls. Behind the fire were three women.

In the centre was the woman who'd spoken to me on the first day. To her left, a girl on the edge of womanhood and to the right a woman who seemed too old, too wrinkled and too bony to be alive, yet her eyes were piercingly bright in the glow of the fire. Behind them on a stone ledge was a long array of skulls, many animals but mostly those of men. In the flickering shadows each dark eye seemed fixed on me. On the cave wall above the skulls was the largest set of antlers I had ever seen by far. What enormous beast had carried those?

The gag was taken from my mouth and I went to speak. The woman in the middle held up her hand with such authority that I shut up before a word came out. Everything fell silent. Then the single flute sounded again and as it did so the younger of the three women stood carrying a small bowl. Using her hands, she smeared my whole body with some ointment. Very soon my skin began to tingle and the many cuts and scrapes to burn. She returned to her place.

The flute fell silent. A drum began a slow beat and the old woman rose. She too carried a bowl and dipping her fingers in drew strange symbols, black or red, I couldn't tell, over my body. As she finished the crowd began a slow keening, then the flute, high and eerie sounded above the drum which beat faster and faster. Then they all beat and whistled at once, the noise was intense as it bounced back and forth around the cave. The old woman sat down and the middle woman stood up. My hair was grabbed from behind and my head pulled back and held firm. Then she walked up to me, pinched my nose and poured a cup of bitter tasting liquid into my mouth. I had no choice but to swallow.

Everything fell silent. My skin burned, my mouth went dry and I found I couldn't help swallowing. I felt dreamy but fearful. My limbs would not obey me. My jaws felt tight and strange spasms passed across my stomach. My vision changed, the cave crowded in on me and all the masked people seemed to become the animals themselves, even to the smell. A wolf snarled at me, a stag bellowed and suddenly my mouth filled with bile. I retched convulsively but the young woman, now strangely coloured, held a bowl under my spewing mouth until I only dribbled phlegm. The hands holding me let go and as I fell to the floor the antlers on the wall got bigger and bigger until they arched across the whole space. The skulls started talking to me but I couldn't grasp the words. I knew they held the key to everything if only I could understand. Then I see a small crack in the cave wall and I fall into it and am squeezed through this tiny space stretched thin until I fitted. I know now that I am dying. I die.

Then like a huge breath, my vision cleared, it was I could see everything everywhere. I was floating above my own body which was writhing on the floor. As I watched it calmed. My head was being held by one woman while the others lay each side of me. I could not tell one from another. I could see that my eyes were rolled into the back of my head. Was I seeing myself in the cave of my own skull?

Then suddenly I was wrenched sideways, floating above a land rushing away from beneath me. Trees, woods, fields, mountains then across a sea until I rose and found I was hanging above an abyss so deep I knew there was no end to its depths. Then I was wrenched sideways again, I tumbled into the abyss and fell for an eternity. I became aware of a very slow drumbeat, boom, boom, boom de boom, boom, over and over as I fell. I became aware that I was not alone, the three women were around me. I could not see them but they were there.

Everything became very clear. Once again, we were crossing a sea. I could see the creatures in it. We talked back and forth. I was leading. I looked around. There were geese all around me, three of which were those women. We came to a land of deep inlets and snow-capped mountains and I realised we were no longer geese but sea eagles circling above a realm of dark forests, many lakes and vast stretches of snow. The trees had odd leaves, needle like, dark and weighed down by their white blanket. I could see every needle, every glistening icicle and then a collection of buildings came into view and I began to circle down.

Outside the town was a forest and in that forest a clearing and in that clearing was a crowd of people around a large ox-drawn cart. On one of the trees a man stood above the crowd supported by a platform with a noose around his neck. His eyes too, were rolled back in his head. Where I wondered was his spirit?

My attention turned to the cart. Three women sat upon it, one old, one in her prime and one young woman. A young woman with dark red hair who I knew well. I flew down and the crowd gasped as I settled before her. It was Moira, my sister, my twin. She stared at me then her eyes widened in recognition.

'Sar, is that you?' she gasped, 'it is you. Do not tarry, go back to your body before you are lost. Know that I am alive and well. Go home, brother, go home.'

I tried to speak but no words came. Then the crowd roared, the platform fell and as I turned, I saw the man thrashing at the end of his rope. A spear was sunk into his side and his body stilled as a rush of blood poured out.

I fell back into darkness.

When I came around, I found myself back in the cave. My mind was full of wonder and I felt, in some weird way, washed clean. I knew what I had seen and knew that I too was meant to be sacrificed, but I felt no fear. I was calm but no-one around me was. The women were talking earnestly to the animal people while the crowd behind strained to hear what was happening. I could not understand a word but could see that I was the cause of their upset.

The middle woman came over to me. 'You are not to die with the dawn. You have a sister, a twin who serves the old God's in the north. We cannot kill you.'

'That was my sister? Was what I saw true?' I mumbled the words out through a mouth so dry my tongue stuck to its roof.

She gestured and someone gave me water. As I drank, she answered, 'You can believe it all. What you saw is real. Your sister is well and she has saved your life and that of your friends. If not for her we would kill you to bring the sun back for another year.'

Even as she talked, I saw the man I'd shared my thoughts of revenge with being painted with symbols and a crown placed upon his head. The woman gave him a cup and he drank. Clearly, I was seeing a hurried form of the ritual I had undergone. Then the man was led through the crowd who hailed him and bowed before him.

Someone wrapped a long fur cloak around me before I was blindfolded again and led out from the cave. After walking some distance uphill, the blindfold was removed. I, and I guessed the whole of this small tribe, were just below the crest of the mountain looking east in the starlit gloom under scudding clouds. The painted man was laid against a standing stone. There was a rope looped once around his neck. He was smiling, his eyes huge and black. As the first grey paleness was seen in the East two masked people took each end of the rope. They pulled against each other and the rope tightened around the neck of the sacrifice. He made no attempt to resist. They pulled, he strangled, and as he passed out the old woman stepped forward, a gleaming copper knife in her hand. She deftly sliced under his breastbone, plunged in her hand and tore out his still beating heart. She held it up in the air and the whole tribe began to sing. As they did so the top edge of the sun appeared on the horizon. The singing rose louder with the sun until the whole glowing disc was visible, its rays underlighting the rapidly moving clouds. When the bottom of the glowing disc left the edge of the world, everyone fell silent and then, still silent, they walked back down the mountain.

Chapter Sixteen

Later that day I was taken back to the home place. I was relieved to see that Maelcolm and Bruni were still there. They'd been tied up for the whole night but were otherwise unhurt. I felt drained and strange lights flickered at the edge of my vision. My mind was full and I did not want to talk. I lay down, and after a while, slept.

I awoke to discover I had slept a day and a night and it was now just after dawn. The small fire in the centre was now alight and I pulled my clothes on by its warmth. A few people were stirring as I climbed out. Snow still lay upon the ground criss-crossed by the tracks of many feet. After relieving myself I went down to the stream to wash. Cold as it was, I stripped off and washed away the marks painted on my body. Dressing, I knew I was being watched and before long the Irish speaking woman came to me.

She made a downward motion with her hand so I sat on my haunches. She stood and looked down on me, 'Never before has happened. The sun rose so our,' she paused seeking the right word, 'man gift accepted but you must go.'

'You're woman priest?' Only men were priests in my world.

'I serve, yes.'

'Will you bless me?'

She nodded, I knelt in front of her, she laid her hands on my head and I heard her, I think, praying.

I felt an unnameable strength flow into me. Her hands left my head. After a short pause I looked up gratefully and was surprised to find that she was nowhere to be seen.

Not long after that a group of men were blindfolding the three of us. I kept asking for our weapons but none of them spoke. I believed that we were being freed so didn't resist and told the other two to do the same. Guided by not too gentle shoves and tugs we found ourselves walking down the stream. Without sight, guided or not, we stumbled many times. At one point I fell hard on my side, the freezing water soaking through to my skin. If we were left out in the cold like this, we'd be worse off than the night before we arrived.

Then we must have been passing through a rock gully as we scraped along rock walls, bumping painfully into unseen outcrops or unnervingly into sodden clumps of moss or fern. Thankfully this did not last long and soon we were out of the stream and crunching through shallow snow. I guessed we'd passed out of a wood as a sudden breeze made me shiver and my teeth began to chatter.

Then no more shoves, no tugs, I slowly moved my hands up to the blindfold, nothing. Taking it off I startled by the whiteness of our surroundings in the still, low sun of a winter's day. Blinking repeatedly, I could hear Maelcolm and Bruni chattering excitedly, me, suddenly I felt the weight of the role I had assumed. To lead our small party.

I'd been right, we were in a broad valley with woods behind us. The shortish grass between the rocks and the missing tips of the small shrubs around us showed that deer grazed this area. Though not recently. There were no tracks in the snow except ours and a few birds. Neither were there any tracks from our captors, saviours? I ran back up to the treeline but could see no tracks but our own under the branches.

Mystified I turned back to the other two. I didn't feel like talking. The valley narrowed as it descended toward the east. Somewhere between here and the sea there had to be a road of some kind and if not, we'd reach the sea and turn north, Dyflin was better than nowhere. To be honest, wet as we were, with no cloaks, no weapons, no means to start a fire and no food, I honestly could not see how we would live through the next night. I pointed downhill.

The strange washed feeling after the ceremony had passed, now I felt low in spirits. I tried to recall the woman's blessing but that too felt lost. Images of my strange visions flashed into my mind as did all the shock and fear of being so helpless, so at the mercy of those strange people and their different ways. I walked on, head bowed, just watching my feet and trying to force my chattering teeth to stay still.

Then I heard an excited shout from Bruni, I looked up to see her running towards a low drystone wall. Maelcolm too was running. I trudged after to find them standing by a small spring bubbling up into a rock lined pool. The wall circled around this pool enclosing it from all sides except the stream that flowed from it. Inside the wall but above the spring, an ancient hawthorn stood, its boughs covered in little scraps of cloth. Below the tree and broad flat stone, and on the stone a pile of our belongings. I found my satchel, the straps repaired, and in it all my money, my whetstones and most importantly my chunk of flint. We'd even been left strips of smoked, dried venison. As I rummaged for my flint, I found a small polished wooden box made from dark bog oak. It was filled with a black, greasy substance. Puzzled I rubbed it between my fingers, then realised, it was to colour my hair. Silently, thanking my benefactors, I quickly rubbed some in.

I didn't know whether to change my clothes or start a fire first. Deciding that the excitement had warmed me up I directed the other two to gather the dead twigs and branches that lay beneath the old hawthorn. While I, after crossing myself, prayed to whatever pagan gods protected this spring and took down the driest and most frayed pieces of cloth from its branches.

Teasing the weft apart until I was left with a bundle of fibres, I rolled them into a small ball with some dry bits of sphagnum I found in the lee of the wall. The other two sheltered me while I chipped away at my knife with the flint until at last enough sparks got entangled in the fibres for me to gently blow them into life. Followed by crumbled bits of bark then small pieces of twig a flame took hold. I slowly fed it until I was sure it would live then began to add the smallest branches. Hawthorn burns hot and before long we had a fire large enough to sit around.

We rummaged through our bags to dig out our spare clothes. Bruni had had no bag but found her ragged clothes clean in a small leather sack placed upon an oddly shaped piece of rawhide. While I watched her sneakily under my lashes through the corner of my eyes, I realised what it was. After she'd taken off the fawn skin dress she'd been given, she put a worn tunic over herself then wrapped the hide around her body. This pressed her small breasts flat and hid her narrow waist. I remembered back to my spear glancing off of her side, a moment I'd forgotten till now. Just before she slipped another tunic over the top, I saw a tear in the side of her protection. Suddenly I felt a rush of affection, pleased that I'd not pierced her body. This thought made me uncomfortable in more ways than one so I got up to check my weapons. Soon we were dry and breakfasted, our wet clothes steaming by the fire. The other two wanted to stay here for the rest of the day and overnight but I roughly ordered them to get up.

Maelcolm just lay there, 'Who the fuck are you to keep telling us what to do?'

I was shocked, I'd not even thought about it. Maelcolm was so pathetic when I found him following Jokul's troop that I'd had to take charge. It never occurred to me to do anything different. Then I was angry, 'Do you think I wanted to look after some failed fucking noble?'

He jumped to his feet, 'Look after? Who have you looked after? Every shitty decision you've made had got us into a bigger and bigger mess.'

'Mess? Mess? You'd never had got through Strathclyde without me.'

'How do you know? How do you know that? I might have done fine without you. I should never have listened to you.'

'Fuck you,' I screamed into his face, 'fuck you.'

'If it wasn't for your fucking dog and your enemies, I might have spent the winter, feet up, ale in hand, in some comfortable Dyflin tavern,' he screamed back at me.

I'm stunned, speechless, suddenly missing my dog terribly. Just me and him. We'd have been fine.

Mealcolm's still yelling, 'We would have frozen to death on that mountain and that was all your fault.'

'You survived because of me remember. It's me that got frostbite, not you.' I held up my foreshortened finger to his face. 'Tell me one decision you would have made different?'

'All of them you cunt.'

I punched him, hard. He went down. As he fell, I saw Bruni's dismayed face. Even though she couldn't understand English it was clear things were not going well. In that moment's distraction Maelcolm kicked my legs out from under me. Next thing we're wrestling madly on the ground. I knew he could fight on his feet but I didn't expect him to be able to gutter fight on the ground. We're rolling over and over getting holds and punches in until we're both bruised and bleeding. Neither of us though is really trying to hurt. Not to maim or kill, and then, somehow, we both come to realise it just as Bruni bursts in, beating on us with my spear shaft. Soon we're much more worried about her attack than each other. I try to defend myself and get a sharp thwack on my forearm. With this I turn and run, jumping over the low stone wall then turning, and dancing backwards, I see that she is now giving Maelcolm a thrashing. I fall apart laughing when a massive blow from behind slams me to the floor. I quickly turn on to my back thrashing out wildly. I soon realise my assailant is large, hairy, stinks and is licking me excitedly.

'Sib, Duw, duw, where did you spring from?' He's so worked up he can't hear me and soon I'm wrestling the huge beast just to get him to calm down. 'Sib, my boy, where have you been?' He licks me some more then rolls on his back offering his belly and throat to be rubbed. He's telling me he's still my dog, that he still trusts me. All of a sudden, I'm crying and laughing all at once. I'm so happy to see him.

Bruni comes running up and gives him a big hug, which he tolerates, then Maelcolm, arrives, who doesn't get too close. Just in case.

'It's alright Maelcolm, I'm done. Don't worry about me.'

'It's not you. It's that dog. I can't touch you when he's here.'

I got up and put my hand out, 'I hope you won't want to. We'll talk, yeah?'

He shook my hand, 'Let's do that.'

We go back to the fire and change our newly sodden clothes into the slightly less sodden clothes steaming by the fire and eat a little more. After explaining what we'd been fighting about to Bruni we decided, between us, to walk east. For all the rolling about on the ground, my first punch had made the biggest mark. Maelcolm's face was swelling up fast. He'd have a massive black eye tomorrow and I didn't mind that one bit.

Before we set off, I looked Sib over. He'd lost some weight, you could easily count his ribs, but his hip bones didn't stick out too far and his legs were still well muscled. He'd eaten, just less than usual. I guessed the crows were picking over a couple of carcasses somewhere not too far away.

It took until way past noon, walking away from the mountains, until we came across a wide swath of tracks and muddy ruts that meant a route from somewhere to somewhere. By now the rain had returned, a soft drizzle mixed with sleet blew from the east. As darkness fell, we'd be in for a cold night. We cast up and down for some shelter to wait in case any travellers passed by. I, well we, wanted to be sure that we would not end up walking vainly away from a warm fire and a roof. I also wanted to be sure we could see passers-by without being seen. I was hoping for a lone farmer or herdsman who would be no threat to us, foreigners that we are.

It wasn't to be. From some way off we could hear the unmistakeable sound of horses and the chinking of buckles and stirrups.

'Armed men,' I hissed, 'Hide.'

We pulled ourselves into a thicket growing around a rock outcrop. As they passed, I peered round a large rock. At least twenty of them, I thought, all carrying lances. I held a hand out, palm out, warning the others to stay hidden. Then the column drew to a halt. I was cursing our luck when their leader called out. 'Child of Strife, I see you.'

I marched out to face them, 'Lord of War, I see you.'

Chapter Seventeen

It was Faelan, Faelan oi Aitre, who, exiled from his home in the north, had led a warband from King Diarmait mac Mael's, Dyflin to raid the enemies of Earl Godwin. His company had turned the tide at the battle of Porloc where I had met him and his fearsome following. His man, Muirchu, had taught me how to fight to my strengths. He'd given me my little shield, I'd learned to call a targe, days before his death. How had I been recognised with my hair black and seemingly without even being seen? You didn't ask questions like that about Faelan. One look into his dark eyes and you accepted him as he was. When I'd last seen him his hair and beard had been long, limed white and piled high. Many of his men, who had an upsetting way of collecting the heads of their enemies, had looked equally as wild. They fought almost naked, relying on speed and strategy to gain their victories, and saw slugging it out in a shield wall under layers of padding and mail as unimaginative and rather dull.

At home they defended the lands of their king and, like the other kingdoms of Ireland laid down their arms in the winter, and raided their neighbour's cattle in the summer. Now his dark hair was only shoulder length and the beard below his long, lean, lined face was neatly trimmed.

So here we were, the three of us surrounded by warriors with intertwined whorls tattooed into their faces and women with laughing, challenging, eyes and the peasants and slaves that served them.

The main settlement itself was only about the size of a large farmstead but the myriad of well-worn trails that led out from its two gates showed its central role in the surrounding community. It lay beside a small river which was joined by a stream bubbling in from a low ridge on the northern side of the valley. It was surrounded by a well-maintained wall of stout timbers upon a high bank. The ditch from which the bank had been dug was clear of bushes and undergrowth. Sheep grazed the scant foliage against the walls while pigs foraged along the muddy bottom. Inside the walls the place was clean and well-ordered but not in streets as in Dyflin or Jorvik instead each family group had a fenced off area within which were the usual variety of buildings. Some were round, I'd never seen that before. Faelen's own hall was one of these, a huge round building with eaves that nearly reached the ground. When it rained the children played under them alongside dogs and chickens competing for scraps. Inside, when serious matters were discussed, the important people of the clan sat in a circle and all were allowed a voice, though it was clear that Faelen's words carried the most weight.

Whatever their ferocity in war this was a moral society, there were no loose women or master-less men. Even among the slaves there were only maidens or wives. Priests, literacy and religion were highly respected. Bruni's womanhood became impossible to hide and her boyish clothes caused many to look askance but were accepted as we were Faelen's guests. What caused more of a stir was her insistence on training alongside Maelcolm and I.

'You promised me this,' she said, 'I've served you have I not.'

I thought about this. She had brought me my food and carried my stuff at times. Once I'd learnt that she was a young woman I'd forgotten our arrangement. That was just what women did, wasn't it? I saw her wry smile as she watched my mind working. She scoffed at me and began to turn away. My mind raced, 'No,' I said hurriedly, 'you're right I did. I did promise you that.'

She'd earned it really. She'd proved really tough and I'd seen for myself how fast and determined she could be. Her face lit up and from that day on she practised every chance she got. Obsessed as I was to overpower Oslaf, this suited me well.

I started her off as Muirchu had shown me. I threw stones at her feet until she understood that to stay still was to get hurt. Her feet were a mess, I'd not noticed before, she'd never complained in the snow or on the stony bits of road. Humbled, I used the purse that Grim had given me to get her some shoes made and to add new soles on mine. Maelcolm grumbled when he realised that I had money of my own I'd not told him about. The piece of rawhide that she'd hidden her breasts behind had caused blisters which turned into callouses on her hips and under arms and limited her movement. We found a man who dressed hides and he boiled the rawhide then trimmed and beat it into a more wearable shape. This not only hid her natural body shape it offered some protection from weapons.

He, fascinated by her ferocity, also made her, from soaked hide stretched over a circular wicker framework, something even more useful in a fight. As the hide dried it firmed into a lightweight shield, not much larger than mine but sturdy enough to deflect a blow. After training with Maelcolm and the Irishmen, Bruni and I would walk up the valley and I continued to throw stones at her until knocking them away or avoiding them became second nature. I expected her to quickly tire of this and demand weapons but she persevered until my throwing arm grew tired.

Weapons were a problem, Maelcolm and I had our own, but we had left our spare blades with Etromma. Any attempt to buy weapons from Faelan's people was politely declined. In the end I borrowed an axe and Maelcolm and I fashioned her a spear from an ash sapling with a fire hardened point and something equivalent to a short sword or long seax out of hawthorn.

As I tried to teach her, I realised how much I had learned but never really thought about. Things like when fighting with blades you never want to receive a direct blow from another edged weapon. A broken or bent blade was a useless tool, the trick is to always deflect or avoid. With her light shield, again, a direct blow would render it useless, so you have to see the attack coming and push it aside. I'd seen heavy wooden shields hacked into wood chips only fit for kindling.

She was small and slight but determined, ferocious, and could move at lightning speed. I taught her how I'd learned to fight by holding on to a throwing spear. It gave me reach to stab, but not enough to pierce mail. So, I had to stab accurately and fast but if the opportunity for a smart throw came, I could take it. As soon as an enemy's blade hacked the staff or he stamped on it, that weapon was done. If I could take an eye, get in the neck or stab an exposed thigh or calf in the first moments of a fight before they recognised my weapons weakness, I had an advantage. After that it was all about speed. For me things had changed, I'd grown taller, and with that my reach had increased but it was now much harder to duck under someone's blade. Bruni could do that, and she was never going to get much taller. Being short, she could not easily hack down, I now could. She was so fast that I learned from her. Until I lived with the Irish, any practice I'd had any was with men who had been taught to hold their ground and to rely on their shields to keep them safe and their swords to attack. The best or richest of them would wear mail over a padded byrnie that took blows which would otherwise maim a man. I could dance around them and sometimes win, but none of them, weighted down as they were, were fast, so I was rarely tested that way. Bruni tested me hard.

It was great for me, I had a companion as fanatical as myself, always throwing our spears, racing, sparring and wrestling. Each of us spurred on by our obsessions, hers to survive and never be a victim. Mine, to survive long enough to get my revenge, and then, who knows?

It was the wrestling, though, that changed things.

It had been a hard days training enlivened by the first signs of spring. Sib had gone off, roaming for something to eat. We'd been trotting homeward teasing, by trying to trip or push, each other off the track. This was a regular thing and before long, we'd throw down our weapons and fall to wrestling. This time though the wrestling got softer, the holds gentler with less desire to escape them. I felt drunk with the musky scent of her sweat as we grappled. I kissed her, she responded and soon we were rutting playfully on the sheep cropped turf. I was about to finish when she suddenly started writhing around giggling. I came, then hurriedly pulled out, abashed and blushing.

She was rolling around in hysterics then, seeing my red face and rapidly shrinking penis, she chortled, 'No, no, it's alright. You didn't have to do that. That was lovely.' She's waving an arm at me still laughing, then just as suddenly she curled up in a ball and started sobbing.

I didn't know what to do, to touch her or not, should I just leave or what? So, I pulled my breeches up, sat beside her and did nothing except feel really awkward.

Next thing she's sat up pulling her clothes on. She grabs up her shield and spear, gets to her feet and runs. Then she turns her face to me, smiling broadly. 'Come catch me then', she taunts, and starts skipping along the valley.

I'm hopping around for a while trying to pull my shoes on then I'm up and off and after her.

For about a week all went well for Bruni and I though we trained less, we made love a lot, as young people do. Then one morning as I came out from the house that I shared with Maelcolm and some other young warriors Faelen called me over. 'It's time we had a talk you and I.'

You don't argue with Faelen so as the others went off to the training grounds I stayed back. He continued, 'Why have you not come to me? Have I not befriended you, given you a place to stay, fed you, let you train with my men?'

I felt like a guilty small boy and hung my head fiddling, as I was wont, with Ealhild's silver spoon I had bent around the torque that hung round my neck. Now, the torque too small, I used a leather thong to keep it in place.

'That wire you have around your neck, is that not the arm ring I gave you in the land of the Cornwaelas?'

I nodded.

'Don't hang your head, you are a man now, man enough to play with women it would seem.'

Startled I raised my head and looked him in the eye. He chuckled, 'Child of Strife, you think I don't know what goes on in my own lands?' He raised his hands and untying the thong he gently bent the torque away from my neck along with the spoon. I was about to protest, but I, not really knowing why, had always trusted Faelen.

'Come with me,' he said putting a hand upon my shoulder, 'and tell me what has befallen you since we last talked.

'That will take some time,' I said as we walked toward his hall. The entrance to his hall had a kind of long porch with benches each side as you sometimes see at an English church though all of wattle and thatch that merged gracefully into the round form of the building. We sat facing each other as light rain softened the view across his steading. Sib settled down at my feet and after thumping his tail a few times settled himself to doze.

Faelen gazed into me with his dark eyes, seeking yet accepting. I took a deep breath, I felt shaky, there was nowhere to hide. 'I don't know where to start,' I said feeling a little frantic.

'Where had you been when we found you?'

'I thought you must have known. We were released so close to you and your men.'

'No, you were captives then? They may have known about us but I know nothing of them'

'Oh,' I said, surprised. I then told him all about our stay with these small dark people. Showed him my shortened finger, how they saved us and why. How I was to be sacrificed and was saved by travelling across the sky with the geese and seeing my sister while I was in the body of a sea-eagle. Then our being freed and led away.'

As I told him our tale his face, usually so unreadable, revealed a whole string of reactions. I read, amazement, excitement, incredulity which held me back, but he encouraged me on, then fascination. He asked for more details. I gave him what I could.

'They lived in a mound; you say?'

'From the outside I suppose.'

'You have met the áes síd,' he said, using words I didn't know, 'the people who live in the hollow hills. He turned his face toward me, eyes wide, 'you have met the fairy people and come back,'

I was puzzled, 'I did?'

'You ate and drank with them?'

'Yes, we did.'

'And yet here you are. Some say they are magical creatures, others that they are the De Danann, the people who were here before us.'

'Old then, very old,' I thought back, 'they had things, things cast from bronze which were looked old, worn but treasured. They were a bit magical. They could move without a sound and you never knew when they were watching you, but then it seems some of your own people are a bit like that.'

'Truth is Sar, I think a herd of cattle could have passed you and you wouldn't have noticed,' he said, a wry smile on his face.

I blushed and looked away.

'They are said to steal children, to put their own in the place of ours. Changelings, they're weak or deformed, they don't live long.'

'A lot of babies don't live long,' I said, feeling a need to defend them, 'but they had very few children.' I looked around, children were running about everywhere, doing errands, carrying fodder, yarn, wood, wool or water. Some boys were finding time to spar or chase each other with sticks.

'It's true, we've lost a few over the winter and we'll lose some more before the crops are in, their teeth lose in their heads or bellies swollen with worms.'

'No, Faelen, I mean really a few. This,' I waved my hand towards the hurrying little figures, 'would be a lot. Whoever those people were, there'll be fewer in the days to come.'

'You think you saw your sister in a vision?'

'It didn't feel like a vision, I was there. She was some kind of a she-priest I think.'

Faelen's voice dropped to a whisper, 'Some of our stories talk of women priests in the old days before the saints arrived.' He pulled me even closer to him, 'some even say that Brigid, was not Christian at all, that she served the Mother Goddess in a grove of sacred oaks.'

I knew why he was whispering, even Faelen was cautious about offending the Church. 'I used to polish a box with a piece of Saint Brigid's cloak in.'

'Ah yes, for that priest, Aethelric wasn't it. He was a fine man.'

'Still is I think, heading back to Canterberie last I saw him. I told him the cloak was the wrong colour'

'What?'

'Well, my stepfather was Irish and he told me a story about Brigid's white cloak but the piece of cloak in the box wasn't white?'

'It's sometimes better not to question these things.'

'Well, if I know Earl Harold at all it won't be in a plain box now it'll be in a casket of gold and jewels and no-one will notice the colour of the cloth.'

Faelen nodded, 'Hmm, you had an Irish step-father then. There's much I don't know about you.'

'There's a lot I don't know about you either,' I said.

He pulled back and it was as if a veil came over his eyes. I wanted to take my words back. 'I'm sorry, Lord, I shouldn't have said that.'

'No, you shouldn't, you don't and you won't.' He breathed out slowly then smiled, 'but don't worry, tell me your story.'

And I did, for the whole of the rest of the day, it poured out of me.

'You've been through a lot in a short time, Sar', Faelen said, putting his arm around my shaking shoulders, 'a lot.'

Strangely those few words made me feel better. It had been a lot, in what? A couple of years.

Faelen stood up and sat back down on the bench opposite me, 'Your father, if that's who it was,' he raised a finger, 'and Sar, I think you might be right, can wait. You've done without him all these years, what difference does it make now? Your sister, believe the vision. Could you have dreamt all that from nothing? It will give you comfort. The lives you grieve. Grief is love for the dead. It doesn't go away but you grow around it. When you can, find your monk friend and talk with him. Maybe not the time in the mountains, he will see them as witches. That leaves your feud, your blood-feud, it may be the end of you.'

'I know Faelen, I know.'

'And Sar, leave the girl alone. You probably have one bastard child already and you barely growing a beard. Leave her alone. She has been used badly and knows no better. She needs a man who can love her truly. Can you?'

I shook my hanging head, I knew I couldn't, wasn't sure I could love at all.

'Listen, from what you've told me you are in my home, in my country, for two reasons. One, you want to find out why Aelfgar's man is in Ireland so that you can tell your Earl about it.'

I nodded.

'Aelfgar's man being Oslaf, who is exiled. Is that not reason enough to be here?'

'I suppose so but I don't trust that snake anywhere.'

Faelen spat on the ground, 'I remember Oslaf breaking that harpist's fingers. Maybe we do have a snake in Ireland.' He thought for a while, 'Secondly, though I suspect it's your first reason for being here, you want revenge. Then you want to get back to Harold and tell him you've hunted down and killed Oslaf.'

I nodded again, unsure where this was leading.

'Let me get this right, you think you can come here, shelter with me and kill a man who will have been granted leave to stay by my own King?' He looked me in the face, 'and then get away and what? Fly to England?'

'Well, not fly,' I answered lamely, my heart sinking at Faelen's words.

'I'm telling you now Sar, if you try to kill him in Ireland, we are no longer friends.'

I jumped to my feet, agitated, speechless.

'But your revenge is justified. The man deserves to die.'

I sat back down.

'Sar, you have to be clever. To think and plan things through.' He laughed then and leant back, 'I do have to say your impulses have got you this far and more or less in one piece.'

'So, what do I do now? If I can't try here what can I do?' I said, a bit resentful.

'Think Sar, think. Do you think Oslaf will want to stay in Ireland?'

'He could I suppose. Carve himself out a space here as you have.'

'What? That flaxen haired Saxon. He probably sees us all as savages. Think harder.'

'No, he'll want his lands and his fortune back just as Godwin and his sons did. He has at least one son in England,' I mused, 'he'll want to go home, but he's outlawed.'

'But rich you say, and he has ships and a following.'

'So somehow, in some way, he will have to go back,' I jumped up, 'and I have to follow him, but how?'

'You have to find out what his plans are.'

'I do, and then I kill him.'

'And then you can try.'

Chapter Eighteen

I told Bruni the next day. It didn't go well. She hit me. In the face. With her spear shaft. Hard. I thought I'd lost a tooth. While I got off the ground, spitting blood but no teeth, she ran off up into the scrub woods at the side of the valley.

By the time I thought it would be a good idea to go after her she was long gone. If she didn't want me to find her I wouldn't. It was easier to go back to the settlement. So I did.

The next day was an important day. Shrove Tuesday, so everyone was getting ready to feast after having their sins absolved. People were bustling around preparing food, benches and trestle tables for feasting and services outdoors. There was nowhere for everyone to fit under one roof. Anyway, anything other than a downpour was considered a fine day here. It was only mizzling gently, a soft day in local speak.

By nightfall there was still no sign of her. I hunted around asking if anyone had seen her. They'd not. After a while I got fed up with the comments, and the laughter, about the livid bruise across my swollen face. I went to bed.

Next morning there was no going anywhere. The whole village was together for a mass confession in front of the priests and leaders. Maybe people like Faelen had made a personal confession but for the rest of us, we mumbled ours as a group. I didn't have much to say. Soon as I could I jumped up on a table and looked over the crowd. I couldn't see her anywhere.

The feasting started but I had no heart for it. I sat for a while moodily watching Sib fighting with the other village dogs over a pile of offal, skin and bones discarded by the cooks. Unable to decide which bits he most wanted to fight over, the smaller, wilier dogs were running him ragged, snatching pieces out from under his snarling jaws. Fuck it, I thought and grabbing my bag from my lodgings I snuck around filling it with food. Sib pricked his ears, gave up the fight and followed after me. Soon I came across Maelcolm. He'd recently got in with a group of young warriors where he could joke and show off his fancy riding and swordplay. Looking at him now, I could see that some of the cocky young man I'd first met had returned. He was even speaking broken Irish. I interrupted his fun.

'Maelcolm, I've lost Bruni.'

He leant back. The smile vanished from his face and his cup dropped to the floor. 'What do you mean, you've lost her?'

'Christ, Mael', I said, taken aback by his response, 'I mean, I don't know where she is.'

He grabbed the front of my jerkin, 'What have you done?'

'Well, nothing really, but she ran off yesterday and I've not seen her since.'

'If you've hurt her, I'm going to beat you shitless.'

'You can fucking try.'

By now his friends are getting interested, mystified because we'd dropped into Welsh. Maelcolm pulled me away from them hissing at me, 'We can fight tomorrow. Now we are going to look for her. Where did you last see her?'

He was right. We quickly picked up a light spear each, my seax and his sword. Not that we expected to meet any danger but you never knew. Then we ran out of the village, through the small herd of overwintering cattle, and up towards the high pastures where I'd last seen her.

By the time we arrived the rain had cleared into watery sunshine, little rainbows in every drop dripping from the sodden bushes.

No sign of Bruni, no visible tracks either, she was light, and it had rained since we parted. I started to call out.

Maelcolm hushed me, 'Seeing as she ran off after you did "nothing really" maybe you should shut up.'

Once again, he was right. We headed up to the ridgeline trying to get a view of somewhere she may have sheltered. I kept quiet while Maelcolm called her name over and over. We quartered everywhere from the ridge to the valley bottoms either side before we heard a faint cry behind us. Sib took off like a hare, divots flying from his paws. Turning, we saw him bowl over her slight, small, figure beside a clump of coppiced hazel.

Maelcolm dropped his spear and ran to her, pushing Sib away he quickly wrapped his cloak, and then his arms, around her shivering body. I held back, unsure what to do while her eyes glared balefully at me out from under his embrace. The sun was dipping down in the west so I got busy. I cut some hazel rods. The clump had been cropped, I guessed, three years before so the rods were tall and strong. I pushed their thick ends into the ground to make a circle, then rived one into thin strips to bind the tops over each other to make a small dome while Maelcolm kept comforting Bruni. I took off my short cloak and covered part of it. Maelcolm looked at me as if I was mad but then, what do these princes fucking know? He, though lord of nothing at all, had somehow got himself a long cloak such as nobles wore. I told him to give it me.

'Why?'

'We need a shelter,' I shot back.

I could see him trying to work it out. I stood and waited. He got there in the end and stepping away from Bruni for the first time he handed me his cloak. I picked up Bruni's shield and crowned the dome with it, wrapped Maelcolm's cloak around the rest, which, with mine, just about covered it all.

I crawled in through the space left under my short cloak. I sat there for a while hearing the other two whispering outside. Then they crawled in too. It was cramped, dark and uncomfortable but out of the wind. We crouched together so close that we had no choice but to be touching each other while Sib panted foul breath and happily forced his way into the middle. Maelcolm was quivering with rage while Bruni sobbed quietly. I remembered my bag and pushed some bread and meat into Bruni's hands, feeling for them in the gloom. After a moment's hesitation she took the food and began to eat. Maelcolm had thought to bring a flask of ale, which he gave her. Soon her shoulders stopped heaving and the tension began to drop.

I think the dark helped too. I spoke. 'Guess we're here for the night.'

'You should shut up,' said Maelcolm.

'We sitting here all night in silence then.'

'Better than listening to you, halfwit.'

'Fuck you.'

'By Allah, the pair of you. Stop this nonsense,' Bruni shouted over the both of us.

'By who?' said Maelcolm and I as one.

'Oh, it doesn't matter. Look we've come a long way together but we can't go on if you two keep fighting.'

'Not that far,' said I.

She sighed. 'Been through a lot then. Sar I could hate you right now. And not because you ended things with me, alright,' said Bruni, surprisingly gently.

Maelcolm stirred but said nothing.

I could feel a small hand seeking mine. I held it. I could hear a similar fumbling on Maelcolm's side. 'Now,' she said, 'You two hold each other's.'

I hesitated, then I felt Mael's hand seeking mine. For a moment we held too hard, then eased, and as we did, so did the tension.

'Boys,' Bruni said slowly but with force, 'boys, we can't fall out. We're three people who don't belong anywhere. We have to stick together.'

'But I do belong somewhere. I'm Earl Harold's man,' I said.

'When did you last see him Sar?' said Bruni'

I tried to work it out, 'I've been away two winters now.'

'And you expect an English Earl to remember you, do you?' said Maelcolm.

You know what, I did, but I felt foolish, so said nothing.

'Maybe he will,' said Bruni, 'Though even if he does, he's a long way away.'

We sat quiet for a while still holding hands. With the four of us squashed in there it started to get warm. There was more food in my bag, so I let the hands go and passed it out, a kind of flat honey cake, and barley bread, thick and wholesome.

Maelcolm was the first to speak. 'It seems to me that it boils down to, why are each of us here, and where do each of us want to end up. I'm here because I ran away. I think maybe I'd like to buy a cantref in Wales and farm.'

I snorted at that, 'I'm here because I want Oslaf dead.'

I heard, or sensed, Bruni catch her breath, 'I'm here because I escaped,' she said.

I felt curious, I don't know why. I'd never really asked her anything about herself. Difficulty with language, maybe, though for a while now we'd settled on a mostly Irish Viking way of speaking with a few English and Welsh words thrown in. Truth is, I hadn't cared.

'So, who did you escape from?' I asked.

'The evil, greedy bastard that brought me to the stinking slave town in this wet cold miserable country,' Bruni spat out angrily. A moment later the quiet sobbing resumed.

These two were more alone than I, I thought, suddenly missing Gyric with a sharp pang deep in my gut.

Bruni spoke quietly, almost a whisper in the dark, 'Since the desert tribesmen sold me from that beach, I have been nothing but a plaything for revolting men.'

She sniffled, choking back tears and snot by the sound of it. 'Coming here I've learnt I'm nothing like other girls.'

Maelcolm shifted and gently spoke, 'You're not so different, Bruni, you just like to fight.'

'You're wrong Mael, I don't like to fight, I have to. Girls here are courted and married. I've been used since I was a little girl.' She was speaking fiercely now, 'I have no idea how to behave. I've been turned into a freak.'

'We all have a story Bruni, tell us yours,' I said firmly.

I heard her take a deep breath, 'I was so frightened, I, and some other girls, were out helping with the date harvest when these wild men on horses swept down upon us with their wicked curved swords. Before I knew what was happening, I'd been swept off my feet and was being held against the side of a galloping stallion.'

She paused, there was no longer any light coming under the sides of our bender. We all shifted until we are all half lying on each other in a circle, heads on another's hip. Cramped but warmer and united.

'I was only a little girl, going on nine, when my whole world changed,' she took a deep, shuddering breath while my mind went back to my own capture. Blood, terror, and catastrophe. 'We were taken to a camp where we were herded in with a score of other captives. The next morning, after our captors finished their prayers, the young women and girls, six of us, were separated out while the rest were tied neck to neck and herded off inland.'

'And then?' said Maelcolm, 'what then?'

'We were taken to the shore where a galley waited side on to the sand.'

'What's a galley?' I asked.

'Does it matter? It's a ship with lots of oars. Rowing from it to us were two small boats full of men armed with crossbows and two young women with yellow hair. I'd never seen that before.'

'What's a crossbow?' I said.

'By Swithhun's eggs Sar, does it matter?' said Maelcolm.

'I suppose not.'

'Well at the time I didn't know either. We were traded, all six of us for those two yellow haired bitches and moments later we were in those boats being taken to the galley. Five seasick days later we were unloaded in a port called Genoa.'

'I've heard of that place, the two-faced city. One face to the mountains the other to the sea,' said Maelcolm.

'Two faced it certainly was but not for those reasons. As we came off the galley, we found ourselves in this busy port full of people shouting in a language I'd never heard before. I'd never seen anywhere so busy. We were led away through crowds of workmen leering and jeering at us. I was so frightened.'

Her head was on my hip. I could feel her shuddering again as she took another deep breath. I put my hand down to stroke her head. She swatted it away, then relenting, held it.

'We staggered along as the ground itself seemed to dip and heave into a cool building of some kind. There we stayed the night and, in the morning, woke to the clamour of bells not the call of the muadhan.'

The what? I thought, but kept my mouth shut.

'In the morning a kind woman came and gave us food and drink, water to wash in, then dressed us up in nice clothes. For a moment we all felt a little better and chatted together. Then men came in again and we were taken out into the bright light of the morning into…' She struggled for a word and gave up, 'Lots of loud noise, crowds of people, shouting. We were put on a, a big table thing. And sold. That was the last time I saw any of those girls and the last time I spoke my own language.'

The wind shifted and a strong draught came under the edge of my cloak. We all shifted around, cramped legs protesting. I pushed the bag into some of the space and wrestled the dog across the rest. He didn't like it. Tough. It was tight in there, very damp but warm.

'I was put into a covered cart and many hours later was let out into the courtyard of a large wealthy home in a town I later learned was called Papia. A woman called Sassia took me into the house. Another day had passed. I awoke to find strange blue eyes staring into mine and a small black hand stroking my forehead. There were three girls. One yellow haired, like the girls on the beach, one with skin so dark it was almost black, and a redhead with white skin and freckles and then me. Ulricus's dolls.' I heard Bruni spit in the darkness. 'What to say? We girls made our own language, while Sassia ordered us about by shouting and pointing. In the day we did chores around the house which was full of the most wonderful things. In the evenings, when he, Ulricus, wasn't feasting with his noble friends, we were washed, scented, dressed in silks, then sent to entertain him.'

On the word entertain, she started to choke up. Quietly, she cried herself to sleep and I dozed off soon after.

We awoke to the dawn chorus. Various arms and legs were sticking out of the now ruined bender. The dog was nowhere to be seen. Blessedly, it was a dry morning, sunny with the promise of spring. In daylight, we found it hard to meet each other's eyes.

Sunny or not, we shivered in our wet clothes. With everything so wet trying to kindle a fire was pointless. Gathering our things, we headed back. I caught sight of Sib slinking along behind us with a fine hare hanging from his jaws. Every so often he would drop it, tear at it for a while then catch up with us. Each time with less of the animal left. They don't like to kill hares here, so I was glad to see it disappear.

As we headed toward the rising sun Maelcolm spoke, 'so how did you come to be in Ireland Bruni?'

'I grew breasts.'

Maelcolm and I exchanged a sharp glance. There was so much I didn't understand about Bruni's story.

'I began to grow breasts and was sent to the servant's quarters. The yellow haired girl disappeared. New children arrived. The servants didn't want me, they said I was spoilt. It was Sassia who told me why I wasn't wanted, "You bleed soon, down there, dirty girl. The master doesn't like that." By now I knew enough Italian to understand her. Long story short. I was taken back to the two-faced city with its wealthy merchants and churches and its sleezy crooked world behind the marble fronts. Then I was sold to a drunken greasy slaver from Dyflin. He put the slave collar on me, then raped and abused me every day of the journey here.'

Bruni wasn't crying now. Now she was raging, thrashing at plants with her spear as we walked on. 'We got to Dyflin where I spent a few days in the slave pens, when Lorcan, that was the worm's name, thought he'd take me one more time. He was stinking drunk when he took the collar off me and dragged me back to his ship. When we got there, he couldn't do it, so he beat me then fell asleep. I slipped over the side and waded to the shore.'

'And then?' I said.

'Then I managed. I slunk about Dyflin till I realised I was being hunted, helping out for food and picking up the language from other strays. Then I ran to the slaughter yards, where you found me.'

'You know we have to go back to Dyflin,' I said, 'you could stay here.'

'I can't stay here. The women think I'm a whore.'

Maelcolm said, 'We could tell them what happened to you?'

Bruni turned on him eyes blazing, 'You really think that would help do you? You're an idiot if you believe that. What's the use?' She threw her spear at me and her shield at Mael and strode off. We meekly picked them up and followed after.

Chapter Nineteen

We got back to find everyone walking around with crosses of ash on their foreheads. Lent had begun. Forty days of people veering between saintly righteousness and grumpy resentment. Those days went faster once I learned that Faelen would be attending his King in Dyflin for Easter. We three would be going. At last, my chance to find Oslaf.

Ploughing had begun so we were kept busy fencing and ditching or leading stubborn oxen for the ploughmen. The boys were taking the cattle further out each day while the dung was turned in on their winter pastures. It was a fine time as the days got longer and the trees came into bud. Despite Lent everyone's mood changed with the promise of better days to come. This land, I so longed to leave, was truly beautiful in the spring.

Then it was time to go. Again, I had to change my appearance, as well as Bruni's. She was looking less and less like a boy. Particularly an Irish boy, with her dark skin and eyes, and long, shiny black, waving hair. I talked about this to Faelen who laughed and said, 'Have you looked around at my warriors and I lately?'

'Well,' I said, 'I had noticed you're all getting a bit shaggy these days. All beards and hair.'

'Not all of us, just those who will be raiding this year.'

It dawned on me. When I'd first met Faelen and his men on the beach at Porloc they'd been half-naked, showing their tattooed bodies, and their hair had been piled up, sticking out in crazy directions, stiff and white with lime. 'You'll go to see your King dressed like that?'

'We will. Our wild looks scare the lights out of those not used to our ways. Diarmait knows this well. We will dress that way and strut around haughtily like we just don't care. Keeps those Norse types on their toes and visitors think twice before crossing us.'

So, I had our solution, we'd all go as Faelen's followers. I still blackened my hair next to my skull, as well as my beard, but would lime the rest. Bruni's hair we cut shorter and, once stiffened with lime, spiked it all out all over her head. No woman would ever do this. Maelcolm refused to dress like a barbarian, which amused me. He was King of the Scots after all. He didn't see the joke.

More men trickled in from the surrounding valleys until we were about forty strong. Others would have to stay behind to protect their own cattle and crops as well as defend their King's borders. Horses are costly to keep so only Faelen, and his two closest warriors rode. The rest of us marched a short distance behind to avoid their flicked-up divots. Two fast hard days later we were in Dyflin where we were housed in a barracks inside the King's compound.

The next few days were spent escorting Faelen to and from Christ's Church, the biggest building in Dyflin, but nowhere near large enough for the leading families and their entourages. We never got to see the King or to even hear a service. A priest stood on a stage outside and we knelt when signalled, prayed when he joined his hands, but couldn't hear a word he said. Still Christ died and was raised and you could feel the passion in the air. There were penitents whipping themselves or crawling on their knees after men dragging huge crosses on their shoulders. Processions of monks, nuns, praying and singing, followed swaying holy figures carried shoulder high through the streets. Then at midnight on the Monday, silence. It was all over.

In the days after, Dyflin was still heaving. Not only the streets. Outside the walls there was another crowded town of tents and rough shelters. All those who could had come to celebrate Easter, in, or at least near, the mother church. For others it was a chance to meet and do business before the many ships crowded into the Pool set sail, either raiding or trading, or both. For Maelcolm and I, our first task was to get to Etromma's home and see if she had kept her word. I wanted to see Jokul as well. Along with Bruni and the dog we forced our way through the crowds. Sib was so tense I had to keep him on a tight leash fearful he would savage some passing dog or worse, child. Behind me Maelcolm pushed Bruni ahead of him, worried we would lose her in the press. I'm strutting through acting like I don't care when I realised. They were no longer behind me.

I'm wrenching Sib around just as some mangy beast half his size decides to have a go. Kicking it away from Sib's slavering jaws, I yanked him after me, going back the way we'd come. There they were. Bruni shaking, her face a strange ashen hue, while Maelcolm tried to make sense of what was happening. I herded them to the side of the street.

I jabbed Bruni hard with stiff fingers, 'What's going on? Eh?'

Bit mean of me I know. 'He's here, Lorcan, the slaver,' she gasped out.

I could now see she was terrified. I spoke gently, 'Where did you see him? Come now, you're safe with us. No way he can know who you are.'

She crooked a shaky finger at a nearby ale booth. Maelcolm and I exchanged looks over her head. 'Come,' I said, drawing her towards the booth.

She faltered but came. We pushed ourselves on to the end of a table. Remembering last time in Dyflin I stowed Sib under the table between our legs. He quieted, just lifting one hairy eyebrow to keep an eye out, his head between his paws.

Maelcolm shouted for some service. 'Bruni,' I said, 'Don't turn your head. Now, tell me where he is.'

'Behind me, two tables over, with three other men.'

'Rough cropped, sandy hair, pointed beard?'

'No, the fat one.'

I should've known. Slack fat, lank, greasy hair flopping into his ale pot, food in his beard. Black scabby patches on the face he was scratching with filthy fingers. His quality clothes streaked with stale ale and other muck. For the first time I really felt for Bruni. Looking across at Maelcolm I could see tears in his eyes. He nodded at me, I nodded back. Bruni, always aware, caught our intention. 'We're going to get him?' she said.

'Yep,' said I.

'There's more of them than us?'

'Only one. They're drinking hard. We'll only have the one, spin it out.'

Maelcolm said, 'Weapons? Bruni doesn't have any.'

Our spears and shields were at the barracks. That left Maelcolm with his sword, me with a seax, and all of us with our eating knives. I also had my handy little blackjack which neither of them had seen in use, and of course, my little axe. I stealthily passed the seax to Bruni with sheath and belt. Bruni raised an eyebrow at me. 'Don't worry,' I said, 'we'll be fine.' I'd never felt so sure of myself.

Maelcolm said, 'We can't do it here.'

'No, be patient, we'll follow them when they leave. We'll only kill if we have to, and if we do, no-one must know.'

Bruni, now fierce, 'He has to be mine. I choose what happens to him, yes?'

We both smiled, glad to see her back.

We were there some time. Long enough for the ale-seller to ask us to go. I gave him a coin to leave us alone. He bit it, gave us a strange look but left us alone. I kept an eye on him. If he spoke more than three words to anyone, I'd be over there, quick as.

They were staggering when they finally left. I handed Sib's leash to Bruni and led the way. They took a side road leading down to the docks. With so much foot traffic the log roads were slippery. Everyone was watching their step, not looking at me. I carefully pulled my blackjack out of my shirt. Now, I was walking behind the last man in Lorcan's group. He was drunkenly struggling to keep upright. A quick glance round and I smacked him. Over his head, bam, with the sand filled leather. His head flew back, eyes glazed. I caught him and gently sat him up in a corner.

'He'll have to sleep it off here,' I said, in case anyone saw me. I loved the look on the faces of my companions. With a smile I headed on.

'Now we're even,' Maelcolm said into my ear.

'Depends on where they're going,' I answered, quickly turning as Lorcan looked back, 'Seems he's lost his way,' he shouted to the others, laughing. They rolled on down the street, grouped closer now.

'One each,' Maelcolm said.

'We've got to get them somewhere out of sight, for Bruni to teach him a lesson.'

Bruni nodded, eyes shining while Sib was all alert. He knew we were on a hunt. Now we were among the slave pens. Miserable captives tied together, tented, tattered sails their only cover. It stank. Streams of shit and piss wound down into the Pool making us all gag. We stopped so Maelcom could retch up his last meal. There were no crowds here. We followed them until they entered a small ramshackle building.

We waited a while then I crept up to the door and peered through a crack. A nearby pen of slaves looked on uninterested. I crept back to the other two. 'I think they're getting food for their slaves.'

I was right. Shortly after one of them came out with a bucket filled with some kind of rank slop. Now they were interested. A low moaning came from the pen as they surged around with wooden bowls in their tied hands. Lorcan's man spat into the bucket then started to ladle the slop into the reaching bowls. I hit him, as before, but he didn't go out cold. He turned, groggy, so I grabbed him round his waist and tipped him into the pen. For a moment the slaves, mostly men, stared woefully at the tipped-up bucket. Then they were upon him, forcing his face into the slime.

His legs kicked out a few times, then he was still. One of them found a knife in his belt and sawed at the bonds of the man next to him. I thanked the newly resurrected Christ that they had the sense to stay silent.

We had to act now. Maelcolm and I burst through the door. The sandy haired man grabbed a chopping knife off the table but Mael's sword was at his throat. Backing off, frightened, he dropped the knife and showed his palms. I kicked the table towards Lorcan who hadn't grasped what was happening. I laughed as Bruni came at him, the seax in his face. He froze. I pushed the table aside and got behind him. I put my left arm around his throat and tickled the back of his skull with my knife. He smelt as bad as he looked.

His arms flailed about but I had him and he knew it. 'No noise or you're dead, got it?'

He got it. Bruni pushed the point of my seax into his fat belly, just a little. 'Remember me?' she asked him.

He shook his head, afraid to speak.

Maelcolm kicked aside the knife on the floor and steered his man into a corner. 'Sib,' I called out. Smart dog. He reared up in front of the man, and put his paws on his shoulders. Baring his teeth, he put his great jaws around the man's head. By the smell I think he shat himself. Sib, point made, dropped back to the ground and sat, watching him, snarling quietly. Maelcolm could now keep an eye out of the door.

Bruni pushed her face up to his, 'You sure you don't remember me?'

Lorcan grimaced, sobering quickly as I tightened my grip around his throat. 'Look harder,' I said, 'look harder.'

He peered at her, seeing a wild boy, then his eyes widened, 'Well, fucking spunk my cock, you're that little bitch I fucked sideways every night all the way from Genoa.' He seemed almost gleeful. Did he really not understand what was happening to him? 'You ran away, cost me a pretty penny I can tell you. We'll catch you now and I'll make you suffer.'

Bruni tutted, 'No, no, no, we're here to make you suffer.' She sheathed the seax and got out her knife and slit his nostrils. He yelped pathetically. Now he understood. She moved the knife up his face, 'An eye, maybe, maybe two. How would you like to be blind Lorcan?'

He squirmed away from the knife but I gave him nowhere to go. 'Go on Bruni. Do it.' I was enjoying this now, from the moment she cut his nose I was fired up.

She wagged a finger at me. 'Or what Lorcan?' she slowly drew the knife down his body, jabbing gently here and there almost like she was tickling him. She reached his groin, the inside of his thigh, 'I could stick this in a hairsbreadth and you'd bleed out. You could watch, wouldn't take long.'

I was proud of her. She'd been listening. A killing wound, one you could do from the ground if you had to.

Then she grabbed the front of his tunic and slit it up fast like a striking snake. He shuddered. He was starting to cry now. She cut his belt, the knife sharp as ever, then she cut his waist string and his parts flopped out. 'Maybe I'll just take these.' She looked him in the eye. Now he's sobbing. 'Would seem fitting somehow, don't you think?' She tickled him again, with her knife just where, in a different setting, a man likes to be tickled. He tried to cover himself. She struck at his arm, slashing it, he drew it back sharply and pissed himself.

Bruni jumped back disgustedly, 'Foul man, foul pathetic creature. Snivelling in front of a girl.' She turned to the sandy haired man, 'What do you think of your boss now, eh? Not so tough, is he?' She looked back at her prey.

'It might be a good idea to get out of here,' said Maelcolm, 'The escaping slaves have been noticed. It's pandemonium out here.'

'It's what?'

'Crazy. A riot. There are men rushing in with whips and clubs but they can't cope. There'll be murders. Trouble. Lots of trouble. By Saint Oswald's head, another pen has broken free.'

Bruni seemed to make her mind up, 'Look at him,' she said, spitting on Lorcan, 'he's done. He won't forget me. I'm done with him.' She shoved her knife in her belt and headed for the door. She looked at me, 'Leave him, let's go.'

She went out the door. Maelcolm followed. That left me with Lorcan, the dog and the sandy haired man. I backed towards the door, my arm still around Lorcan's throat. 'Go Sib go.' Out he went. The man moved from his corner, sidling crab-like, eyes flicking around seeking a weapon. He found one, a short whip. He cracked it menacingly. I kept an eye on him but was still running over Bruni's choice. I hadn't thought she'd leave him alive. Not me though. I shoved the knife up into the back of his skull. I tried to pull it out but it stuck fast. I heaved the bloody faced corpse towards the whip cracker and, snatching my axe from my belt, backed out the door. As I turned to run, he threw Lorcan's still twitching body to the side and came for me. I back-swiped him with the axe, slashing his face but not deeply. He flinched back and I got away. Now he was shouting, 'Murder, it was those three, with the huge dog. Them, they freed the slaves.'

We frantically pushed our way through the throng of slaves and slavers. Most of them didn't care about us, keener to get their slaves back into the pens. Some did, some caught sight of the shouting bleeding man, and then us. Now we were the hunted.

My mind raced. I knew we'd messed up. No one should have died, except maybe Lorcan, and then only if we weren't seen. No slaves should be running loose about Dyflin. Now what? Where to go?

We ran on. I got Sib's leash from Bruni and on him. I let him lead. Uphill. Pushing people out the way. Stay together. Elbow, duck, wriggle. The crowd seethed. Men rushing downhill. Women, children, dogs, slaves pushing in all directions. We fought against the crowd. Then I saw a building I knew. 'This way, come on,' as I shouted, I saw armed men were following us. 'Get low,' this really was for me and Maelcolm. We crouched hoping to get lost behind the crowd. 'This way.' I pounded on a door. Sadb Hosvir's door.

'What if no ones in?' says Bruni

'I don't know. We fight. I don't know. Jesus, let us in.'

The door opened so fast I nearly fell in. It was Hosvir.

'Let us in. I can explain. Just let us in please.'

He stood aside without a word. We pushed through his house. Past his wife, Aideen, with her baby at the breast. I stammered some apology as we went through. As we did the door started to shake under the blows of many fists.

I was crouched behind their back door watching Hosvir as he calmly opened the door, turning the good side of his face to his unwelcome visitors. It revealed a bunch of sweaty, dirty slavers carrying the tools of their trade. Clubs, whips and short seax's.

'We want the men who just ran in here.'

Hosvir leant against the door jamb, smiling gently, arms crossed, 'No men in here apart from me. You should stand back. My wife is nursing our child.'

'They had a huge dog. Big, grey beast. Three people. At least one Irishman, one a boy,' gasped a man who appeared to have taken charge.

Hosvir laughed and reached for his sword which hung behind the door. 'Do you think I'd have missed three men and a huge dog running through my home?'

'Then we're coming in,' shouted a man from the back.

Hosvir turned, showing the scarred side of his face and bringing his sword into sight, he said, 'I think not.'

I could see a couple of them recoil at his face while others looked warily at his sword. I tensed myself ready to hurl myself across the room. I had no need to. Hosvir slowly and calmly raised his sword to the level of their leader's eyes. 'You owe my wife an apology.'

'We owe you nothing. You're hiding fugitives.'

With a quick flick of his wrist, Hosvir, shifted his sword from the man's eyes and smacked him in the temple with the flat of the blade. He reeled back, dizzily, into his followers. 'Any one of you can apologise.'

By now Aideen had stood up in the centre of the room, her robe closed, her shawl over her head and the baby in her arms. I couldn't believe it but one after the other those rough men touched their forelocks and told her they were sorry to have disturbed her. I was sniggering into my hand and as the door shut, I couldn't hold my laughter in any more.

'Hosvir, whoa, you certainly showed them,' I chortled, then tried to explain it to Bruni and Maelcolm. They looked past me, not even smiling. 'Oh God, Hosvir, I'm sorry.'

'Yeah well, I'm glad you find it so funny,' he said to me sternly.

I looked back, unsure, 'No, I shouldn't have come here. We'll go.' I nodded to his straight-faced wife. 'Is there a back way we can leave.'

She grinned wryly. Then it was Hosvir's turn to laugh, 'Ha, ha, your face. I do believe you felt shame for a moment there Sar.'

Soon after that Aideen's sister and a servant girl arrived, excitedly talking about the scandal in the town. Aideen hushed them as they took their bundles through to the cooking hearth. They gazed at us and the dog, wide-eyed, but shyly, said little. After feeding us Aideen said we'd better stay for the night. We bedded down where we could in their small home, grateful beyond measure.

Chapter Twenty

I woke with a start, hands leaping to my weapons. It was only the servant girl, breathing life into the fire. I lay back, watching her, reminded again of Ymma. It was all so long ago. Maelcolm was deep asleep, but I could tell, by Bruni's cat-like pawing's above her face, that she would wake soon. As her eyes opened, I placed a finger on her lips. She nodded, and gently woke Maelcolm. As it was her and not me, he didn't grumble. The dog stretched, startling the girl. I hushed her, 'Thank Aideen and Hosvir for us. We need to leave. Is there a back-way out?'

She nodded, and crooked her finger at us. We followed her through the house into a small yard. She went to a solid looking fence at the back. She wrestled with a board to open a small gap we could just push through. I turned to thank her. She shook her head, 'Those poor slaves and that disgusting man you kil…'

I put my hand over her mouth, 'Say no more…'

She smiled, not so shy now, and, pushing my hand away, grabbed my face then kissed me full on the mouth. As Bruni scowled, the giggling girl ducked back inside the fence. We turned to go.

'Which way?' whispered Bruni. We'd found ourselves in a winding alley between high fences, with yards each side and houses beyond. Here and there other alleys branched off. A maze, another Dyflin behind the streets. Having no idea where we were, I had to perch up on Maelcolm's shoulders to see over the fences. Feeling stupid, we snuck around until I finally caught sight of the roofs of Diarmait's hall. With a direction to head in, we got through the maze without meeting anyone. Emerging, we had no choice but to walk through a main street. Despite the early hour people were already out and about. It started with whispers.

'That's the dog all the fuss was about.'

'Two men and a boy.'

'Yes, one young bald man.' Maelcolm winced at this.

Then the whispers got louder until they turned to shouts, 'It's them. Those that caused all that trouble yesterday,' and worse, 'After them. Don't let them get away.'

For all the shouting they were loath to get close but their numbers grew. We walked faster and faster, trying desperately not to run. If we ran, the mob would pull us down. The odd lump of mud was thrown our way. I felt sick, desperately pulling Sib's head to face forward. We didn't need him to attack anyone now. At last, we came to where the street rose towards Diarmait's compound.

Two of Diarmait's own housecarls guarded the gate. As we drew closer, I could see one of them call out. More armed men appeared until they filled the space left by the open gates. Now we had an increasingly angry crowd behind us and, in front, a row of levelled spears.

Only one way to deal with this. I'm one of Faelen's warriors and I don't care. I drew myself up as tall as I could, 'I am Faelen oi Aitre's man. Why do you bar my way? Can you not see this dog? I am the man that everyone is looking for. Clear my way.'

The spears parted and we walked in. For a moment I felt like Moses. I strutted on towards King Diarmait's hall doors. I had no plan at all. In the corner of my eye I saw what looked like a small group of English housecarls. Odd, I thought. Then Faelen himself stepped out from the hall. His face showed nothing but by the quivering tension of his body, I knew. I knew he was furious.

I kept up the pretence as we followed him round the outside of the hall. Once we were out of sight of the courtyard, Faelen turned, and punched me right in the side of my head.

* * *

I came too, spluttering, with a searing pain in my left temple. I opened my eyes just as a second bucket of very cold water sloshed into my face. I sat up to see Maelcolm stepping back with a sly grin on his face and a bucket in his hand, behind Bruni was pulling back a very confused looking Sib. Then I remembered, and there was Faelen, stood above me.

Iesu Mawr, what was I going to say now? I looked up at him but couldn't hold his gaze. 'I'm sorry Lord,' I mumbled.

He knelt over me and grabbed my face. His voice was low, steady and hard, 'Sorry, doesn't really cut it Sar, does it? Escaped slaves, dead Irishmen, slavers hunting you through the streets. Then to cap it all you turn up here claiming to be my man.'

'We needed to get in.'

'You needed to respect what I told you.'

'You told me not to kill Oslaf,' as soon as the words left my mouth, I wanted to take them back.

'Don't insult me Sar, you're not stupid'. With that he grabbed my face again, heaved me off the ground and pushed me against the solid log wall of Diarmait's hall. I didn't even try to resist, awed by his strength. He put his face close to mine, 'Anyone else, I might kill them now, but you, I need you alive.' There was a strange look in his dark eyes as he said this, 'Alive, yes, if I can keep you that way.'

He let go of my face, God it was sore, my neck too. As I stood there wondering at his words, he turned to the other two, 'No use you two smirking either. He didn't cause all this mayhem on his own. Now all three of you have to meet my King. You are all going to walk in and kneel before him. Be aware, one wrong word and you won't walk out. Get me?'

We all nodded shamefacedly. I looked at the other two with their mud-stained clothes and tousled hair and realised that my hair was dripping limewash down my clothes. I must look a sight, unwashed, filthy clothes. Black hair by my skull, dark red hair from there, and greyish white ends. No proud Irish warrior now, just a bedraggled fool. And now I was to meet a King.

Faelen hustled us into Diarmait's hall through a side door. Central to the room was a platform with upon which was a tall chair silhouetted from behind by light streaming in from an open shutter. Each side of the chair stood a fully armed, helmeted and mailed warrior, both huge men. The chair was empty.

'Over here, this way,' came a voice from a shadowed corner of the hall by a small hearth. Coloured by the flickering flames a slight figure sat beside a small table.

Faelen pushed us towards him. As we entered another beam of sunlight, he said one word, 'Kneel'.

We knelt. I signalled to Sib to lie down. Maelcolm and Bruni looked down at the floor. I found myself staring straight at Diarmait, for that was who he must be. No long beard like King Edward of England, no clothes embroidered with gold and silver, no crown, not even a jewelled band across his forehead. Just an ordinary looking man wearing a couple of very fine rings.

Faelen's strong hand grasped my hair and forced my head down, 'Respect my King boy, show some humility.'

'Let him stare,' said Diarmait, 'not the kingly figure you were expecting, eh?'

I shook my head, not daring to hold his gaze.

'You'd do better to speak. Your lives are on the line.' As he spoke, he rose and stood before us.

I swallowed hard. My mouth went dry. I managed to speak, 'No, Sire, not what I expected.'

'You've seen a King before then?'

'Two, sire.'

'Two?' He drew his head back in surprise.

'I was at Wincestre with my lord when I saw King Edward, and I saw a prince crowned King of Alba.' I could feel Maelcolm stirring uneasily beside me.

'Lord? I thought Faelen was your lord.'

'I'm sworn to Earl Harold of Wessex.'

'Hmmm, and yet here you are. Harold, I liked Harold, we did each other a good turn.' Diarmait was pacing back and forth, 'Doesn't mean I won't take your lives for the trouble you have caused.'

Maelcolm spoke for the first time, 'We are very sorry, Sire. The slaves escaping was a mistake, not our intention.'

Diarmait seemed to pounce, 'What difference do your intentions mean to me? Who are you anyway? I can barely understand your uncouth Irish, so, tell me where are you from and why?'

'I'm a Strathwaelen, my cousins want me dead.'

'Some sort of renegade then.' He turned to Bruni, 'And you, look at me. You are not even a boy, are you?'

Bruni squirmed, 'No sire.'

'And you are from?'

'Al Qayrawan,'

'You've come a long way.'

'You know it?' asked Bruni eagerly.

'I know of it. A Holy city, from what I've heard, but not for Christians.'

'I was a child when I last saw it,' Bruni said, 'Just a girl.'

'But not baptised. We'll see to that.' With that he clapped his hands. Immediately two servants came out and placed a large platter of breads, cheeses and cold meats on the table along with a jug and five cups.

'Eat with me,' said Diarmait as he and Faelen sat one side of the table. We three sat side by side on a bench opposite them relieved to be off of our knees. Along with the others, I reached for my eating knife. Shit, I thought, remembering where I'd last seen it. Everyone else began to cut up their food.

We were all eating off the board, peasant fashion. Diarmait cut a piece of cheese and gave it to Sib, who delicately took it from his fingers, 'You not eating then?' he said, looking directly at me. 'Your name is Sar, is it not?' I nodded. 'Not hungry then, Sar?'

I was hungry, truth was I could eat a horse. Then he snapped the trap.

'Would this be what you're missing?' He had my knife in his hand. 'It was found in the back of a slaver's head.'

As the breath went out of me, I heard Bruni draw hers in, sharply. In a flash Bruni's own knife was pricking the side of my neck. I drew back stiffly, swivelling my eyes to hers. Diarmait sat calmly watching us, as my eyes passed his to Bruni's I noticed for the first time that his eyes were different colours.

'You agreed that what happened to Lorcan was down to me,' hissed Bruni, angrier than I'd ever seen her. Sat between me and Maelcolm she was struggling to get up from the bench.

'Sit down girl,' commanded Faelen, 'Sit!'

Visibly shaking, Bruni pulled herself together and stabbed her knife into the table. Now I could see that Maelcolm was also staring at me, with a frown on his face.

'He deserved it,' I shouted, 'he fucking deserved everything he got.'

'Not your choice, Sar, mine,' said Bruni.

Diarmait's level voice cut in, 'Well, I now know which one of you should die for these murders in my town.'

Oh God, the end of the road for me. Without my revenge. Alone. I couldn't take it in as I forced back tears from my eyes. Oslaf would still be alive, while I. I would be dead.

'Perhaps you need to eat.' Diarmait passed me the knife.

I took it unthinkingly, my mind racing. Won't see my sister either. What was wrong with me? I'd faced death more than once but never shook like this. Duw, help me. I pulled myself together, looked at the knife in my hand, still scabbed with Lorcan's blood, then reached out and cut a wedge from a small round cheese.

Wedge shaped too were the colours in Diarmait's irises. Blue, green and brown. I looked straight into them, pleased as I, untremblingly, took a bite of the cheese. I put the knife down, reached for the jug, and poured wine from it into a cup. After taking a sip, I smiled at him, 'Very fine wine, sire. It has kept well considering the season.'

One corner of Diarmait's mouth rose briefly, 'It has, it has indeed. Full of surprises you are.'

I could see him taking my measure, not at all fooled by my act. I realised I was dealing with a very clever man. 'Don't want to die crying, is all,' I said.

'Faelen tells me you're an Englishman, and you speak Welsh and clearly you've learned Irish. Is this all true?'

I nodded. Where was this going?

'While you were causing a riot in my town, a seagoing drakkar with thirty pairs of oars arrived here, flying the flag of an English Earl.'

'Aelfgar, at last.'

'Why do you say that?'

'Oslaf is here, he's Aelfgar's man.'

'Oslaf has been here for some time.'

'Seeking ships for an Earl,' I said.

'You seem very well informed. Why?'

I looked at Faelen, he nodded. 'I came here to kill him.'

His eyes narrowed, 'Your friends should leave now. You,' he pointed to Maelcolm, 'back to the barracks. And you, girl, you will stay with the women of my house. A priest will see you tomorrow. Your disguise is clearly no longer needed.'

Bruni gave me another ferocious stare before a young woman led her from the hall. Maelcolm walked off without a backward glance. Sib whined and put his head between his paws. Didn't they care if I was killed?

'Your dog is sad to see your friends go. Tell me where did you get him?'

I told him.

'A very fine dog, trained?'

'Mostly, catches anything that runs'

'Hmmm, well that dog belongs to me now.'

'What the fuck? No way, you're not having my dog.'

Diarmait shrugged, 'Your life or your dog. Either way the dog stays with me.'

I was going to live. The relief must have shown on my face.

'You have a chance to live. For some reason Faelen is very keen that you do. I want a service and I want your dog,' said Diarmait. 'I want the dog for two reasons. Firstly, when my people see the dog, they will know that I have dealt with the criminal responsible for all the trouble you've caused. You are lucky that Lorcan has no family here.'

'And secondly?'

Diarmait laughed, 'It's a very fine dog. Now, down to business. Oslaf has been trying to assemble a fleet but without the visible backing of a man of power he was never going to get far. He now has that man. He will get the fleet he wants. For the right price.'

'So, what do you want from me?'

'As is usual, the destination for any raid is kept a secret, except from me. I have to be told before anyone can recruit. From now on all that is said here remains between us.' He took a long swallow, refilled our cups and signalled for another jug. 'Earl Aelfgar has arrived here, he says, to take a part in Welsh affairs.'

My dog, I was thinking, but my mouth said, 'What part?'

'Never you mind,' said Faelen, sharply.

Diarmait raised a hand, 'What I want to know is why he felt the need to come himself. An English Earl or a Welsh King could easily have sent an emissary to confirm Oslaf's story. If there's more to this, then I want to know. That's where you come in.'

'You need a spy,' I said, 'Can't do it. Oslaf knows me.'

'Knows you how?'

'He put this scar on my face for starters.'

'You need to tell him Sar,' said Faelen.

I drank some more of Diarmait's wine. I felt wretched, my dog was going. I'd escaped death but had just turned Diarmait down. What was I thinking? Should've lied. No point. Faelen knows my story anyway. I told Diarmait what was necessary. I drank some more.

'Faelen, if he's found out. I've lost nothing,' I heard Diarmait say, 'We disguise him. A monk, servant, maybe. Hmmm, how about he's a guide around Dyflin?'

'Servant might work, but Aelfgar's an Earl, he arrived on a large ship. He'll have his own retainers,' said Faelen. 'Guide might work, but I can't see him hearing anything useful.'

'I could demand he uses our servants. It seems petty though, not like a King.' Diarmait paused, his brow furrowed, 'I can, and have, limited the number of armed followers a visitor to my Kingdom is allowed. Faelen, I'm going to hide this man where anyone can see him.'

'You what?' I said, 'Oslaf will kill me on sight.'

Faelen laughed, 'No Sar, I think I see where this is going.'

Diarmait nodded, excited, 'Yes, I will provide him with his own honour guard. A troop of my wild Irish mercenaries from the west. You take the same disguise you came here with. We use some of Faelen's men, and some who really do come from Munster, not that any Englishman can tell them apart, and you Sar.'

'Me?' I said, reeling a little with the wine.

'Yes you, we'll whiten all their faces, get you all similar enough that they won't know who is who. You will always be the one closest to which of them you think you can learn from.'

'Sure, but how can I be in their quarters?'

'You'll always enter first. You won't leave. Stand each side of the doors and when they ask you to move, you don't understand a word.'

I didn't really have much choice. Disguised or not, the idea of Oslaf staring into my face was not a happy one.

Then it dawned on me, 'Look you, Sire, you need someone who speaks Welsh and English. Yes? Irish, enough to tell us what been heard?'

Diarmait looked at me askance, 'Yes, we have you.'

'But we also have Maelcolm.'

'Your friend, you selling him out now?'

I shrugged, 'He's never met Aelfgar, I have. He's never met Oslaf, I have. Change his appearance, job done.'

Maelcolm looked very much the English warrior. He'd shaved his beard and kept his long moustaches. I laughed out loud and said, 'Shave his whiskers, trim his hair. His bald patch gives him an instant tonsure. Dress him up as a monk. Ha, he can even read.'

Diarmait narrowed his eyes at me, then turned to Faelen, 'Your boy here speaks some sense.' He got up and slapped his hand down on the table. 'You'll both go in. Faelen you sort them out.' He left and Faelen went to seek Maelcolm.

Chapter Twenty-One

So, there we were, that same afternoon, both of us part of the welcoming party ceremonially greeting the arrival of an English Earl into the Kingdom of Leinster. It had been decided that Aelfgar's people were to be housed in a local monastery. Its abbot would be able to converse in Latin with Aelfgar's priests, how ideal. And, among those monks, a very humble novice, Maelcolm. And, in the honour guard, keeping English warriors from straying, and Irish folks from interfering, an arrogant young warrior, me.

Diarmait was right, some of the Englishmen clearly resented our presence, but to most of them we were just ignorant savages, only good for fighting. We were quickly ignored. As for Maelcolm, every court was full of priests and monks scurrying about. So much so that they were barely noticed as they brought food, candles and drink in and out. The lay servants served the monks and soldiers, and the monks served the leading men among our visitors.

The first time I saw Oslaf I shook with hatred. I controlled it, my knuckles white on the hilt of my seax. He, Aelfgar and his advisors kept close counsel along with a couple of Welshmen, by their accents, from the north. Maelcolm had far more opportunities to get close to them than I did but all soldiers gossip and much could be gleaned from their boasts and rumourmongering.

At the end of each day, once everyone had bedded down, we had to report to Diarmait. To Aelfgar's vocal chagrin, he was kept waiting for a week before he was given an audience. We'd learnt a surprising amount, Earl Siward, that great grizzled warrior lord, had died, stricken with the flux but, they said, most of all by the loss of his son. His only heir now, the young Waltheof, was too young to inherit the great Earldom of Northumbria. Diarmait already knew this but it was news to me. I'd confirmed that the Welshmen were indeed from the north of that country, being followers of Gruffudd ap Llewelyn. Their plan was to engage Aelfgar's forces and an Irish fleet to defeat Gruffudd ap Rhydderch which would make ap Llewelyn the King of all the Welsh.

'Why would Aelfgar help the Welsh unite, any thoughts on that?' asked Diarmait.

'Odd, there's bad blood between his father and the Welsh, being as they share a border,' said Maelcolm, 'but Sweyn Godwinson once allied with one Gruffudd against another.' 'Aelfgar lost out to the Godwinson's when they returned from exile,' I said, 'there's a lot of younger Godwinson's who will, all in time, want a piece of the pie. Maybe he wants a powerful ally.'

'That fits with something I heard,' said Maelcolm, 'if it's true. Aelfgar has been exiled himself. Really he's no longer an Earl at all.'

'What do you mean?' said Diarmait, 'be clear.'

I was yawning so hard I nearly missed the next bit.

'In early Lent King Edward called a council to determine who would succeed to Northumbria. Aelfgar had high hopes here. He'd previously lost the rich Earldom of East Anglia when Harold returned. He got it back when Godwin died but maybe it still rankled,' said Maelcolm.

Diarmait gave him a shrewd look, 'You seem to know a lot about the affairs of the English state, but go on.'

'Well, it seems that the council declared for Tostig. This would mean that Godwinson's ruled both the rich Wessex and the vast Northumbria. Aelfgar got angry.'

My head was nodding, I was struggling so hard to stay awake.

'Then to everyone's shock and surprise a young ragged housecarl forced his way into the chamber and engaged Harold in a fierce whispered conversation. He was particularly notable because he wasn't wearing any shoes.'

My eyes shot open, I blurted out, 'No shoes, he still wasn't wearing shoes.' It was Gyric. It had to be. Why had it taken so long for him to get there and why was he still without shoes? Diarmait shot me a sharp look. I shut up, but I was grinning from ear to ear.

'Aelfgar was getting more and more angry as people stopped paying him attention. Then Harold accused him of having a man in Ireland.' Maelcolm went on, 'Aelfgar lost it, yelling at Harold about him getting his own fleet from Ireland to challenge his King.'

'And Edward just sat through all this?' asked Diarmait.

'No, not at all, from what I heard the King went a livid white stood up and bellowed at the whole hall to shut up. He then demanded from Aelfgar an explanation. Aelfgar blustered for a while then revealed that he'd been in touch with Gruffudd ap Llewelyn. Many there didn't see much of a problem with this but the King did. He challenged Aelfgar on this. Aelfgar really lost his temper now and started raving about the Godwinson's. Sweyn had done it, Harold had got a fleet in Ireland now Tostig had taken Northumbria while his family was the last of the noble families left after Cnut's purge so why not him?'

'I wouldn't tolerate that in my court,' said Diarmait.

'Nor did King Edward. It was clear that Aelfgar had poked the fire. Now it was Edward's turn to lose his temper.'

'I've heard he has a bad temper,' said Diarmait, 'and that he's vengeful.'

'It would seem so. He got so angry he turned from white to purple and exiled Aelfgar on the spot.'

'And so here he is. In need of a friend. You've both served me well. Get some sleep.'

'Does that mean I can have my dog back?' I asked.

'Don't push me boy.' Diarmait got up to leave.

'No, don't leave,' said Maelcolm, 'there's more.'

'Don't leave sire,' said Diarmait, pausing.

'Sire, they plan to attack Hereford, once they've beaten ap Rhydderch.'

'Hereford, hmmm, that's an English town is it not?'

'Wealthy, they say. It walls are fallen into disrepair, they say. Ralph of Mantes is the Earl.'

'Edward's French nephew. Aelfgar agreed to this?'

'I don't know whose idea it was but Aelfgar seemed keen. Historically the town had belonged to his ancestors.'

'Maelcolm, I suspect there's a lot I don't know about you, but you've made a good spy. Though now, you two present me with another problem.'

We looked at each other, surely, we were out of the woods.

'You can't leave Ireland until this is all over.'

'Why not? We've done everything you've asked, and more.' I almost shouted.

'For which you stay alive. How can I let you go? You could warn the English and put my men at risk.'

'I'm never going back to England, ever,' said Maelcolm.

'Back? There's me thinking you were from some remote fading Kingdom,' Diarmait scoffed, 'and you Sar, you serve one of England's great Earls.'

My heart sank. I now knew Gyric was alive and back with Harold. That was good but, what about me?

Maelcolm and I were kept away from everyone while Diarmait met Aelfgar. With what he'd learnt from us I bet he drove a hard bargain. Two days after that we were released back into Faelen's service. This was the day that Diarmait would publicly recognise Aelfgar and other men who were allowed to recruit ships or men to the shipmasters and war leaders of Leinster on The Mound. Following that anyone seeking a berth could approach those leaders still seeking men.

The Mound was a large man-made hill with a flat top on the far side of The Pool. To get there you had either to cross the neck of The Pool or travel all the way round. Crowds of excited men made their ways there. Younger men flexed their muscles and boasted of their prowess. Older, or wiser, men were quieter, more concerned with the purse they'd bring home, or that they returned at all.

Somehow the last few days had brought Maelcolm and I closer than we'd ever been, maybe it was the job we'd done, or, maybe, Bruni's absence. Either way I'd begun to like him. He'd shaved his head completely now, looked good, better than a young baldie. Face looked naked but the first shadow of a new 'tache was growing. We swaggered our way on to a boat and crossed the neck of the Pool arriving at the Mound before the crowds arrived. At one end of the flattened top a massive column stood made from a single tree. Before it stood the chair we'd last seen in Diarmait's hall, along with its two heavily armed guardians.

It was soon made clear that the flat top was for the use of men of consequence. Faelen, of course, but I also saw Jokul make his way up there. Somehow in the milling crowd we met Hosvig. As the notables arrived, I pointed Oslaf and Aelfgar out to him. Diarmait arrived and took the chair. On his lap was a boy, looked about five to me.

'That's Murchad mac Diarmata mac Mael-Na-Mbo King of Leinster. He's been brought from Fern to be introduced to the people of Dyflin as Diarmait's heir,' said Hosvig.

'Fern?'

'Diarmait's capital, south from here, where the Kingdom is ruled from.'

'I thought Dyflin was his capital,' said I.

Hosvig's lop-sided face contorted into a laugh, 'This place? Town of raiders and slavers. The Irish are not who you think they are. Fern is a large town of monasteries, churches and fine halls. A place of learning and power.'

He was right, I'd not seen that Ireland. Meanwhile behind Diarmait was his hounds-man struggling with a huge grey dog, my Sibhirt, who was not behaving well. Either fighting his leash or sitting down refusing to move. Behind these great affairs Diarmait was still attending to the day-to-day concerns of keeping his people on his side. They would see the great dog and know that, although they had seen no visible justice nor received compensation for their losses, in some way Diarmait had dealt with the culprits.

After Diarmait's spokesman had announced who was allowed to raid where and when his company left. I asked Hosvig whether he was going to sea with Jokul again.

'Jokul's staying at home this year to attend to his farms. Besides one of his ships is laid up for repair and the rest rented out to men I'd rather not follow. I'm going to sign up with Faelen if he'll have me. I arm more heavily than most of his men, but I'm also a trained bussecarl and a good fighting man. There's a need for a man in a mail coat as much as for fast runners and scouts if only to guard ships. Aideen is with child again. My household grows faster than my fortune.'

I told him we weren't allowed to leave Ireland but somehow, I had to be on those ships.

'Diarmait will leave soon. You're just a complication. Talk with Faelen again when he's gone.'

With that he left to find Faelen while Maelcolm and I set off to find Jokul. We couldn't get a boat to ferry us back so walked around the Pool. We wended our way to his house to find ourselves arriving just as he came back. He greeted us warmly, we met Etromma and got all our money and weapons returned. Why we'd never met her boy that day at the church remained a mystery. We all ate, drank and swapped stories until dusk when I thought it wise to head back before Faelen sent a search party out for us.

Diarmait didn't leave but was so pleased with Aelfgar's gifts that, on Faelen's request, he allowed us to swear ourselves to Faelen until the campaign was over. We were free to go. Maelcolm was still not happy, 'We've not seen Bruni this whole time. Do you think they've put her in a convent or something?'

'How would I know?'

'You don't care?'

I thought for a moment, 'Sorry Mael, I do care, just don't know what to do. No way am I risking Diarmait's displeasure again.

One, I still want Oslaf's head. For me, and because he killed Earl Harold's cousin, Bjorn. Two, I want to live more than I want to see Bruni.'

We spoke to Faelen. He didn't know where Bruni was. He did have this to say, 'You two want to come with me on the campaign? Sar, you were born in Caer Dydd. The King we will be attacking was, in name, your King.'

'I owe him nothing, Lord. He neither helped our village nor protected it. I'm sworn to my Earl who has done both for me.'

'Maelcolm, you should consider another name, more Welsh, less Scots. Both Diarmait and I know who you are, neither of us care. We will keep your secret. You can swear into my service for the campaign, or for always. What do you say?'

Maelcolm thought, 'I'd like to find a home in Wales, Faelen. I have wealth enough to find a place. I can speak the language well. My accent is close to that of those men from the north who came with Aelfgar. I would be delighted to serve you for the campaign. I would ask for no reward.' With that he knelt and swore fealty to Faelen.

'Diarmait said we had to stay,' I said, stupidly.

Faelen stirred uneasily, 'That's for me to worry about, Sar, but I need you to swear the same loyalty to me as you have for Harold, until I choose to release you.'

It wouldn't be Faelen's worry if Diarmait caught us leaving I thought but said, 'I owe you far more than that. I owe you my life. Returning to Harold without proof of Oslaf's death is unthinkable anyway.' I too knelt and swore a solemn oath tying myself to Faelen's service.

From that moment on we worked from dawn till dusk. Either helping prepare the ships or training as a fighting troop. I was happy to learn that Hosvig would be joining us. Whenever we were going to or from the barracks, we would find a way to pass near Diarmait's hall and try to talk to any of the women or girls who served him. Though most ignored us, the odd one would talk. We learnt no more of Bruni save that she had been baptised but that in their eyes she was no Christian girl, but a rabid heathen.

That sounded like the girl we knew, but it got us no closer to finding her. The bustle around the Pool became frenetic. Aelfgar would be leaving with a fleet of eighteen ships, a large force indeed. As many other ships were also leaving. along with the usual working fishermen, the place heaved. The day came for our fleet to leave. As we filed down to embark, parading past Diarmait and his nobles, Maelcolm and I kept our heads covered. No sooner had we passed them when a roughly dressed boy with a large pack bashed into us.

'Pssst, don't say anything, it's me Bruni.'

We instinctively moved each side of her. We hustled her down to the dock and smuggled her into Faelen's ship. It was so loaded with provisions, men and weapons that one more bundle went unnoticed in the cramped ship. As our ship pulled away to take its place in the fleet a great commotion began on the crowded wharf as a huge grey shape, barked, bayed, snarled and bit its way through the crowds and threw itself into the sea.

'It's Sib,' I shouted, missing my stroke and crossing with oars each side of mine. We nearly collided with another ship as I further disgraced our crew by turning to appeal loudly to Faelen. With a wry smile, he signalled to back oars. Sib swum out to us and I heaved his sodden body over the bulwarks. Bruni sprang to help. I saw Faelen see her, and then, pretend not to see. Laughing wildly, I got back to my oar as that crazy dog shook himself all over my protesting shipmates. Once again, our troop was back together as we headed for the open sea.

Part Three

Chapter Twenty-Two

As soon as the water turned from blue to brown, I knew we'd entered the Safearn sea. The huge tides made anchoring near the shore difficult. One moment, you are in deep water, a short while later, stuck in deep mud. For this reason, our fleet, as many had done before, beached on Fleet Holme island. From here a fleet could be aiming to attack almost anywhere in the western parts of England or the southern and central parts of Wales. We would have been seen but no-one could guess our intentions.

It was hard to be here, where I'd pleaded with Harold for my life while Oslaf aimed to take it. Where I'd first met Gyric and Jokul while I was tied to a post. Where I'd last seen my twin being herded aboard a slave ship, while I skulked, hiding on the shore. My gut twisted with that old shame.

Soon after dawn, the ships captains and the leading men met together in the centre of the island. I was taken along to listen for Faelen. Sib would not leave my side, so I had to take him along. As plans were discussed I learnt that we were planning to create havoc in the south of Wales to divide the enemy's forces as they tried to repel attacks from the north. I squatted behind Faelen, whispering words the translators missed or the muttered asides of the speakers who thought we'd not understand. My hair was now straggling over my face in long thick black locks. My scanty beard, dyed, was enough to cover the scar on my face.

The first attack they planned was a feint on Caerleon, an important settlement on one of the approaches to Caer Went, Gruffud ap Rhydderch's main fortified town. I'd learned a lot about raiders. Most important, greatest reward for the least risk. Every man wounded was a burden. Everyman dead could not be replaced. Joining expeditions like Siward's was very much the exception. Caerleon could be approached up its own river, the Usk, but not far from the mouth it was blocked by a log boom, guarded at each end. Left intact, this was almost insurmountable for ships. Breaking it from crowded ships would provoke a massacre. We'd be exposed to plummeting spears and arrows while wrestling to free rusting chains fixed to slippery twisting logs, from the decks of moving ships. Landing to seaward would leave the ships at the mercy of the mud and the tides and any chance of surprise would be lost.

'I know a way to attack one side from the land without beaching ships in mud,' I whispered to Faelen.

'You do?' he said.

'I do. It depends on tides, skill, and running fast through the night.'

'What about all the sucking mud?'

'If you know the secret, there is a bay beyond the tides.'

Then I heard that hated voice, 'You two. Care to share with us, eh?'

Fucking Oslaf, I steeled myself not to react as Faelen answered, 'No secret, my man here has some local knowledge.'

I looked down at the ground as Oslaf crossed the central space. He addressed Faelen, 'You're the Irish warlord who flanked the battle at Porloc, are you not.'

'I am, shipmaster, we served alongside each other under the Earl Harold.'

'You had local knowledge then too. A Welsh boy, wasn't it?'

'Is that what he was? Possibly,' Faelen shrugged, 'more importantly moving fast, far and quietly is what we do.'

Osalf narrowed his eyes at Faelen, 'Hmmm, so is this the man?'

I stood up reluctantly, as I did, Sib did too, stretching himself like a bow before letting loose a low, threatening growl.

Oslaf stood back, looked hard at me, 'That dog, I've seen that dog before, twice, in Dyflin. Once with King Diarmait, and before with a surly Irishman, could that man have been you?'

I stared at him from behind my long black locks. 'Many people ask about my dog. You are not so memorable,' I answered, foolishly, as well as untruthfully. His translator blanched but told him what I'd said.

Oslaf sucked his teeth, shook back his long yellow-white hair, and swallowed the insult, 'Come, talk with Aelfgar.'

We walked to where Aelfgar stood with his housecarls. A handsome man, as tall, dark and brooding as I remembered him. He moved with the sure authority of an English Earl. Even among all these Norse and Irish warriors he clearly saw himself as not just a leading man, but the leading man. He impressed me.

I told how the bay beside Caer Dydd was always full of water. How three rivers flowed into it, and how its clear waters were fresh. There were murmurs of doubt once my words had been put into English.

'It's a trap. He's a traitor.'

'How can that be? This river is as muddy as a field drain.'

'Irish stories, they're all mad.'

Oslaf didn't stop staring at me but spoke to Faelen, 'This man. What's his name?'

'Muirchu, his name is Muirchu.'

'And he knows all this how?'

'Many of my people trade over here. His father dealt in dried fish and hides,' lied Faelen, smoothly.

Oslaf's lip curled in disgust. I'd have loathed the arrogant fucker even without our shared hatred. Memories of killing his father swamped my vision. I so wanted to do the same now, to him, here, in front of everyone.

'I beached at Caer Dydd before. We spent hours in the mud.' Oslaf was staring at me now, 'My father was killed there.'

I ignored those last words, 'You beached upriver of the spit. There's a way into the bay, but if you don't know it, your ship breaks.'

'And you know this secret? Then tell us,' said Aelfgar.

There's no way I'm telling anyone I thought, sorry I'd opened my mouth at all, 'I can't tell you. I can only show someone willing to trust me.'

'Faelen, here, trusts you?' asked Aelfgar.

I nodded, and to my relief, so did Faelen.

'I don't trust him,' said Oslaf, 'I think he's hiding something. He's not who he says he is.'

Diw Sant protect me, I prayed to myself. Does he know who I am, or just suspect? 'I can get two ships ashore at the height of the tide. No sooner, no later. We'd need men able to run through the night, and arrive ready to fight.'

Aelfgar thought for a while. 'We'd want to follow the river up past the boom on a rising tide towards Caerleon. You'd need to get there, fight, cut the boom and be ready to fight off a counter attack in time for us to ride the tide up the Usk.'

One of his leading housecarls, a burly giant of a man with a long walrus moustache and yellow teeth, said, 'That's not a lot of time. Tides as they are. Our men could not do that. Could not run through a strange land all night and fight before dawn.'

'But mine can,' said Faelen, proudly. 'We'd wear no mail, no heavy shields, take no provisions, trust our guide here,' he swept his arm towards me. I gulped inwardly. Truth was I'd explored that way, once, as a boy, with Moira, and it only got dark on our way back. It was a long way and what if I got lost?

The burly giant looked impressed, 'You fight without mail or shields?'

'If we jump them before dawn. They will have no mail. Just the shields they can grab. Has to be said, these won't be staid English warriors fighting rooted to the spot. These are Welshmen, more used to fluid fighting but I have some ideas,' said Faelen.

'We'll need to know when, if, you've succeeded. I'm not taking this fleet into a trap,' Aelfgar said. 'You'll have to signal, you'll need smoke, enough to be seen upriver from here. We'll ride the tide from here in the early dawn. It's not that far to the mouth of the Usk my own local man tells me.'

A short grubby man stepped out from behind, stooping humbly, ''Scuse me your lordships. I'm that man,' he paused, wiping a rheumy eye with his sleeve. 'I know all the waters, and all the shoals, from here to Cas-gwent. I've heard of your sweet water bay, even know where it's meant to be. I've looked that way from the river. There's no way to it, always shoals, no deep water, not ever. Your man there,' he said, pointing at me, 'he's full of shit.'

Everyone looked at him, then me, then Faelen, who said, 'We'll burn things, there'll be some kind of guardhouse at the boom. Can you see Caer Dydd from here?'

'You'd see smoke,' said I, turning on the little man, 'Why would I lie, you scrote. Stick to what you know.' I drew my finger across my throat. No-one bothered to turn my Irish to his tongue but I think he got my meaning.

'A fire then, before dark, at Caer Dydd. Then you'll know we've landed and another when the boom is cut as the sun rises,' said Aelfgar. 'Work it out between yourselves.' With that, like a true commander he walked off, leaving the details to us.

The details took some time. Everything had to be said, then explained two or three times, from Irish to English and back again. Then into Welsh for Gruffud's men, who clearly feared betrayal. Then their words back, then the Norse Irish would want to clear up a point or two in their own dialect. Drove me crazy as I could understand them all but was pretending to understand none.

The tides decided for us. If we didn't hit the bar at the right moment it would be too late. Faelen and I boarded after a quick word with his other ship's steersman, then we headed across the water to my childhood home.

I knew as we approached the reef, we might not survive it. All we could see was a bank of stones and mud. When the tides are high here the waters rise faster than a man can run and soon the bank disappeared leaving a wall of whitecaps and frothing seas. I'd never actually done this before but I'd talked with some that had. At the very height of the tide, I saw a small patch of sea that had settled into smooth waves.

I was on the prow of our ship and yelling, pointed the gap out to Faelen who was hauling on the steering oar, 'There,' I yelled, 'there,' pointing with my whole body, leaning out over the twisting waters.

Faelen could not have heard but his eyes followed my arm. He could see now where to steer. The other ship, so close I feared we'd crash, followed his lead. We lurched into the gap. For a moment all was fear. The keels groaned loudly as they ground over the ridge. The oarsmen pulled for their lives. If we lost headway now the ships would break. Then, from one moment to the next, we were in calm water, clear water.

'Taste it,' I yelled, 'Taste it and eat your words you doubters.' I was beside myself with glee capering about on the small platform behind the prow then swinging around under the carved dragon-head in triumph.

Men were tasting the water and it was sweet, beguiled, they looked at me with the gleaming smiles of men who'd seen their lives flash before their eyes. I laughed out loud, 'How about that. You can catch a cod over there or a trout just here.' At this point I nearly fell off the boat. Time to calm down.

From there it was only a couple dozen long strokes to the shore where we saw people running away as they realised we were not the traders they'd expect from across the clear water. I jumped ashore and shouting in Welsh assured them we would do no harm. Mostly they still ran. After a quick word with Faelen, Bruni, the dog and I ran up through the scattered village to the massive heap of decaying brickwork that had once been a Roman fort.

The doorway was still the same, I stooped under the lintel, through the goat pen into the cave painstakingly hollowed out in the depths of the wall. Although the hide covering the doorway was pulled back it was still gloomy in here. It smelt of sickness. There seemed to be no-one here.

A bundle of frayed rags and goat skins stirred at the back of the room. I went over and pulled them back to reveal a smelly old man. Christ, it was my Step-Da. He was in a bad way, sweating and shivering. He cowered back as I tried to speak to him when a row erupted behind me. I caught a glimpse of a shape slipping out of Bruni's grip as a wooden bucket smacked me in the face.

'Get away from him you. Get away,' she said, as she, for it was a she, swung the bucket back for another go when Bruni snatched it, pulling her backwards to the floor.

'Don't hurt her,' I shouted, 'that's my sister.'

Bruni stood over her, 'I thought your sister looked like you.'

'That's my half-sister, Elena.'

Elena looked at me puzzled recognising her name although not knowing our tongue. As she sat up, she said, in Welsh, 'You know my name, how?'

'Don't you know me, Elena,' I asked in the same language forgetting what I looked like.

She looked at me keenly, seeing me, 'You look like a savage, but you sound like Sar. You were taken when our Ma was killed. I saw you. I saw you stab that huge man in the neck.'

'You saw that?'

'Yes, I saw that young man with the long white hair carve your face. You pissed yourself.'

Three years ago, she must be about nine now, maybe ten.

'We were hidden under Meurik's coracle, me and Adaf,' she added guessing what I was thinking.

I'd last seen Meurik when Oslaf's father Eardwulf had lopped the top of his head off with an axe, not long before he killed our mother.

'Where is Adaf?'

'He's gone. He went with Gruffud ap Ryhderch's men. They came here, said they needed everyone, even boys, to beat the red devil from the north.'

'So, they've all gone north, all the men?'

'There weren't many. Most were taken when you were. We went hungry for a long time.'

'And him?' I pointed to the bundle of rags.

'He came back but he wasn't much use. Drank a lot. Couldn't get over what happened to our mother.'

I spat in his direction, 'He didn't have much trouble getting over her when she was alive.'

'Oh Sar, he's still my Dad.'

She'd been a sweet child in a hard family, seems she still was. 'You could come with us. Leave here. Get on one of our ships and I'll see you soon. Leave him here.'

'What about Adaf? He won't know where I've gone.'

'I'll find him.'

'No Sar, that's not likely. I have our goats, they're in the wood now. We'll manage. We've had to,' Elena said.

Babes and suckling's, it was true finding Adaf in a war-torn country wasn't likely and what would this wise little girl do in the company of raiders who spoke another language? I had a few coins on me, her eyes widened as I passed them to her forgetting that she rarely saw coin. 'Here, these are worth a lot in a place like this. Find someone you trust, only ever show one at a time. Make your life better. I must go.'

As I got up to leave, she asked, 'And Moira, what happened to her?'

I cupped her face in my hands, tears in my eyes, 'Oh sweetling, Moira is doing well. She misses you more than you could know.'

Bruni looked at me askance, not understanding my dishonesty. Thing is, I believed my vision, and of course she missed our siblings, of course she did.

I went back to the ships, tears running down my face, to find two of the village hovels burning.

'Our signal,' someone said to me, 'Faelen paid them.'

A few sad looking villagers sat next to a pile of their belongings. They'd been given time to clear them out. Probably gained by the exchange.

I joined the raiding party with Bruni. Maelcolm and Hosvig would be staying with the ships. For this job we needed the light and the fast. I led the way up and around the old ruins and into the roughly grazed scrub behind.

We set off at a ground covering trot. As we sweated, the sun descended, bringing a chill breeze from the sea. A bright moon rose with black clouds scudding across its silver surface. At times sharp showers cooled us, if we crossed a stream we drank like animals. The woods grew thicker but the path seemed clear to me. Recognising a landmark or two I was satisfied my memory was true. Branches snatched at our clothes, roots at our feet, brambles gripped and were shrugged off. We ran at a crouch, our spears low so as not to catch in the trees, we ran and we ran. Just when I thought I could run no more Faelen would call a halt by a whispered command. We'd wait as stragglers came in, but not for long. There were about fifty of us running through those woods, over rocks, through scrub and grasslands. You could not have cleaved us from the sounds of the night. Apart from the odd swish of a branch, or a rare snapping twig, we ran silently, unspeaking, untiring, remorseless, wolves in the night.

Chapter Twenty-Three

We arrived close on the banks of the Usk still in the dead of night. Were we above the boom or below? Faelen sent scouts up and downstream. There was nothing downstream before the river got too wide. Crouching low we flitted upstream between wood and shore. The river had more twists than a blackthorn then it made a hard sharp turn to the right. Running round the long side of the curve, we saw the glow of a small fire and a dark line snaking across the river. The boom. Pulling back into the woods for fear of the moonlight we adopted Faelen's strategy. We all stripped, silently cursing the clumps of nettles. A dozen of us blackened our bodies and faces with charcoal, the rest striped their limbs and chests with white stripes of lime and painted their faces with the same.

We all admired each other in unspoken merriment. Then the work began. We that were blackened crept along a few yards from the foreshore. There it was, a small stone and wood construction, maybe large enough to house twenty men. Tethered to a rail behind it were a couple of small horses. On the shoreline half a boat stood prow to the sky, almost certainly a shelter for pickets by the small fire that glowed before it. The horses would be the most alert, they could also quickly carry a messenger to seek help. Two men silently picked up their tunics and crept out to them. They got to the beasts and, with gentle hushes, covered their faces with the tunics and led them up into the woods. While they were doing this, two men and I slithered down behind the boat-shelter. One of our white painted men came out further down the shore. His white stripes lit by the moon, he looked spectral, skeletal. I could hear voices muttering in the shelter.

'What is that?'

'Trick of the light, no, a spirit.'

'You sure, are you? Don't look human.'

'Ever seen one, people talk but you ever seen one?'

I was trying not to snigger as the figure started contorting his body into grotesque shapes. His skull like head seeming to be peering out from under his arms. The guards couldn't help themselves. They moved tentatively forward from the shelter, two of them, still muttering. As soon as they got clear I got up behind one of them, and hand over his mouth, slit his throat. I braced to support his weight and silently lowered his body to the ground. Another man had done the same with the other guard. We paused to listen, no sound came from the building, but I felt rather than heard faint sounds from behind me. In the dark a furtive figure was attempting to push a small rowboat into the river. More concerned with survival than warning his fellows he didn't call out. I'd left my spears behind the shelter. I ran, retrieved one and turned to see the boat already on the water. I threw at the black moonlit shape. With a sharp cry, he slumped oars cock-eyed, my cast was true. The boat, my spear and the man all floated away slowly downriver. The tide was still ebbing, but not for much longer.

A shutter clattered in the building, someone had heard something, a horse whinnied. We crouched low, more dark shapes joined us on the shore. Heads poked out from the shutter.

'The horses have gone, who tied them up?'

'Are you blaming me?'

'I thought I heard a shout from the shore,' a third voice.

'Me too,' said another.

I crouched, listening, we needed them out. I called from the darkness, 'There's boys stealing the horses. Come help us.'

I knew my Welsh would sound the same as theirs as I grew up not far from here. How well did they know the guard's voices? Not well enough. A few men rushed out, then a few more, that must have been most of them. Spears flew from the forest edge which suddenly filled with dancing skeletons. They'd erupted from their building expecting to be chasing boyish thieves now they faced death from mysterious silent spectres. Suddenly the cavorting shapes let out a loud eerie howl followed by high cackling laughter.

Their poor victims milled about fearfully. Too scared to fight, too fearful to run. Only a couple had died when I'd seen enough. These men were clearly armed churls, not trained soldiers. I called out in Welsh for them to lay down their weapons, and again in Irish so my companions would understand what I was asking. For the defenders my voice came from the dark shadows. They dropped their weapons and showed their hands. We quickly gathered round them and herded them back into the building. Not one of us had even a scratch. Some of us were severely stung. By nettles.

Now, the boom. We stirred up the fire to see how it worked. Chains ran from under massive rocks on the shore to be firmly stapled into whole tree trunks with iron brackets. Each log was connected to the next in the same way, snaking down the beach and into the water. There had to be a way to release them. We floundered around in the mud and then attacked the chains but could not break them.

I yelled to Faelen, 'Get me one of the prisoners.'

He ordered that done and soon a trembling older man was brought to me. 'How do you let ships in and out?' I demanded, suddenly fearing that it had to be freed on the other side of the river.

He feigned ignorance so I whacked him with the shaft of my remaining spear. He mumbled something while my mind whirred, it can't cross the whole river in one piece. It would swing way too far.

'It breaks in the middle, yes?' I poked him hard.

He nodded, 'You have it, boy.' He grinned wryly, 'but too late for you,' he said waving towards the dark shape of the rowing boat drifting down a moonlit path in the water.

I cursed and grabbed his throat. 'How does it work, tell me or I'll cut your ears off.'

'Agh, what difference does it make. If you could get out there, you'd find the logs joined to boats, one from each side. The chain goes from the boats into the deep. You have to haul it up to part it,' he laughed and then spat, maybe losing his ears didn't bother him, 'and you've no boat to get out there.'

I quickly translated for Faelen then saw there was only one answer. I ran down to the first log in the water and jumped on. It twisted instantly and threw me into the mud. I took my shoes off and tried again. I had more success this time and only got thrown into the water on the second log. I couldn't get back on. There was no grip on its slimy surface. I decided to swim the rest. There was almost no current so I knew the turning tide had reached the mouth of the Usk. Here it was still slack-water, the eerie time before it would sweep back upstream. It would not be long before the waters rose and Aelfgar would need to get his ships upriver.

It was cold but I struck out furiously alongside the boom. I'd not swum far for a long time and with that and the cold I tired quickly. Then I hit something attached to a log, it was a small boat. I heaved myself in and saw a thick length of chain dropping into the water and beyond my boat lay another. I still had a knife with me and quickly cut the rope that joined the two. They tried to drift apart but the chains weight held them together. I started to haul on it, shivering and sweating at the same time. Whose bright idea was this? Then I came across a kind of knot, the chain seemed to be twisted around itself. Looking up I saw the moon was fading as the first glimmer of dawn broke in the east. I yanked, pulled and twisted the chain as I saw how it joined and then, with a great splash, one end fell away and dropped into the water. The boat I was in wallowed as I pulled the remaining chain aboard. A gap appeared between me and the centre of the boom.

I heard shouts in Welsh from across the river. They'd seen or heard something, I yelled out that there was no problem, just checking. If they didn't believe me, they'd be casting off their own boat now. I felt the first drift of the boom as it began to float upstream bending slightly towards the shore. I crumpled exhausted and lay flat, my job was done. Their boat could do its worse, the boom was broken. The river was open.

I drifted to the shore and dragged myself back to land, already bare-chested and shoeless and somehow, I'd also lost my keks. With all the charcoal washed away, I pathetically shivered my pallid wrinkled body back to my companions. Here I warmed myself on a blaze made from the guard's shelter, their shields, spears and any tables and benches found in their building. Sib and Bruni joined me. Soon after that we had to move away from belching clouds of acrid smoke as old mouldy thatch was added to the flames. A thick black pillar soon wound its way into the rapidly lightening sky.

We dressed, shared any food that had been found and stretched ourselves between shore and wood in case we were attacked. But no attack came. Then Aelfgar's fleet passed us, as he'd hoped, riding on the swelling tide. We rested for a while more then set off after them, hoping our own ships would find us later. Our prisoners we left behind, harmless now with no-one left to warn. We left them to sneak back to their homes.

We strolled into Caerleon way past noon to find the whole town taken. What was meant to be a feint turned out to be a conquest. The place was as well defended as the boom had been. The attacks from the sea had come as a complete surprise as every spare man, had indeed, gone north. The town had a harbour with room for most of our ships, the remnants of a defensive wall and a fair number of provisions. For now, this was home. The campaign could not have got off to a better start.

Chapter Twenty-Four

Caerleon was a strange town, full of Roman ghosts, bits of stone walls everywhere and a big circle of stone benches where the priests held a service, Saint Cadoc's church being way too small for an army. The harbour had stone wharves. We treated the inhabitants well, orders from above. We'd all get paid at the end of the campaign. Huge rewards, we were told, but only if the Gruffud of the north did not end up ruling a wasteland. That meant only killing those who fought us and no burning and looting of churches. We still needed to eat.

A few miles away there lay another town, Caer Went. We marched over there and circled the walls. Stone walls, high stone walls. I'd seen big walls around Lundenburh but they were mostly wood. Aelfgar decided to leave the town be. He'd have liked to have brought the fleet to nearby Porthsgiwed, but a raid from Caer Went could destroy it in a day. Even from outside the walls, it could be seen that the garrison was not just boys and old soldiers. There was no way the ships could be put at risk. Without them there was no way home.

As we raided the surrounding country capturing horses, pack ponies and herding in cattle, we started coming across groups of refugees seeking shelter in the south. These sad people were shocked to find us instead of safety. Aelfgar sent them into Caer Went but never let them back out. 'They can feed them,' he'd say, 'not my problem.'

As we probed northward Gruffud ap Rhyderch's forces had to start fighting both north and south. Mostly small skirmishes, ambushes, sometimes just wicked arrows from the dark. In this wooded hilly country, you rarely saw your enemy before you fought him. The enemy might be only yards away, in woodland or beyond one of the many streams, for us to pass each other unaware in the dawn or the twilight. Casualties were low but regular. The need to be constantly aware was exhausting.

This almost led to disaster. It had been a useless day. We were still going out in our ship's companies, in our case two ships, leaving behind guards, clerics, and the shipwrights. So there were about fifty of us, wending our way back, tired and hungry with only two scraggy cattle to show for our pains. Two scouts ran ahead followed by Faelen on horseback. We were straggling out through a narrow, wooded valley, the stupid cattle either refusing to move or leaping from the path. Vicious little beasts with small sharp horns. Would have been easier to cut them up and carry them.

Yeah, I was in an ugly mood. Even Sib was dragging his feet as the light fell. Hosvir and Maelcolm were falling behind, along with most of the men who wore mail and carried shields. They made the core of our troop while men like myself were meant to act as a screen, to scout ahead, or run alongside the column to reveal hidden attacks. This steep sided valley pushed us all into its centre splashing in and out of its muddy bottom. We were wearily watching our footing when a tree crashed down through the middle of our column, splitting it in half. Idea was that, when ambushed, the light soldiers fell back behind the heavily armed. In the chaos I saw Faelen's horse rear in fright as shadowy figures rose out of the alders that roped and twined in the stream running alongside the track. Stabbed in the throat, it fell backwards, screaming, blood pumping in a gory arc across the dying sun filtering through the trees. Its thrashing body trapped Faelen underneath as it crashed into the mud, I threw myself towards him just as a thickset man raised a club over Faelen's head. Faelen lay, stunned and helpless, with an odd, knowing, look in his eyes. I straddled Faelen and thrust my spear into his attacker's chest. As I did so something tore across my shoulder, a burning cut sliced into my back just as I was speared in the thigh. A moment of intense pain then I faded fast, drifting to the ground, slowly, gently as if in a dream. I could see Bruni fighting ferociously, her blades flashing everywhere as she ducked, twisted, twirled and stabbed. Then, with a loud crack, the world went black.

I never did find out how that fight ended. We lost men, the Welsh lost men, our troop reunited, darkness fell, we got back. I'd been carried, mud slapped into my wounds, draped over one of those cattle I'd so loathed earlier that day.

I drifted and I wondered. Why had my mother not come to warn me, not come with a message, as she always had when my life was threatened? I felt deserted by her spirit, or was I, was I in fact, free of her now? Free of her reproaches. I sunk into the sky of my vision, my twin, how I missed her. How I missed our days, when like two peas in a pod, we scavenged our way into life. How people would cross themselves when we ran off with stolen fish, a loaf or a piece of cloth, with our long unkempt, red hair the colour of drying blood and our white, freckled faces. I knew now, we were feared as much for our own strangeness, as for our wild rebellious mother.

I dreamt too, of Morwed, in her woad blue dress, her clear chant as the sunlight faded from my eyes on the Wincestre field. Morwed, the woman I feared I would always want, but knew, could never want me. Would never want me. If I ever got to see her again.

Gytha too, Lady Gytha, hard to even think of her without her title, stroking her wolverine fur as she sat, the spider in the centre of the Godwinson's web. More than King Edward, more than all the Earls I'd seen, she was power in a person. She oozed it, born to it, married to it, mother to it and taking it for her own.

Sweet Ymma too, who I'd happily deserted. To be fair she had told me to go, despite carrying my child. Born a slave, the least to look at, she was stronger than them all. She bent like a willow wand, then unbroken could snap back and cut you. If I ever got back to England, she could have my wealth I swore, as the world started to creep back in.

'Can you drink, Sar, can you drink this?' Bruni's voice, need to talk with her too. Shouldn't have killed Lorcan, should've listened. Don't even know her real name, never asked. She was here? She was tugging me away from my dream place, please don't, please leave me here, let me go.

'Come girl, move, he's not lost, Sar, wake up.' Faelen? No. He's gone already. Under that horse.

'Don't shake him, he'll start bleeding again, he can't lose any more blood. Faelen, fuck off. I mean fuck off, sire.' Well, that was Bruni. She'd stopped trying to hide her sex. They'd burnt the rawhide she'd hidden her breasts behind. Now she dressed how she wanted when she wanted. Mostly like a man, because we were doing things men mostly did, she'd say. People can think what the fuck they like, she'd said. I smiled at the memory.

'He's smiling,' a third voice, Maelcolm's, excited, pleased. Seems in this place we're all here and they all like me. Very odd.

'For Brigid's sake,' a rough hand shook me again.

'Fuck off the lot of you,' another voice, 'leave me be.' I knew that voice. It was mine. My eyes flew open.

I was weak, weary and very sore. It was much harder being alive. I'd been gone for a while. So long that monks and priests wanted to know whether Saint Peter sat equal to or below Christ and was it dark in Purgatory. I couldn't help them. Those conversations were odd but I had an even odder one with Faelen.

He looked ashamed, even guilty, 'Sar, I didn't know you might die.'

What was he talking about? 'We are at war, aren't we? Of course, I might die.'

He squirmed, Faelen always so collected, squirmed, 'I too had visions, Sar. I won't tell you how they came about, but I knew our lives were entwined. I had seen that place before.'

It came to me now. That odd look in his eyes as I threw myself at his attacker. 'You mean, in the wood, at the ambush?'

'Yes, I mean then.'

'I'm serving you, sworn to you. I did what a loyal warrior does.'

'I knew you Sar. I recognised you when you were that boy on the pebbles at Porloc.'

'You did?' I thought back to that day. It still made no sense. I remembered the dark faraway look and his all-black eyes, no irises. Remembered how I knew he was dangerous, how he listened, how I led him and his men and how few questions he asked.

He went on, 'When I felt your presence in Ireland, I knew the time was coming where my life would meet a fork in the road. That you being at that fork meant I would live.'

I felt uneasy, 'So, you did all that you did for me, so I'd save you when the time came.'

His frank, dark eyes met mine. 'Yes,' he nodded, briefly.

'That's why you pleaded for me with Diarmait?'

He nodded again.

I didn't really know what to make of this. What would I have done? 'I'd have done the same,' I said, 'I would have.'

'Maybe, Sar, but you have saved my life. And I did, deliberately, put you between me and my fate. He sat quietly for a while then, reaching into his pouch, he said, 'Remember that I took your torque and that spoon from you?'

'Yes, there never seemed to be a right moment to ask for it back.'

'I was always going to return it Sar,' he said gently, 'and here it is.' He passed me, not a thin wire torque, but a thick arm-band. Someone had cleverly joined the spoon and the wire into a beautiful, wonderful thing. It felt heavy in my hand so I knew there was more silver than before but what was most startling was the spoon bowl had been turned into a snake's head, with green jewelled eyes. The silver band made a circle then wrapped around itself behind the head of the snake allowing the band to open wider or close.

He took it back from me and slid it over my left wrist to up above the elbow where he gently tightened it. 'This is Jörmungandr, the serpent that holds the world together. It's an old pagan story from the Northmen. You kept my world together. May this talisman do the same for you.'

'Hmmmm,' was all the thanks I could manage.

As I was fading away, I heard him say, 'I release you Sar, and your companions, from your oaths to me. When you recover, you can leave whenever you wish. Go home if you like.'

'Home? But Oslaf still lives,' I whispered, slipping back into the dream.

I hovered between the worlds for some time. It turned out I'd been shot with an arrow, slashed with some kind of blade, speared in the leg and whacked round the head with a club. It was a blessing I'd been out cold when those wounds were treated. I was weak for a long time, then slowly, slowly I was able to build myself up. Although I'd been battered a lot. I'd never been cut deep, except by Oslaf. In my mind I'd come to believe it was only him I really had to fear. I knew better now.

The war between the Gruffuds only ended with the death of ap Rhyderch in September. Unable to fight off the invaders and unable to return south to his strongholds he'd been hunted down like a dog. As the campaign dragged on it had got more and more cruel. More nasty bitter fights in dark valleys or on bare hills, more captives tortured and killed. When I saw my friends, they were weary to the bone. These Welshmen knew how to move far and fast, striking hard then fading away. No wonder no one had become King of Wales before. Now, at last, Gruffud ap Llewelyn could make that claim.

Caer Went surrendered to Aelfgar, disgorging troops of the living dead. Hunger drove them out, too many mouths, not enough to put in them. You could get anything from a good pair of shoes to a shag for a small piece of bread. Some of them wanted to sell themselves into slavery their plight was so pitiful. Nobody wanted them. We moved our army there and our fleet to Porthsgiwed. Now we were moored at the mouth of the Afon Guoy, the river that snaked up into the borderlands. All of Wales was under Gruffud's control and our way into England secured.

The army rested, our patrols went unresisted, returning laden with newly harvested grains, fattened sheep, cattle and pigs. Life was good, my dog got fat and I got better. Bruni and I had that talk. She'd wanted Lorcan to live with his humiliation as she'd had to live with hers. She'd hated me for a while but Lorcan wasn't worth the grief. Her real name was Sawdah, but don't call her that because it made her cry. We made our peace, became friends again but nothing more. She told me her and Maelcolm had got close. He cherished her tenderly and she liked that. They'd see how things went. That stung a little and explained a lot.

'You know she saved your life?' This was Maelcolm when Bruni had left.

'She did?' I answered. I think maybe I knew that.

'Yeah, after you protected Faelen, she flew in there like a demon, and afterwards, when the fight broke off, we all thought you were dead.'

'You did?'

'All of us did. She insisted on packing your wounds with moss and mud, wouldn't leave until we'd tied you onto that cow. Then she nursed you after we got back to camp.'

Hosvir, who was there too, nodded, 'You were badly cut up. Having fever dreams and gibbering. She wouldn't let the monks near you until you were already healing. Between her and that dog, no-one could get near you. It was her that cleaned your wounds and somehow, they never went bad. We all thought you'd had it.'

'I owe her then, I do,' I said lying back, drained again.

While I'd been unconscious Maelcolm had taken all of our money from where we'd stowed it in the ship and now, it turned out, it was under my bed. He'd had an idea, why not share it between the four of us?

I blanched at my wealth disappearing before I remembered just how much it was. There were gold mancuses in there. He was right. They'd earned it, especially Bruni, and Hosvir had been far more than a good friend. Maelcolm had already divided it up. So now all four of us were enriched by monies stolen by the King of Alba from the King of Alba.

My hair had returned to its dark red, as did my scraggy beard. I hadn't seen Oslaf in weeks, he had no reason to be around our wounded. Earl Aelfgar was easy to admire as a leader but hard to like. His English followers, mostly kept apart from us, divided by language and their distrust of us as mercenaries. We laughed at this, for surely, sworn to their Earl or not, they were worse, rebels to their King. I took to tying my hair back and always wearing a hood, just in case. Released from my oath, I could try and kill him now. Then warn my own Earl, Harold, of their plans, if I could escape. Now though, I had friends, split loyalties and anyway, how could I kill him, on my own, in the middle of an army?

Chapter Twenty-Five

Then just as the winds were beginning to bite and the trackways became slippery with falling leaves, we were ordered out of Caer Went and sent, grumbling, to camp beside our ships. Aelfgar and his men stayed in the town to welcome Gruffed ap Llewelyn to his new maedref or royal town. Many roads met there and soon those roads were filled with Gruffud's horde, as well as the dejected, beaten remnants of the other Gruffud's forces coming in to lay down their arms before their new lord.

Only one road led from Caer Went to our ships. Gruffed ap Llewelyn came down that road to meet our leaders. We formed up behind them. Nineteen ships crews are an impressive sight, especially when paraded as we would fight. The hard mailed, heavily armed, axe-wielding warriors of the Norsemen and the firm shield wall of the English spearmen flanked by the wild, weird, lean, fast troops of the Irish was an impressive sight. A small complete army on its own. We were all curious to see who we'd been fighting for. Soldiers soon get bored and, since we'd been sent out of the town, we were more bored than ever.

They rode across our front, later I learned who was who. Gruffud was a brute of a man, barrel chested with a circlet of gold in his sandy, red hair and a beard, grizzled with grey. Cruel eyes and a cruel mouth gave him the look of an old badger who'd been baited and put back in the sack a few too many times. He rode with his half-brothers, Bleddyn and Rhiwallon, half a length behind him.

Two very tough looking characters. Behind them a man rode under the banner of a great red dragon with huge claws and teeth. Now the banner of all the Welsh. Then came Aelfgar, dressed as darkly as his looks. Beside him rode Oslaf, who, once again, had found himself a long white cloak, to match his long white hair. With them, Rhys Sais of Faelor. Sais means English, maybe he had an English parent, certainly that he could speak it. He came from the borderlands around the River Dee. He was a powerbroker, clearly known and trusted, by both Aelfgar and Gruffud. His face, all angles, with an arched nose and deep-set eyes was hard, like a falcon. His dark hair was swept back. Like most of the Welsh, he was bearded, but it was neatly trimmed, while his moustache was long like an English warrior's. His lands adjoined those of Earl Leofric, Aelfgar's father. This man then was the bridge between the English Earls and Welsh Princes. Must have some skills. Gruffud had killed Leofric's brother, Aelfgar's uncle. No morals these powerful men, by rights they should be in a blood-feud now, like me.

Gruffud made a speech which most of us couldn't understand. It amounted to that he wanted to see what he was paying for. Do as he ordered and afterwards, he told us, we could sail round Wales and he would pay us a fortune in Deverdoeu. He looked very disgruntled when there was no response but then Rhys shouted, 'Fight hard, win, wealth, money, Chester,' in English, then that was translated to Irish and from that to Norse. Then there were the rousing cheers he wanted. Nodding and grunting he roughly rowelled his horse with his spurs and rode away.

Finally, we were on the move again. Gruffud's forces would lay waste to the Ircingafeld, a rich land in long dispute, which lay between the Afon Guoy and Wales. If you spoke Welsh you would live and keep your lands, English, only death or slavery awaited you. I was grateful to be on the ships. They would be wending their way up the river towards a real fight rather than the vicious ruination of harmless farmers.

I wasn't grateful for long. It was a hard, back breaking row. The tide helped for a few miles, some of the day. After that it was sweat all the way. With strong hard currents working against us, we constantly fought with the many bends in the river, seeking deep water. Aelfgar's drakker was a beast, a beauty in the sea, but a bastard on the river with its deeper draught. Often, we were towing it, sometimes getting out and pushing it through shallows as it wove its ungainly way inland.

'We should burn the fucker,' said Maelcolm, who rarely swore.

I seriously thought about it, 'and all who sail in her.'

'You're fools the pair of you,' said Bruni, playfully pulling Sib's ears. She could do things with that dog that would make me think twice.

Hosvir stirred amiably, 'It's just a bit of work. Who cares? The ship won't kill us.'

I lay back and stared at the sky, we were resting, anchored, waiting to be fed. 'Christ would you look at that,' I pointed to the sky. Palls of black smoke were raining ash down upon us.

'See,' said Hosvir, 'Gruffud's army is near and that is the smoke of burning farms.'

Bruni held her palms up to the sky in an odd gesture I'd seen her use before. 'God help the poor children, God help them,' she said, weeping gently.

I looked around at the tall cliffs to one side and the narrow fields beside thick woods on the other. 'If I swam over there now, I'd be in England. I could warn Hereford or rush to Wincestre and find Harold. I'd be a hero.'

'Maelcolm laughed, 'We'd have to stop you, wouldn't we?'

'You would?'

'What's that,' asked Hosvir. We'd been speaking in Welsh. Maelcolm told him. In a flash of polished iron, Hosvir's sword was at my throat. 'We would,' he said smiling his twisted smile at my shocked face. Just how did he do that?

I returned to Irish, 'I've not spoken English for so long I'm not sure I am. Grew up Welsh after all, except for my mother's ideas.'

Bruni frowned, 'You could stay with us then? You know, if you wanted.'

'I'm certainly never going back to England,' said Maelcolm, 'not sure I'd be well received if I did.' He grinned, 'Might have some explaining to do eh?'

'When I've killed Oslaf I will go back,' I said, 'I'll go back to Harold, I'm sworn to him.'

'But why?' said Bruni, 'why?'

'He saved my life, I suppose. It's hard to explain. I miss him you know, but when I'm part of his household I'm just another man. But when he looks at you, you know, you'd follow him anywhere.'

Bruni scoffed, 'Bit like Faelen then. Got to be someone has it, Sar? Someone you have to follow, yeah?'

She didn't understand, in England a lordless man is nothing, but it wasn't just that. Harold was the first person to see, me. No, even that wasn't true, Moira had been, my twin, but did we see each other, or just feel the same? I retreated back into silence, confused as to who I really was, whose side was I on and why?

At that point Faelen stepped down from the steering platform. 'Sar, you know anything about Hereford?'

'Not really, got a big church.'

'Yes, and a big church means an old town and an old town usually means walls.'

Maelcolm said, 'I've heard about Hereford, it does have walls. Ralph of Mantes was supposed to be building a castle there. Something they do in France.'

Faelen frowned, 'Castle?'

'A tower really, place for soldiers to hold up in.'

'A castle, and walls, and it's October. So, how're we going to take it? They want our ships so as we can assault the town from the wharfs. If we can't overrun the walls then we'll trying to besiege the town in the winter with the whole of England behind it.' Faelen shook his head, 'I'm not convinced. All Earl Ralph has to do is sit behind the walls and wait for the winter.'

'Well, we'll just have to scale the walls then,' I said brightly.

'That Sar, you have never tried to do,' said Faelen, frowning. 'If a sturdy wall is well manned many more die in the assault than die on top of the wall. If you can get over it at all.'

Maelcolm thought for a moment, 'This must be for Aelfgar. He needs to prove his power to King Edward. Prove he can be more trouble in exile than it's worth.'

'Or Gruffud doesn't really have the wealth to pay us. Meaning we have to win it for him,' said Hosvir.

Faelen grunted, called for his boat and went off to talk with the other shipmasters.

We carried on chatting, 'Oslaf, when are you going to kill him then?'

'I don't know Maelcolm, if there's a siege I've got some time. We'll camp. Might be able to creep up on him, slit his throat.'

'And escape?' said Bruni. 'How?'

'What if there isn't a siege? What if the city surrenders?' said Hosvir.

'Then I'll have no time. Bloody hell, I need a plan but I don't know what will happen. Once Hereford is sacked who knows where Oslaf will go. And I will have to follow.'

'But aren't both him and Aelfgar exiled from England?' said Maelcolm.

'Oslaf's outlawed. As for Aelfgar's exile, the entire Godwin family was exiled and look at them now. Aelfgar's father's an Earl, from the old nobility.'

'Hmmm,' said Maelcolm, 'King Edward's maybe under a lot of pressure to forgive Aelfgar.'

I laughed, 'Yes, and Aelfgar'll make that happen by attacking his kingdom. Crazy don't you think. The ways of the powerful?' So how was I going to get to Oslaf before the campaign was over?

We ate and soon after Faelen came back and we bent to our oars.

We rowed on upstream. Slowly the hills grew less steep, and the land flattened out around us. We had rounded two huge bends when we came across an armed party on our left bank. One of our ships approached warily, to find Rhys Sais waiting for us. We shipped our oars and dropped anchors. Off our leaders go and back they come.

'Rest up lads, tomorrow you'll be fighting. We're assaulting the town from the river. There are walls around the town but only a low wooden rampart on the river bank. They have many warriors so it won't be easy,' said Faelen, bluntly.

'What will the Welsh be doing?' someone asked.

'There's a lot of them, some will ford the river above the town to work around it drawing defenders away from our attack.'

I stood up and said, 'So, we're the main attack on the town, are we?'

'There is also a low bridge into the town beyond which our ships cannot pass. The Welsh will take care of that, which puts them on our left flank. From the bridge they will attack the gate and its defences.' Faelen continued, 'Should you succeed in your attack do not go into the town. The Minster will be dead ahead of you, go and secure it. That is where the most wealth will be. It mustn't leave. No priests or monks leave. Have you all got that?'

'And what of Ralph's castle?'

'It's not much of a concern. We will pass what there is of it on our right. It's barely started. We're going to ignore it. Our two ships will attack between the bridge and the main assault. Your job is to harass the defenders in support of the Norse and English troops.'

There was more detail but our work was to notice any sudden weaknesses that speed or ferocity could exploit to relieve pressure on the heavily armed centre whose task was to scale the wall.

Now all there was to do was to wait and prepare. Out came the whetstones, every blade sharpened until you could shave with it. I plaited my hair, checked my targe straps, pulled my seax in and out of its sheath, made sure my throwing spears shafts were still straight and their heads true in their sockets, knowing that I would check it all again in the morning.

Chapter Twenty-Six

I flew awake, sweating, remembering nothing, but by Bruni's odd stare, I knew I'd been talking in my sleep. Embarrassing, but better than having a head full of strange, riddling bloody visions but with waking up came those first gut-felt twists of fear. We broke our fast in a tranquil landscape rich with flocks of twittering songbirds. No one talked and for a while I lost myself watching them fluttering amongst the trees along the river side. Then I checked every buckle and strap, again, sharpened every blade, again, as I'd known I would, as I knew everyone else would.

We were ready long before the other ships. We waited while their warriors struggled into padded byrnies and mail. It's hard enough moving around a crowded ship carrying weapons let alone mailed, helmeted and hefting a heavy shield and a long war spear. I didn't envy them their protection. They would bear the brunt of the attack. The wait gave me time to settle Sib who'd twigged that something was going on. Sneakily I set up a rope under the steering platform to tie him to when the time came. I could see no way I could fight my way over a wall with a dog. He wouldn't like it but it had to be done.

Finally, we were all ready and as one fleet we leaned into the oars. At a slow steady pace, we rounded the last bends to where a large tributary joined us on the starboard. The smudge of smoke from morning fires grew above the town we couldn't yet see. Then the first mill appeared, a shocked carter ran into the building, shouting a warning. We rowed on, some chatted, many were silent, lost in their thoughts. Our two ships led the way, we had the furthest to go.

Then we saw the Minster towering above the morning mist. That's where we were to head for once in the town. The town's first corner was walled around the base of an unfinished tower. Heads started to appear along the parapet. Then murmurs began, this was a serious obstacle. We rowed on feeling very alone when we heard loud high pitched horns sound not too far away. It was our Welsh allies. Although the banks here were low, we could not see much beyond them. It takes time to row against the stream and as we crept on the tumult on the larboard grew into a roar of drums, shouting men and the scream of trumpets. We'd only heard them used for signalling in short bursts. In numbers they made a terrifying sound. Then they died, maybe signals after all. Deeper horns sounded to our right, and as we rowed on, we passed the defences we would be attacking. Rhys was right, there wasn't a true wall along the river. A mound, topped by a low wooden wall, about a man's height, set back from the banks. Behind it we could see helmets moving back and forth. Ahead of us a bridge crossed the river, another mill under one of its arches. This was fortified on the town side. Our job was to land near the bridge and harass the defenders as our main party stormed the walls.

Suddenly there was a great commotion ahead of us, the clattering of armed men on horses. Hundreds of them were crossing the bridge, hooves drumming loudly on the wooden boards as they poured over. I could hear Faelen curse in delight, 'Christ's blood, they're leaving the town. The fucking idiots.'

Faelen famously didn't curse. I knew from his delight that our task would be easier, but that didn't mean men wouldn't die and as we steered for the bank, I readied myself. Then, before the turn could begin, English voices roared at us from behind. 'Get out of the way. Move your ships, move your fucking ships!'

I looked over my left shoulder as Faelen yelled, 'Drop your oars, drop them now.'

My God, Aelfgar's drakker had somehow raised a sail and was ploughing past us, splintering our oars as it went. Our oar leapt up in the air giving Maelcolm a sharp blow in the face as it went. The whole ship rocked violently. Shocked, I looked up to see Aelfgar's ship crash into the bridge, its mast snapping and, held by a rope to the sternpost, twisting sideways, crashing down in a tangle of rigging and sail. In that moment I could see the last of the horsemen leave the bridge and warriors from Aelfgar's ship climbing up and over the wreckage onto the bridge itself, passing up war-spears and shields.

Faelen, had the best view from the steering platform, 'Clever bastard, look what he's doing.'

'He's just wrecked his ship and our whole plan of assault,' I said to Maelcolm's bleeding face.

Bruni, too slight to row, wiped Maelcolm's face while he said, 'Faelen's right. Aelfgar is a clever bastard. Get a shield-wall across that bridge and none of those horsemen will be coming back into the town.'

I was just thinking how smart that was when we grounded on the Hereford bank. I grabbed my targe in my left hand and a bundle of throwing spears in my right. I kissed my arm band for luck then, just in time I flicked away one of the few arrows fired in our direction. I scrambled over the side into shallow water and sticky mud. For a moment I panicked, stuck, suddenly aware that without Aelfgar's troops, our attack was much weaker. As I stared around another ship passed behind us to run alongside Aelfgar's. I saw a white-cloaked figure lead his men across and then on to the bridge; Oslaf. A spent slingshot knocked a spear shaft and brought me back to the task in hand. I threw my bundle towards the bank and high stepped my way out of the mud feeling very exposed. Where was the storm of missiles we'd expected?

Getting to the bank I threw myself on all fours and scrambled my way to solid land, then turned to help my companions onto the shore. We grouped to watch our Norse allies on the bank to our right. They'd grounded properly, bows on, unlike us with our smashed oars. Most of them could jump onto firmer ground, and, quickly fanning out their foremost ranks, present a formidable wall of shields and helmets. They formed themselves into a blunt boar's snout formation and headed for the wall. We ran to join their left flank. Now the missiles started as the foe reacted to the assault. This was where we came in, as any man appeared above the parapet to drop a rock or cast a spear, a spear from us sought him out. We were good at this and soon no more faces showed themselves.

Lucky for us really, as we now had little to throw at them. The front of the snout reached the wall, their men kept on their feet by the men behind them, barely a sword drawn at this point. We ran in behind them, seeking thrown spears or rocks small enough to throw back over the wall. Already there were a few men on the ground, faces smashed by rocks, pierced by arrows or spears. I stepped over a screaming man and pulled a spear out of the ground and turning to throw it, saw the first of our men raised to the top of the wall. A war-spear thrust out at him and, unbalanced rather than wounded, he crashed back into the men beneath him. They roared at the sight as more men clambered up and were pushed back or hacked down by the defenders. We could no longer risk throwing spears at them for fear of hitting our own men.

I felt a sharp tap on my shoulder, it was one of Faelen's lieutenants. He signalled us to go left. Wide eyed I stared around frantically, as we regrouped. Faelen came to our front and with a mixture of signals, and yelling above the din of the attack, he pointed us to a length of wall between the gatehouse and the assault. There were few faces showing above the wall here. Shoving a few of us who still had spears to support us from behind, Faelen led the rest of us into the attack.

I sucked in a deep breath vaguely aware of Hosvir's presence to one side and Bruni's behind me. I puked, then an icy calm came over me. This had happened before and I welcomed it, as I pulled my small axe from my belt. I felt my legs move and, as one, we rushed the wall. Some grapnels were thrown, a couple of defenders tried to remove them but were quickly despatched by thrown spears. Everything seemed bright, clear-cut, sharp to my view. I grabbed a rope with one hand and hacking repeatedly into the soft wooden wall with my axe, and kicking my toes into the rotting wood, I hauled myself up. Being unencumbered by shields and mail we could scale the wall far more easily than our allies so long as we were unopposed.

I was atop the wall. I paused, drew my seax, no time to get my targe off my back. A man came at me, helmeted, shielded, thrusting a war spear at me. I sensed his hesitation, ducked under the point, grabbed the ashen shaft, pulled on it and, rising up over his shield, stabbed him in the face. Easy, too easy, this was no trained fighter, probably a farm hand or artisan, conscripted in the fyrd. He dropped his spear, clutched at his face with his free hand and fell from the walkway over the parapet and into the mass of our men at the base of the wall.

Hosvir grabbed up the spear, 'Could have done with his shield, as well,' he said grinning at me with his macabre smile.

I grinned back, totally alive, 'You could jump down and get it,' I answered, stupidly.

Then Faelen was beside us. 'You, you, you and you, fight towards the gatehouse. We must not be attacked from behind. The rest of you come with me.'

Hosvir, Maelcolm, Bruni and I with about fifteen Irishmen turned towards the force on the gatehouse. The walkway was only four men wide, a rampart of rammed earth a few feet above ground level. I fisted my targe and kept an eye out for arrows but none came, a couple of spears did. Easier to see them coming, we flicked them aside with the ease of practice. The defenders between us and the gatehouse nervously backed along the rampart. Eyes wide above their spears and shields.

Someone shouted, 'Look at them. They've never seen a fight. Charge them.'

We did so. Screaming like maniacs. A couple tried to fight but were quickly overwhelmed two to one. The others dropped their shields and spears, jumped down into the town and ran for their lives. Now there were only those left on the gatehouse which was in a better state than the wall. It had a tower at each end and spanned the road to the bridge. The doorway leading from the rampart to the tower was closed. No wonder they'd jumped, they had nowhere else to go.

Maelcolm and Hosvir both picked up shields as we backed away. 'Do we attack the gatehouse?' said Maelcolm.

I looked outside the ramparts onto the bridge to see Aelfgar's troops filling the bridge with a shield wall across it opposing the gatehouse and a longer one curving out beyond the other end of the bridge. Nothing was getting in and out of the town while they were there.

From my vantage point I could see the battle beyond. A stampede of horsemen was flowing across the front of Aelfgar's men seeking a way to cross the river. They were followed by the screaming trumpets of the Welsh and a small horde of archers firing, running, stopping, stooping for spent arrows, then firing again. The plain in the bend of the river was filled with fallen horses and isolated warriors being hacked down by troops of ruthless Welshmen.

I stared, aghast at the sight. So much death in so short a time. It looked like Earl Ralph had tried to attack the Welsh using cavalry and it had gone badly wrong.

'Look at them,' said one of the Irishmen, staring down at the bridge 'they're doing fuck all. Why should we attack while they just sit there?'

He was right. My blood surging with excitement I jumped up on the rampart. 'What are you lot doing? Going to give us a hand or what, fucking wankers?' I shouted in English.

Some faces looked up at me and shouted back, not kindly. Then I noticed, one of those faces was Oslaf's. I saw him and he saw me.

I saw a look of dark fury cross his face. He shouted something at me then turned to bawl at his men. They were already forming up around their ship's dismounted yardarm about to start their own assault. Then they started to batter the gates with it. The men in the gatehouse had more to worry them than us.

I didn't want to hang about for Oslaf to break through. 'Let's leave them to it lads,' I shouted, and jumping down from the rampart I called the others to me. They followed. We ran back towards the main fight. Though there were few of us. we were now behind the defenders, something every fighting man dreads. Seeing us coming they broke and ran into the town. We had won.

The Norse and Irish force, full of bloodlust and triumph, poured over the wall and into the town. Raiders at heart, they wasted no time pillaging houses but headed straight for the main prize.

We swept into the space in front of the Saint Ethelbert's Minster to find a group of priests and monks in front of the main doors, praying and waving crosses.

One of the Norse leaders rested his battle-axe on his shoulder and signalled us to stop. We paused, curious to see the outcome of this encounter.

One of the priests stepped forward holding a silver cross on a long shaft, 'Heathens, you shall not enter these holy precincts.'

The Norseman, took off his helmet and looked around, 'What's this fool talking about?' he asked.

I yelled out a translation in the Norse-Irish dialect.

'Thank you,' said the Norseman, politely, then turning to the priest he asked, 'Do you think I'm a savage?'. He beckoned me over, 'Tell him what I said.'

I stood there, almost naked, seax in hand, covered in blood and translated for him. The priest didn't answer.

'Cat got your tongue? You want to be a martyr? I know my saints like a good Christian. Saint Ethelbert's head cured a blind man, didn't it?'

I translated as quickly as I could and added, 'Back off you fool, he'll kill you, back off.'

The obstinate priest certainly was a fool or wanted to be martyred. He raised one hand in a blessing and tapped the Norseman on the head with his cross.

A look of fury crossed the axeman's face. 'Let's see what miracles your head will perform,' the Norseman shouted. Then he whirled his axe around and sheared the stupid priest's head from his shoulders. 'Now that's what I call irony,' he said, kicking the priest's head across the cobbles.

'It would be if he answered you back,' someone shouted.

I didn't bother to translate. Some of us laughed. Then we murdered them all.

Chapter Twenty-Seven

We stepped over their twitching bodies and crowded into the Minster. Then we paused, awed by the sheer size and magnificence of the building, its rich hangings and its beauty. Then the mood broke and we turned to an orgy of looting. The hangings were ripped down and spread out and soon piles of golden crosses and croziers, embroidered vestments, richly jewelled books, sacks of coin, precious stones and metals grew upon them. The Minster was where all the wealthy locals bank their wealth and the taxes of the Earldom stored. This was riches beyond belief.

Even as the sack continued our quartermasters sought bread, cattle and ale to feed our ravenous hunger. Before long the outside of the Minster was like a shambles and various cuts of meat were roasting inside. Fires were lit where the people of this town usually said their masses, smoke filtering up to the wooden vaulted ceiling. Soon we were all drunk on an easy victory, roast meats, wheaten loaves and the fine fresh ale the clergy drank.

We'd reached the point where agreements turned into arguments.

'Let's go sack the town.'

'Someone has to guard all this,' the voices of our leaders.

'Why not share it all out now?'

'We're sharing it with our allies.'

'Anyone fancy finding some women, eh?'

'There's a whole town out there to enjoy.'

'What happened to the defence?'

'Or the Welsh?'

'Breach another cask why don't you?'

'Are we here on our own?'

'Aelfgar's troops weren't far behind us.'

'So, where fuck're they?' I shouted, stumbling around with a monk sized flagon in my hand. 'Still shitting uh bridge, shouldn't wonder.'

'You want to know where we are. We're here.' The firm loud voice cut across the noise of our squabbling. In the flickering light of the fires, and the Minster's entire supply of beeswax candles, we could see Earl Aelfgar dressed in his usual dark clothes. Behind him, from one side of the nave to the other, stood a wall of sober disciplined warriors.

Those who could stumbled into rough lines and faced them. It was clear, if it came to a fight, we were screwed. Some, sensing this, tried offering the Englishmen food and drink. They stood, silently ignoring our overtures. Our resentments grew, insults flew, mostly in tongues they didn't speak which was just as well. Aelfgar's ship had damaged ours, he'd left us to do the assault without his men. He couldn't have known there'd be little resistance.

Faelen pushed his way into the space between the two sides, dragging a reluctant Maelcolm with him. He still feared he'd be recognised. Faelen spoke, Maelcolm translated as best he could, shouting so that all could hear

'Lord Aelfgar, clearly some here did not understand your actions today. Could not see how you seized the moment to prevent the return of our enemies trained forces.'

Aelfgar nodded, 'At least one of you savages can see what's under your noses.'

Faelen, who understood more English than he spoke, 'There is no need for rudeness sire. We are all allies here.'

The Norse leader with the axe stepped forward understanding Maelcolm's Irish translation, 'I'm called Ulf, I thought we had settled this question of savagery earlier.'

'By slaughtering priests,' Aelfgar retorted.

For a moment silence fell, maybe that hadn't been such a good idea.

'They died soon after the assault, blood was up, tempers high,' said Faelen. 'You must know how men are after such an assault.'

Aelfgar replied, almost casually, 'I can't say that I do.'

'Of course he can't,' shouted Ulf waving his axe about. 'He's never been in one. Leaves that to other men.'

'You know nothing of me, Ulf priest killer. Have you forgotten that you command a ship while I command an army? Your murderous soldiers besmirch my reputation. You and your mercenaries have slaughtered men of God as if they were swine,' said Aelfgar, now visibly furious.

'The fool priest hit me,' shouted Ulf, 'What was I meant to do?'

'Show some dignity perhaps,' said Aelfgar.

Ulf humbled, backed down rather than start a fight he couldn't win, only to be taunted by some of Aelfgar's men. Tempers started to fray again. While some resorted to drunken bluster, those with sense tried to cool things down. I just sat to the side, sucking on my flagon, enjoying the arguments. Then there was a commotion in the ranks of the English and a huge grey dog appeared, muzzled with leather ropes and held fast by two men. Beside them stood Oslaf.

Christ's blood, I'd forgotten the dog. Now Oslaf had him. Unthinking I leapt to my feet, 'That's my fucking dog. Give me my fucking dog,' I screamed at the hated figure.

'Come and get him, goat boy, come and get him.'

I tried to but was grasped from behind, tripped and thrown to the floor. First Bruni, then Hosvir, and then Maelcolm, joined in and forced me, foaming at the mouth, to stay where I was.

Oslaf scoffed at me, 'I've not done with you, bastard. I know who you are and I know you are here. I will find you, catch you, and slowly, I will kill you.'

This ruckus nearly led to an all-out fight, until myself and some others were dragged to the back. Then the leaders began to argue about who should take charge of the huge pile of riches we had accumulated. There were rules about these things but with all that wealth in front of us, feelings had changed. Men started pushing and shoving each other, more tried to come in through side doors while others were trying to leave. It was chaos and only one drawn weapon or thrown fist meant mutual slaughter. Then more figures appeared, behind and above the English. Men on horseback had forced their way through the great doors of the Minster and were breaking through the lines of the English.

It was Gruffud and his brothers, followed by Rhys Sais, and other Welsh leaders. Pushing in behind them came a troop of archers, arrows on strings, who formed into a screen around the horsemen.

Gruffud's voice boomed out above the din, 'It is I who lead here. It is I who have brought you all to this place. And it is I who will pay you when the job is done. Do any of you wish to oppose me on this?'

There was no denying his authority or the size of his army which would now be surrounding the Minster for sure. Even before his words were translated his meaning was clear.

'Earl Ralph and his men, those who survived, have fled in fear and disgrace. My men are already pillaging the town, whatever or whoever you can take. It is yours,' added Gruffud. After being loudly repeated by Rhys and Maelcolm, pillaging the town and its defence-less residents appealed to everyone. The crowd quickly thinned.

Seeing Oslaf, and Bruni's slapping me about, sobered me up quickly bar a throbbing head, a thick tongue and a marked inability to control my feet. She and Hosvir dragged me through a refectory attached to the Minster and out into the chill of the night. Maelcolm followed with our weapons, some food and a small bag of coin he'd pilfered from the main hoard.

'At last, Maelcolm, you're learning,' I slurred at him, the fresh air making me reel all over again.

'It's good that one of us is,' he said. 'Look at the state of you.'

'We need to get out of here fast and hide,' said Bruni, breathlessly. 'Oslaf may be hunting you down already, Sar.'

'Let's start by getting out of sight,' said Hosvir, 'come this way.'

He led us back the way we'd come. Any houses here were ransacked already. We pushed our way through a broken door into a small home. Sure enough, it was empty, a small fire still smouldering in the hearth and, miraculously, a still upright bucket of water. I raised the heavy wooden thing to my mouth, drank deeply, then tipped the rest of the contents over my head. 'Aaah, that feels better. I was so thirsty,' I said with relish, staring around at their shocked faces.

'Yeah Sar,' said Sahb Hosvir, not so sweetly, 'Piss on the fire, my toast is done.'

Bruni muttered something in her own language then added, 'Why do we bother with you Sar? You're such a selfish bastard.'

'So why do you eh? Did I fucking ask you to? Did I?' I shouted at them, weirdly realising that I wanted to cry. I felt a tugging on my belt, then, before I could react, a crack on my skull. I blacked out.

I woke, shivering and feeling very sorry for myself, knowing I'd been an arse. I wanted my dog, another drink, oh God, I wanted my mum. Opening my tearful eyes, I could see my companions sat round the fire. I crawled over and pushed myself between them seeking warmth. That of the fire and that of friendship.

Bruni was the first to speak, our peacemaker, 'Do you remember anything Sar?'

I nodded miserably, 'I do, I'm so sorry.'

'Say that again, Sar, say it loud and clear,' said Hosvir.

Maelcolm stared at me, nodding slowly. He was slapping my blackjack in the palm of his left hand while gripping it firmly with his right.

'I'm sorry, Hosvir, Maelcolm and Bruni. I'm really sorry,' I said shakily. I meant it. I really did feel sorry 'Have you all slept?'

'For a while, Sar. We've also been talking,' said Bruni, 'talking about how to deal with Oslaf. Either we abandon you to your fate.'

'Or we help you kill him,' added Maelcolm.

'And get my dog back?'

'The dog might have to wait,' said Hosvir. 'We have to get Oslaf away from the army and the only way to do that is to use you as bait.'

First, get back to the ships. We went out through the smashed unguarded gates and down to the riverbank. Our ship had been brought into the bank and a ladder placed over the bows. As we went, I realised I was limping, my leg and shoulder wounds sore after yesterday's exertions. I'd not felt a twinge during the assault. We greeted the guard and gave them eagerly awaited news. Then we dressed warmly, checked our weapons and collected our possessions. Who knew when, or if, we'd be back?

Second, get horses. This was easier than we expected. The dawn revealed many riderless horses clustering about the bridge trying to get back to the stables of their dead riders. Many of them were skittish, some terribly wounded and disfigured, a sight that disturbed me far more than that of wounded men. Eventually we rounded up six that seemed not too frightened, led them down to the riverbank, watered and fussed them. Bruni had never sat a horse. I could ride but not well. Maelcolm and Hosvir were skilled riders.

Third, bait the trap. The plan was to get Oslaf to chase us into the countryside. He wouldn't come alone, but he couldn't bring an army. Then we'd see what would happen. Not much of a plan, but needs must when the Devil drives.

By mid-morning we were as ready as we'd ever be. Bruni and I crossed back over the bridge and climbed up onto the parapet above the ruined gate. Looking over the town we could see pillars of smoke rising from behind the Minster. Too thick for hearth fires we guessed that houses were burning too.

'How're we going to get Oslaf's attention?' said Bruni. 'It's chaos out there.'

I looked at the rising smoke doubtfully, 'He's an experienced war leader who would have learnt a lot from his father. His men would have to know where to find him.'

'I could go and look for him. Give him a message from you.'

'Oh Bruni, he'll keep hold of you. He'd slice you to pieces just to spite me. His mother killed all my kin and most of a village to get back at me.'

'Then what?'

I turned to look at her and noticed the ships beside the bridge. He would have left a guard on his ship, so would Aelfgar.

'Follow me.'

After walking back onto the bridge, we climbed down to Aelfgar's ship, still wedged under an arch, where we were quickly challenged. I said we needed to talk to the guard on Oslaf's ship which was tied alongside. They asked no questions, gave Bruni a funny look then let us onboard.

A single bleary-eyed guard unrolled himself from under a bench. 'What you want? He said, 'You bringing me some victuals?'

'No, we need you to take a message to Oslaf,' I said.

'Now why would I do that?'

'Well, there's a town full of food, drink and women out there just waiting for you.'

'That's true, while I'm just left here,' he thought for a while, 'But Oslaf don't take kindly to those who disobey him.'

'There's enough guards on Aelfgar's ship aren't there. Anyway, who's going to raid our ships. They've all run away.'

He rubbed his hairy chin, 'Yeah, he's meant to be setting up in Saint Guthlac's monastery. Shouldn't be too hard to find, but, well he's a right bastard that one.'

'Look, he'll want this message. He'll probably reward you,' I said. He probably wouldn't I thought.

'What message is that then?'

'Tell him Sar Nomansson will meet him on the other side of the bridge if he cares to come.'

'Uh? What kind of message is that?'

'Tell him the man who killed his father and his brother is waiting for him,' I said.

239

His eyes widened at that, 'Ooh, I don't know as I want to carry that message.'

'Do you want to be the one who didn't?'

Bruni, who didn't understand English but wasn't stupid, had slipped round behind him. She placed the point of a spear against his spine.

'A message you're going to carry I think, or my friend will have a word,' I said, handing him a silver penny as I did so.

He bit the coin looking unimpressed, had a word with the guards on Aelfgar's ship, then headed off towards the town. In truth he was probably glad for the excuse. We re-joined our friends and prepared the horses ready to leave. Now all we had to do was wait.

This was easier said than done, restlessly I paced about then headed back across the bridge. There were still horses milling around. I had an idea. I killed three of the horses with the worst wounds. It was a mercy really and now they blocked the road.

'I like horses,' I said to Bruni, 'I've ridden a couple.'

'They make me nervous,' she said, gently holding the head of a horse with its entrails poking out from a savage cut in its side.

'They used to me, but I think they have a quiet place inside them. If you stroke them and whisper, they seem to understand you mean no harm. I think they have a soul.'

'You mean they go to heaven?'

'I've never thought about that, but they're innocent. Not like the men we've killed.'

'But then so are pigs. Where I come from no-one eats pigs.'

Pigs in heaven, this was too much for me. As I betrayed those poor beasts by cutting their throats, I felt more upset than after any fight.

'They'll slow down a pursuit if only for a short while. Oslaf didn't come with horses so he'll have to borrow or catch them. We need a head start, far enough to draw him away, but near enough for him to follow.'

I decided to watch from the gatehouse. The fires in the town were spreading, even up to the Minster. This could work in our favour. Aelfgar would not want to spare many men if it meant the Minster burnt down.

The wait seemed to go on forever. Where was he? Had my message even been delivered? I paced up and down. Looking westward, I could see my puzzlingly loyal friends waiting to leave but on the town side, the road to the gate remained empty. Until, it wasn't.

My eyes narrowed with hatred as I saw him approach along the street. My grip tightened on the shaft of my spear. For a moment I was tempted to risk all on one throw. One well aimed spear cast and it could all be over. His eyes caught mine, as I raised the spear, he raised his shield. I lowered the spear and took in the whole picture. There was Sib, still muzzled, but no longer struggling. Behind then there were about fifteen men on foot, helmeted, mailed and armed.

Oslaf tucked his helmet under his arm and yelled out, 'You going to fight me then goat boy? If you hadn't been rescued, I'd have killed you last time. What makes you think you can beat me now?'

'I killed your brother, didn't I? He died slowly Oslaf. He died as I stabbed him over and over, while he flailed around in his mail unable to land a blow. I stabbed him in his face, in his eyes, in his neck, anywhere I could get my seax in, until he slowly bled out. Think I can't do the same to you?'

Oslaf was furious, 'He was sleep befuddled. He'd come out from a burning hall blinded by smoke.'

'Yes, your parent's burning hall where your mother was killed to avenge her crimes. Have you killed the man who did that?' I knew he hadn't. That had been Grim, making her pay for commanding his brother Toki's death.

Beside himself Oslaf's voice rose to that high pitched screech that I remembered from the day my mother died at his father's hands, 'I will fucking kill you. Get down off there and fight me.'

I stopped for a moment, enjoying his foam at the mouth fury, then hurriedly ran down from the gatehouse and across the bridge. There were still many horses milling about, mostly saddleless as we'd cut the girth straps of those, we could get close to. I jumped on the horse that had been saved for me and we waited long enough to see Oslaf standing on the corpse of a horse, demanding that I wait.

'I will meet you Oslaf, on the ground of my choosing. Chase me if you dare.'

With that we turned our horse's heads to the west and rode.

Chapter Twenty-Eight

We headed roughly southwest along a wide trackway through wide swathes of riverside pastures. Everywhere in the torn grass lay the bodies of dead men and horses like mushrooms sprouting after autumn rain. Behind us pillars of smoke billowed skywards from the burning town. We rode into a brisk wind as the clouds darkened ahead of us. Our tracks lay clear in the soft ground as we crossed the direction of yesterday's wild fight.

Once the pasturelands passed, we came upon smouldering farmsteads and then, to our surprise, we found a group of boys setting alight a completely intact group of buildings. We slowed to give the horses a break and I hailed them in Welsh, 'What are you doing lads? Why are you still burning? Was this an Englishman's farm?'

'Nay sir, this one was our own, but we have to leave.'

'Why's that lad,' asked Maelcolm, 'Gruffud has beaten the English here and their farmers have gone. Could you not farm them too?

The boy, a small dark lad, about twelve maybe, pulled a wry face at Maelcolm's accent, 'My Da says, that Gruffud, who we must now call King, knows jack shit sir. Easy to burn the farmers out but is he going to stay here? 'Course he ain't.'

Another boy, spit of the first one, adds, 'Then the English will come back and kill us all.'

'Better to go now,' said the first boy, 'As long as Gruffud thinks this land is his and Earl Ralph thinks this land is his, no farmer will thrive here. This is fine land, and the English and us got along fine too.'

'Yeah, so our Da says the doings of powerful folks is stupid,' says the second boy. He thinks for a while then squints up at us, 'Are you powerful folks, on horses and the like?'

I laughed, 'No boys, don't worry, we'll not harm you. Where's your families?'

'Up ahead sir, we're working our way to Abergafenni. We'll catch them on the road.'

They turned back to whooping at the rising flames. What boy doesn't love a fire?

A few miles up the road we came across crowds of refugees herding a huge mass of beasts ahead of them. Sheep, cattle, pigs and geese swirled around squawking, hissing, baaing and bellowing while dogs barked and howled behind them. In the centre of all this were ox-carts being hauled through the ever-thickening mud.

Hosvir swore, 'How are we ever going to get through this lot?'

It was a good question. We came to a halt behind a stricken wain. The wide-open countryside had narrowed in, and with a small river to our right and rising ground to our left there was no way through or round.

I dismounted, as did Bruni, looking very uncomfortable. 'God, Sar, I'm sore already,' she said, wincing and tugging her breeches away from her crotch, 'if this is what horse riding is about you can keep it.'

'It gets easier I promise.' I said, passing her the reins of my horse and walking to the stranded ox-cart which was surrounded by a group of women struggling to heave it from the mud.

The cart was piled high with churns, buckets, cheese presses, cloths and so on. Much more than could be found on any one farm.

'Been doing a bit of looting of your own, have you ladies?' I said.

A broad, stocky woman with arms a blacksmith would have envied, pulled herself upright and put her hands on her hips. Then she spat in the mud and spoke, 'Any business of yours, lad, eh?'

'No love, I wish you all the luck.'

'Don't you 'love' me my lad. Now why don't you do something useful with yourself 'stead of making remarks,' said she.

Despite the efforts of four harnessed oxen and these formidable dairy women, this cart was going nowhere. Hosvir and Maelcolm joined me leaving Bruni to hold all six horses. We heaved on the wheels, threw brushwood under them, whipped the oxen but it didn't budge. Reluctantly we roped the horses in to help. You need a collar for a horse to draw properly but by tying ropes to the saddles we got just enough traction to get the cart moving. At the very last moment it tried to slide into the river but, catching it just in time, we kept it to the road.

We walked alongside while the women rewarded us with bread and cheese, 'We'd give you milk and curds but it's all been spilt.'

'Thanks anyway, we'll be fine.'

'You seen any boys on the way here?'

'We did, joyfully burning down a farm, they yours, were they?'

'Ay son, they are,' tears burst from her eyes, 'that's our home they was burning, our home.'

Helplessly I watched this stalwart woman give way to her grief and soon the whole group were keening even as we walked. 'Still, we're all alive eh lad? Alive and free, not like our neighbours.' She looked at me suspiciously, 'I suppose you were among those running them down, eh lad?'

'Not me missus,' I answered quickly, 'not me.'

'So why are you here?'

I noticed Maelcolm and Hosvir sniggering at me being bested by a farmwife and said, 'Truth is, we're being chased by some Englishmen.'

'Thought they'd all gone.'

'Some of them fought with Gruffud, did you know?'

'Heard such, yes.'

'Well, this is some of them, but still English, you know. While I'm a Welshman.'

'Hmmm but your friends aren't, are they?' She pointed at Hosvir, 'He's Irish for a start and what's that little brown one eh? And him with the funny accent. What about him?'

'He's from Cumbraland.'

She looked him up and down, 'One of our northern cousins, then. Pleased to meet you sir.'

'Look, we're being chased which is fine, we want to be caught,' I held up a finger, 'but only by a few of them. And off their horses, if possible.'

She smiled, 'You've helped us lads, so how can we help you?'

'I think it likely that a small group will be ahead of the main troop. Led by a man with white hair.'

'Old guy?'

'No, white like so yellow it's white, like sun-bleached straw. He'll be well dressed and well-armed, long white cloak.'

It's him you have business with, eh?

'No flies on you love?'

I jumped back as she gave a friendly slap. 'A bit ahead, after we ford this river, there's a way up to the right. Stick with us and I'll show you. It gets narrower and steeper, with wooded sides.'

'Sounds good, sounds really good,' I said, for the first time feeling real belief in our crazy plan. Maybe it could work.

'We'll wait at the ford and direct white hair after you. If there's another party we'll tell them you forced your way through with no manners. Being soldiers, they'll believe that.'

'Oh, I could kiss you,' I said, 'you're a life saver.'

To my shock she blushed and, after bashfully pushing me away, she got back to the task in hand.

We followed that massive mixed herd for a few more miles then turned off to the right as directed. I opened my bag and gave the woman some coins.

'You don't have to do this son, you did us a good turn.'

'I know,' I said, 'don't be offended, you'll need all you can get by the look of things.'

Just then a small horde of boys turned up and these women's thoughts all turned to their children. We rode off up the valley.

'We need to get moving, Oslaf must be close on our heels,' says Maelcolm.

Him and Hosvir had already swapped mounts being heavier than Bruni and I. Not only were they heavier than us but they were both wearing mail and carrying shields. I only had my little targe and throwing spears. Bruni had never found anything to replace her wicker shield so now fought with a seax in each hand. She also carried spears.

'I want to keep him following till nightfall,' I said.

'Yeah, he'll have to stop when he can't see our tracks,' said Hosvir, 'These paths are tricky enough even in daylight.'

'I have some ideas but it means we won't get much sleep,' I said.

'Let's get ahead somewhere and camp,' said Bruni, 'then plan.'

The valley floor widened for a while then narrowed steeply and we began to climb, the stream beside us got angrier and the darkening clouds released their first flurries of rain. We couldn't camp in the floor of the valley in case they caught us up. We dismounted and pushed our way through the undergrowth until we found a flat enough place to spend the night. I'd left two horses tied at the bottom. After a brief rest and a bite to eat, Bruni and I took only our weapons and walked back down in a blizzard of falling leaves. Under the clouds it was almost dark, once in a while a gap let the moonlight reveal the stark black and white criss-crossing of branches over a silver stream.

We mounted and carefully, slowly, letting the horses find their own footing, retraced our path. I had to admire Bruni, as she managed her horse. She'd not fallen nor complained once and here she was doing something a skilled rider might balk at. The wind was on our side, blowing up the valley. We'd hear them before they heard us.

It didn't take long, they were very close behind us, but camped. Unlike us they'd lit a fire. For while all we could see were the leaping shadows of men and horses crossing the firelight. Worried that our horses would whinny to theirs we walked away, tethered them, then walked back. I crossed the stream while Bruni went wide on their other side.

After muddying our faces and hands we crept around them. For me the stream helped cover any missteps that made a sound. Bruni could creep like cat. I could see her in my mind's eye, carefully placing, each foot, and testing, every step.

Getting as near as I could while keeping a watchful eye on the clouds, I counted the men and the horses. Seemed to be about the same amount of each. I crept on round and met Bruni below the camp. We were upwind from them now so we carefully spoke in whispers and signs, very close to each other because of the gloom.

'Men?'

Bruni flashed up eight fingers and nodded at me.

I flashed nine. 'Horses?'

She flashed nine, probably nine men then.

She whispered, 'Too many men?'

'Tired horses, hungry,' They would be, like ours, they'd been ridden to war the day before we took them and there was no grazing here except the ends of leafless twigs.

'Guards?'

'Didn't see any.'

'I thought they were arguing, couldn't understand them,' said Bruni.

'Yeah, I thought so too but stream.......'

She nodded. 'What now?' she mouthed. 'Men, horses, dog?'

'Dog?'

'They've got Sib tied up with them. Still muzzled.'

I resisted the impulse to rush in and free him. He'd lasted this long. He'd have to wait. 'Horses, kill them or run them off?'

'Maybe one man, then run off some horses.'

I nodded. We'd have to wait longer. Then the opportunity came, one man separated from the group and walked into the trees. We smiled at each other; men are so predictable. We crabbed our way sideways low to the ground, knives out. A flash of moonlight. He was fighting his byrnie and mail, struggling to squat. Couldn't be better.

I sneak up behind hearing him make straining noises, too much meat, I thought, the penalty of the victors. There was just enough time for my nose to wrinkle as I threw my left arm round and over his mouth. With my right hand I tried to force my blade through the rucked-up mail and padding. He was struggling furiously then Bruni appeared in front of him and cut straight through his wind pipe then stabbed him in the side of the neck. Dropping her knife, she laid over his legs as they thrashed in the leaf mould. He still had a sword in his belt, I pulled it free. We paused, listening, no alarm.

The horses were tied up randomly wherever a suitable branch gave enough purchase. The first three we came across, we stealthily freed. Apart from one other there was no way we'd get near enough without getting seen. I signed to Bruni and she crept back away while I crept up on that horse. Then I stuck the sword through its guts. The poor beast screamed horribly. The free horses bolted downstream while the remaining tethered beasts reacted with horror, rearing and panicking.

Commotion complete, I ran round the way Bruni had come, trusting my feet to find their way in the dark. My heart was beating furiously and I nearly crashed into Bruni when she stopped me with a whisper.

'Our horses are here Sar, over here.'

She'd already untied them. They were skittish, they'd heard the noise. We had to calm them before mounting while every fibre of my being wanted to run. No-one came, we mounted.

'Eight,' said Bruni.

'Eight,' I said.

We found our way back to the others and crashed, exhausted. This time I did dream, horrible dreams of terrible wounds and bloody vengeance. Of the ease with which I stabbed that farmhand in the face. His ruined face cursed me just before my mother's, even more ruinous, pushed his aside.

I'm crying, 'It shouldn't be that easy, Mum. I'm not like that, I'm not.'

'But you are, my son. You are the cold killer you are meant to be. You avenged me, you did well.'

For a moment I felt warmed by the approval I'd so rarely received.

'Now avenge my sister. Avenge your sister,' she hissed savagely in my face. 'Tomorrow, my son, your journey ends. Blood flows in the water. Blood flows down the stream.'

'Tell me whose, Mother, whose blood Mother?' I pleaded, diving into the dawn. I'd yelled the words out loud.

The others looked at me, questioning. 'Don't want to talk about it,' I said, breathing hard to come back into myself.

'Eight of them, that's long odds,' said Hosvir, 'two to one. They're all veterans.'

'So're we,' I said, 'so are we.'

We carried on upstream, a long climb for tired hungry horses.

'He'll be having a harder time of this. Either some of his men are walking or they're doubling up,' said Bruni.

'He'll kill his horses under him if he has to,' I said, and so would I, I thought, so would I.

A strange feeling came over me. Whatever happened next was simply fate. I felt calm, unhurried, clear thinking. I considered our resources. Two mailed men, expert swordsman, one still carrying a long war spear. Two fast, lithe, lightly armed fighters with five throwing spears between them. The only certainty; Oslaf would follow me to the death. The hate between us ruled the day to come.

After a narrow stretch, where we forced our way up the stream through over-hanging trees, we found the right place. Where the stream had levelled out beavers had dammed the flow. The pool behind it gave a clear view for a spear throws distance.

The riders approached, the clopping of hooves grew nearer and nearer. I stood at the far end of the pool. Then they appeared, 'Oi, you there, Oslaf with you?' I shouted. 'Come and get me, you tossers.'

'That's him!' shouted the leading horseman, spurring horse from walk to a gallop. 'Get him.'

He rushed into the narrow stretch when Hosvir stepped out from the brush, crouched and raised the head of our war spear. Its base was firmly rooted in the twisted branches of the dam. The horse frantically baulked, but too late. It drove its chest deeply onto the head of the spear. Its rider pulled uselessly on the reins. Hosvir hacked through his right arm with one stroke, then leapt away. Beside him the next horse was pushing past. Its rider urged it over the dam behind which Maelcolm was crouching. He jumped up, the startled, panicked horse twisted away. Maelcolm stood back and sliced the beast's hamstring as it crossed the dam. The horse collapsed, thrashing wildly in the pool, screaming horribly. Bruni rushed out, spear in hand but Maelcolm shook his head and dodging the flying hooves hacked into the fallen rider's neck. Bruni turned, ran to the top of the beaver's lodge and threw her spear high over the carnage. It plunged down into another of Oslaf's men who was running up on foot. As for Oslaf himself, he was calling his men back, furious at their stupidity, he laid about them with the flat of his sword.

I wanted to spend time taunting him but with none to waste we ran to our horses and rode on up the valley.

'That leaves five,' said Bruni.

'Yes, some throw that, girl,' I said, 'some throw.'

We grinned at each other, happy, united in slaughter.

I was thinking hard. Five of them, two horses. We still had all six of ours though two were clearly going lame. The going was getting tougher, steeper, rockier.

'I want to abandon the horses,' I said.

'But Oslaf will get them,'

'They're carrying our stuff.'

'Put all our bags on the fittest horse,' I said, breathing heavily, 'Go on, on foot, lead the horse. One of us is going to fall at this rate. This country is only fit for goats.'

We had no choice but to stop to do this. We could hear Oslaf shouting below us. Continuing up the valley it got so steep we had to let the last horse go. Shouldering our bags we trudged on. After a last kink in the stream and a waterfall, we pushed up through a thicket to our journey's end. The stream ran over a small platform from a spring gushing out from under a low cliff. A fitting natural arena for what was to come.

We waited, dry mouthed, weary, alert to every noise. At the first rustling in the thicket, we let loose a barrage of stones. There was at least one hit, a sharp cry and curses made that clear. Then they pushed out into the clearing, spreading out in front of us.

They were all mailed, helmeted and carrying shields, except one who held a battle axe. They looked us over. Maelcolm and Hosvir stood, easy and confident in their mail, with their shields held high. Bruni and I, both on our toes, with spears ready to throw, were not so formidable, but no soldier who'd fought with or against the Welsh and the Irish would take us lightly.

Oslaf spoke first, 'I only want him,' he said, pointing at me. 'Give him to me and you other three can go.'

I translated this for Bruni and Hosvir.

Hosvir took a step forward and gave Oslaf the benefit of his sweet smile and spoke to him in Norse.

Maelcolm called out in English, 'He's telling you that the odds are in our favour. You delicate English flowers don't stand a chance.'

For a brief moment Oslaf looked doubtful, maybe he'd remembered he'd only four men left. Then he laughed, 'I could take you all on my own,' he scoffed. 'Come on men, attack them.'

They didn't move. One of them, blood seeping down his face, spoke, 'Maybe that's what you should do Oslaf. Fight them on your own.'

Oslaf exploded, his voice rose, 'You're my men, cretins, you do as I order.'

'You told us it would be easy, hunt down some renegades, back by nightfall revelling in Hereford, but here we are.'

'Aelfgar will have your guts.'

Another man spoke, 'Aelfgar's not here.' He made his mind up, sheathed his sword, wished us luck and walked off, along with the other speaker.

We four were stunned. 'Well, Oslaf, looks like the odds are in our favour now,' said I, 'even your own men hate you.'

Whatever else Oslaf was, he was a brave man, and the outcome was by no means certain. He hitched up his shield as he and his two remaining men formed a defensive triangle, backs to each other.

The last fight, this was it. I felt immeasurably weary as I looked up into the racing clouds and prayed. Then it rushed into me, the God given ferocity of my hatred. I threw a spear. I'd hoped to cast it past the man facing me into the back of the axeman's head. The man in front of me was short, but swift enough, his shield caught my spear. It stuck hard, but swiftly Oslaf cut the shaft off. My first blow was wasted, one spear lost.

It was a strange fight, no more insults were exchanged, no shouts or cries only odd grunts of exertion or pain, the rasping as metal glanced off metal or thuds as blows hit shields or bodies. Even those sounds were snatched away by the stiff wind. We were fighting in the void.

After that first cast it quickly turned into an all-out ferocious skirmish. While Hosvir and Maelcolm fought feet firm, Bruni and I dipped in and out, stabbing with our spears if openings appeared. I was aware that blood was dripping down my face but I'd felt no wound. My second spear broke, I drew my seax, now I had less reach than the swordsmen, I dove, ducked, sidestepped, trying every trick to get a blow home, with seax or targe. The fight so fluid, the faces before me seemed to blend into one. The fight so close, we risked the blades of our friends as well as our foes.

Then everything slowed down. I saw Maelcolm fall to his knees as the axe smashed down on his shield. Bruni, with both hands holding her last spear close to her body, pushed it into the axeman's side. As he crumpled, Oslaf's shield smashed into her head and she fell, horribly limp, to the ground. I saw my chance and stabbed Oslaf in the back of his thigh. As he twisted away, his mouth open in a silent scream, the seax was wrenched from my hand. This was enough to distract the other swordsman. Hosvir, seizing the moment, smashed his shield into the man's body. He fell backwards onto the churned sward, beaten. Hosvir disarmed him then finished him off.

Maelcolm was now keening over Bruni, his shield was gone but his left arm hung lifeless by his side.

Oslaf was trying to stand, my seax still sticking out of his leg. He let go of his shield and half crawled, half hobbled, to the back of our fateful arena. He dipped his left hand in the water, cupped it, drank, then wiped his face. He stared at me defiantly. I limped over towards him. My old wound was making my leg stiffen. I felt dazed. I felt sore all over.

I stood in front of Oslaf. He was beaten, I knew it, he knew it.

'Give me time to pray.'

I nodded, still keeping my distance, he could strike like a snake. He watched me as we both remembered Conor's camp. 'I'm not that boy now Oslaf.'

'I know that now, Nomansson.' He thought for a moment, 'You spared my son. Why?' As he asked me this, he threw his sword to one side and un-buckled his helmet shaking out his long white hair.

'I don't know, he was just a boy,' I paused, 'No, Oslaf, I do know. I didn't want to be like you.'

Oslaf shifted and said, 'Have you any children Sar?'

Even now I didn't trust him with that knowledge. I said nothing.

'You have, you bloody have. He sneered, 'Can't believe I missed that?'

Rage courses through me, I pull out my knife and grab his face. Suddenly there's a knife in his hand too. He stabs at my chest. Once again, I'd fallen for his tricks. I was still moving. It cuts deep, painfully deep but doesn't stick in. I slash his wrist. His knife drops to the floor. I thrust mine into him, forcing it through the mail, over and over again in a mindless frenzy. We wrestle wordlessly. We're writhing around in the water. He stills. I stare into those strange pale blue eyes a hand's span away from mine. He's smiling. His eyes fix on mine. He takes a deep breath, 'I used your sister, goat boy. I used her before I sold her.'

I jump to my feet, sickened by his words. I lift my foot to stomp on him but his eyes have closed. He looks peaceful. I fall to my knees defeated. His body slumps across the stream. Hosvir pulls me to my feet.

I look around, Maelcolm is sobbing over Bruni's prone body. Hosvir, seeping blood from his right shoulder where his mail is crushed into his flesh, collapses exhausted to the floor. It was over, Oslaf's blood was in the water, not mine. We'd won, I'd won, but I felt no triumph, only bitter emptiness. I cry to the sky, 'Killer enough for you Mother, killer enough? Am I done? Are you avenged? Are you satisfied?'

I swear I heard a voice in the wind, blessing me, soothing me, releasing me. I knew better. I was twisted far, far, away from the boy I'd been when I first met Oslaf. I was now more him than me.

A thought comes. 'I need proof,' I say out loud, 'I need proof to take to Harold.'

Taking my knife, I cradle lift Oslaf's head in my lap and scalp it. As I tug his body around a wall of water wells up behind it, marbled with his blood. I peel the scalp free of his seeping skull and as I do, the water pulls his body away. It tumbles over the edge and out of sight.

I see myself, half-crazy with a bloody scalp in my hands, crawling about on my knees in the water, screaming, 'What now?' into the emptiness of the endless sky. No answer comes back. Empty, wrung out and shaking weakly, I ask Hosvir, 'Sadh Hosvir, my friend, what now?'

'We need to get home, Sar,' he says gently, 'all we need is to get home.'

I nod, not too sure what that means. I know I would like to see Gyric. I look around, 'And that dog of mine. Where in this hell, is he?'

Epilogue

'And then what happened Sar? Did you find the dog? What happened to Maelcolm? How did you get back here?' asked Gyric eagerly.

'Come now. I've told you enough of my story. What about yours?'

'You know some of it. I got our news to Harold just in time.'

'But you were still not wearing shoes. That's how I knew it was you they were talking about.'

Gyric blushed to the roots of his hair, 'Ah well,' he squirmed a little, 'I had more to atone for before I got home.'

'Tell me,' I said, amused at his embarrassment.

'Hmmm, well it took an age before Burgric would leave Alba. Then we had to stay in Jorvik for the Earl's funeral.'

'Yes, and?'

'And I had to find somewhere to stay.'

I laughed, 'So you found Hilda.' It wasn't even a question. Gyric's face was so readable.

He smiled to himself, 'Yes, I found Hilda. Her and Lodin had found a new place down on the dock. It had an inn for eating and an open fronted bothie for the passing trade. They were doing well.'

'And you shared her bed?'

'Let's just say I felt my penance should continue.'

'You're wearing shoes now.'

'I am,' he said, admiring his well shod feet with pleasure, 'I met Aethelric. He was at the King's Lenten council.'

I felt a stab of jealousy. I'd love to see Aethelric again.

Gyric went on, 'He told me that excessive penance was a form of vanity and that I should confess my sins and put some shoes on, so I did.'

'But you are still a housecarl. Not a monk.'

'No after staying with Hilda I started to feel a lot better about things. Besides what would my father say?

I could guess, he wouldn't be pleased, 'Does that matter?'

'You wouldn't understand, Sar. I have a duty to my family. Anyway, I love my father.'

I changed the subject, 'Did Hilda ask after me?'

He frowned, 'No Sar, I told her about Einvar's death. That was all she needed to know.'

I took that in, why was I even bothered? 'It took you a long time to get south, to Harold.'

Gyric squirmed again, and as he looked up, I could see tears in his eyes, 'Once Burgric released me Sar, I fell to pieces. I missed you, I had no family or friends and without orders I had no purpose. It was hard. If it wasn't for Hilda and Lodin I don't know what would have happened.'

I could have asked more questions but I think I understood. Silence fell between us as we picked at the remains of our meal.

'Turned out Bruni was just stunned,' I said, to fill the silence, 'she was stunned and Maelcolm's arm though numbed was not broken.'

'And Hosvir?'

'He was alright, after we'd rested some. We were all well beat up. We had to peel Hosvig's mail out from the flesh of his shoulder. Maelcolm's left arm was useless for hours. Bruni, we'd just about given up on her. Her skin went ashy and she seemed not to be breathing.' I shuddered at the memory, 'Maelcolm was beside himself with grief when her eyelids fluttered. She was alive but did not seem to know where she was. Then she was sick, tried to get up and was sick again. Slowly, very slowly she came to her senses but with a headache so bad she could barely think or respond.'

'And you?'

'I had no serious wounds, my left wrist swelled up with the blows I'd deflected with my targe. I'd twisted my knee painfully, the wound in my back had opened and was sticking my tunic to my back but otherwise I was just sore and bruised. God, I felt rough though. Worn out, every movement felt enormous. We all felt the same, but we had no choice but to move. Maelcolm's shield was wrecked and Hosvir abandoned his. Our spears were all damaged and useless. We gathered up our things and struggled back down the valley. I picked up Oslaf's sword, a beautiful well-balanced weapon with a fine Rhenish blade.'

'Aye, I've noticed that, beautiful hilt, plain scabbard,' said Gyric.

'When we passed Oslaf's body lying face up in the cold waters I could not face stripping his body. His fine scabbard and his quality mail lie rotting and rusting along with his mouldering corpse.'

'And the dog? You don't have him now.'

'Oh, we found poor Sib, tied up where we'd last seen him. He was in a bad state. Very thin, still muzzled and with deep cuts in his neck where he'd tried to free himself.'

Gyric's face fell, 'You didn't kill him did you Sar? Please tell me you didn't.'

'I didn't kill him. On our way back down the valley we managed to recapture a few of the horses. They were past riding but we loaded our belongings onto them. We camped for another night and Sib helped himself to the carcass of the horse I'd killed. With us all together and a full belly he soon cheered up, but he wasn't fit for a long haul across England.'

'Where is he now then?'

'He always loved Bruni, doted on her truth be told. She and Maelcolm took their share of the money and some horses and headed off into Wales. They've chosen new names and hope to make a home for themselves in some quiet valley. Sib has gone with them.' I took a swig of ale, 'I'd always imagined bringing him back to impress Harold as a gift. He'd have made a great stud for his own hounds.'

'Harold seems to be very impressed by you anyway? Everybody's talking about it and trying to guess why.'

'Yes, when I told him his cousin, Bjorn, was finally avenged and showed him the proof he was greatly satisfied. I also told him of the battles and the campaign. Remember I left out Maelcolm's real identity. You must keep that to yourself.'

Gyric nodded, he knew I trusted him.

'And about the priests at Hereford,' I added, urgently.

'You've not really been very clear about that yourself.'

'No.' That was a subject best forgotten, I'd been very vague about my part in attacking Hereford as it was. 'He said he's going to gift me some land, Harold did. What will I do with that?'

Gyric shrugged, 'Get someone to run it for you I suppose. Means you'll be responsible for your own upkeep.'

'I will? Bloody hell.'

'Yeah, you'll have to get your own horse, clothes, mail.'

Truth was, I could easily afford all that without the land and I still hadn't received my share from the northern campaign. At least once I got some land, I'd have somewhere to hide my heavy purse.

'I might ask Ymma to manage it for me. I wonder if she and our baby are both alive,' I said with more than a twinge of guilt.

'Ymma, freedwoman, run an estate?'

'I realised when I was away that she's tougher than all of us. She'll probably turn me down but if not, she, and my child would have a home.'

I stared thoughtfully into my drink.

We sat together in silence for a while before Gyric spoke, 'By the way, what happened to Oslaf's scalp?'

'I still have it,' I said, and pulled out the shrivelled skin with its long white locks. I thought of turning it into a purse.'

'And Hosvir?'

'He re-joined Faelen's men. I said my goodbye's to Faelen, who paid me well before he bade me farewell. Then, now a wealthy man, I rode to find Harold. Luckily for me I followed rumour to find him here at Glowecestre, less than a day's ride. The rest you know.'

'And the rest I know,' said Gyric raising his jug.

My mind drifted back to that Welsh hillside and Oslaf's body lying face up in the cold waters we'd crossed on our way back down the valley. It was over. It was really over. I looked at the scalp in my hand and getting up I placed it in the fire. It fizzled wildly for a few moments then subsided into bubbling ashes. The acrid smell of its burning was the last evil thing Oslaf could ever do to me or mine.

I sat back down across the table from my friend as we sat together among Earl Harold's housecarls. The faces of my recent companions passed through my mind's eye. Sibyhrt, both the man and the dog, Hosvir, Maelcolm, Jokul, Faelen and Bruni, sweet Bruni, all took their turn but there in front of me was the friend I valued above all others. My dear friend Gyric. I was exactly where I wanted to be.

Historical Notes

The Battle of the Seven Sleepers is perhaps the most well-known event in my book as it is the battle described in Shakespeare's 'MacBeth'. In Shakespeare's play the Malcolm who Earl Siward supported was Malcolm Canmore but was he? There are many Mael Coluim's at the time and in one source he is described as 'son of the kings of the Cumbrians' so not a prince of Alba (read Alex Woolf's 'From Pictland to Alba' for a discussion of this issue). The Maelcolm in my book is a scion of the Cumbrians. If such a son was the man who Earl Siward supported then he has disappeared from history; which makes him fair game for an historical novelist. Maelcolm's father or grandfather, was Owain the Bald, hence the premature baldness my Maelcolm endures.

The battle itself was huge by the standards of the time and its duration reflected that. The survivors left with a great deal of loot. Earl Siward's son and nephew did die in the battle and Siward himself soon afterwards. The last Viking Earl of England.

We do not know the location of the battle but Shakespeare has it at Dunsinane. This is a large hill not far from Scone, the traditional home of the Alban kings. Folk memory is a tenacious thing and often holds elements of truth. So why not Dunsinane?

The Orkney lords, Thorfinn and his sons, have been described as enemies of MacBeth. They have also been written of, as his allies in the battle. I think given the fluid alliances of the time, both positions are possible. This has allowed me to place Erland in this context. He appears again at another strategic point in recorded English history and we will meet him again. Did a son of Thorfinn the Mighty cruise round England in his youth? Why not? He comes from a seafaring people but nothing of his youth is recorded so I've made it up.

Dolfinn, son of Finntor is mentioned in the Irish Annals and he died at this battle. The Irish Sea was more of a community than a division. Settlements on the north west coast of England may well have been more connected to the Isle of Man and Ireland than the Earl of Northumbria who was their nominal lord.

The Kingdom of Alba eventually grew to become Scotland. The Kingdom of Cumbria was not the Cumberland of modern times but was a surviving British Kingdom straddling the River Clyde.

My description of the Stone of Scone is mischievous. I once came across a reference to another possible Stone of Scone; a lump of meteoritic iron with strange whorls on it which was found in Scotland and taken to the British Museum. The Stone in legend fell from the sky and was reputed to be Jacob's Pillow. Why then has a piece of ordinary red sandstone become so significant? It has little to distinguish it from many other stones in the region. On the other hand, meteoritic iron does fall from the sky. What if it was hidden many years earlier from some other invader and replaced by a fake?

In Ireland my hero has a strange encounter with 'the fairy folk'. These stories abound in Ireland and I view them as a folk memory of earlier peoples who possibly survived hidden amongst their supplanters. I have chosen to give them dark skins because 'Cheddar Man' was found to have had a dark skin and he definitely was a member of a people who predated the many dominant cultures that have since prevailed. Communal homes constructed in the same manner have been described in North America. I have borrowed that idea to create a 'Hollow Hill'. The making of bronze in Ireland from the deposits I described is historical. The three women combination occurs frequently in Western Mythology.

My Irish warriors put lime in their hair. This was supposed to be a habit of much earlier Celtic warriors. The warriors who were later described as Irish kerns were still recorded as taking heads well into the Middle Ages; a decidedly conservative custom. In that case maybe they continued other habits of their ancestors? However they dressed for battle they earned a fearsome reputation as light, highly mobile troops. In my book we meet Irishmen and Norsemen in Ireland who are all fighters. This is a very distorted view of a country that was also home to a thriving Christian scholarly tradition. In culture, if not in wealth, the equal to England.

Earl Aelfgar's expulsion from England is historical but the sources are unhelpful as to the reason. He very quickly assembled a large force in Ireland to attack South Wales and then England. I wonder if he already had an alliance with Gruffud ap Llewellyn to defeat his rival and may already have had communications with the Irish which could explain the speed of his retaliation. This may also explain why he was exiled for 'having committed hardly any crime' in that he had, at that time, not actually supported a Welsh prince in his ambitions, but only intended to. King Edward was no fan of the Welsh and had a very bad temper despite the saintly reputation he has garnered since.

The sack of Hereford did take place with the alliance of combatants I describe, It seems a strange way to regain your place in the English nobility but that is what Earl Aelfgar did as had Earl Godwin before him. The murder of the priests was seen as a great crime at the time. I suppose everyone else was fair game. Saint Ethelbert did have his head severed and it was reputed to have healed a blind man. The rout of Earl Ralph's mounted troops did take place. Exactly how and where is not known. We don't know if they crossed the bridge. It certainly meant there were few fighting men left to defend the town. By not forcing a siege Earl Ralph may well have made a huge mistake. The event cost him his reputation, earning him the title of Ralph the Timid. The bridge at Hereford was moved to outside of the town soon afterwards. Alfgar's ramming of the bridge is my own invention.

Archaeologists have never found a wall along the riverbank. Possibly the city relied on the river itself as a defence as they certainly walled the rest of the town. In my tale I have therefore not placed a stone wall in the way of the assault from the river.

Cardiff Bay was indeed once a freshwater lagoon, and remained that way until it was destroyed as Cardiff was turned into a port. The assaults of Caerleon and Caerwent are again my own invention but they were important places in the Kingdom of Gruffud ap Rhydderch.

Portskewett guarded the entrance to the Wye valley and may have been the place Aelfgar's fleet assembled. We know nothing of the war between the two Gruffud's except who won but it does say a lot about the winner's ability to coordinate an international coalition to achieve his aims.

The result of this campaign was that Gruffud became the first, and so far, the last King of all Wales. A great strategist and a ruthless eliminator of possible competition. Read 'The Last King of Wales' by Michael and Sean Davies for a much fuller picture. We will meet him again in my next novel in the series.

There is a tendency to regard late Anglo-Saxon England as a land of the free before its enslavement under the Norman yoke. I'd love to adopt that view but Anglo-Saxon England was a land of terrible inequality with the many slaves, bottom of the social heap. We find remains of people from this time whose bones are distorted by extreme hard work and abuse. Almost certainly the remains of slaves.

It is impossible to avoid anachronisms in the writing of historical fiction, especially in the language used. I've used the word gunwales on a boat for example long before guns existed. I'm sure there are other examples throughout the book, my apologies, the story has to come first.

Spelling of both names and places varies enormously from source to source. In some cases, particularly names, I have tried to use the form most accessible to modern ears but different enough to remind us that they are not of our time. In some cases, place names have not changed at all, in others they are unrecognisable. I've tried to use a form as near to the time of the events as I can find. There will be mistakes.

After reading the first novel many people have assured me that the Anglo-Saxons didn't swear or use words like fuck or mate. In that case I don't suppose anyone used the word 'fuck' before the 1960's. Nearly all, possibly all, of our literature from the time was written by clerics and consists of scriptures, histories, the lives of saints and a few poems in a form of our language we no longer speak. Because we have no records doesn't mean it didn't happen. I'm sure 'coarse' people used 'coarse' language, the more 'refined' wouldn't have written it. Sar will be cursing his way through a few more years to come.

It is impossible to truly enter the minds of the people of the past but I hope you have enjoyed this little tour of their world and if it inspires any of you to study the real history, so much the better.

Simon Phelps

COMING SOON

Book 3 –
Death in the Borderlands

Chapter One

I'm standing at the back of the King's Hall in Glowecestre on a broad wooden platform. Also here, sitting around a sturdy plain table there is Earl Harold with some of the kingdom's most powerful notables who are picking over the remains of a meal. In the hall below long trestles are lined by all the lesser thegns, reeves and aldermen from the surrounding shires. There is no merriment. No minstrels entertain. No young women are serving wines or ales. The mood is sombre. The purpose of this meeting? War.

All the men here will soon leave to levy the fyrd. Every man available will have to take his war spear, his helmet and whatever mail he owns or is issued and converge on Glowecestre. The majority will be armed peasants but every landowner will have some trained warriors to steady the rest. Chief amongst them are the elite housecarls of the Earls. Men like my friend Gyric. but not, ignobly born, me. The reason for all this tumult? A combined force of Welshmen under King Gruffud ap Llewelyn, the army of the English Earl Aelfgar and Irish Viking mercenaries have captured the borderlands up to and including the great city of Hereford. They have burnt down its cathedral, stolen its riches and enslaved many of its inhabitants. Not long ago I had been one of those mercenaries.

It's cold, the shutters are down letting in what little winter light there is along with a steady chilly wind. The ochre-stained walls are bare of tapestries, the rusting heavy iron hooks to bear them jut out at intervals, grim reminders of the King's absence.

I cast a bored and weary eye at my Earl's company. There's Earl Ralph, his tall, once elegant, figure slumped in shame at one end of the table. It was his forces that ran before the Welsh, abandoning Hereford to its fate. Assisted by a young priest, Bishop Athelstan, bishop of Hereford, trembles as he searches around with sightless eyes. No longer active in the church, he's here because his deputy, Tremerig, died soon after the cathedral burnt. Athelstan doesn't look far away from his heavenly reward himself. Ralph the Staller is here too, a formidable presence, representing the King. Earl Tostig, my Earl, Harold's brother, ruler under the King of Northumbria is not here. His huge restless Earldom keeps the Scots at bay. Also notable by his absence is Earl Leofric, although his lands border Wales to the north, Aelfgar, who is his son, fights with the Welsh. Should he have to fight against his own son? Can he be trusted? Aelfgar fights alongside Gruffud ap Llewellyn, now King of all Wales. Yet in the distant past, Gruffud killed Leofric's brother. One of England's most powerful Earls; nobody is certain where Leofric stands.

Harold's brother Gyrth is here, as too is Thorkell, commander of Harold's housecarls, a Dane by birth. Next to Harold sits his chaplain, Leofgar, a priest, but one who sports the moustaches of a warrior as well as the tonsure and robes of a religious man. All I know about him is his name. Thegn Skalpi is also at the table, Gyric's father, half Danish like Harold himself. All the other great men are strangers to me.

My guts rumble noisily, God, am I hungry. My mind wanders to visions of bowls of curds, fresh baked rolls.......

'Sar, here!' It's Thorkell's voice, 'Here, your Earl wants your views.'

I leap upright, my pale face blushing, 'I'm here sir.'

'Yes, I know you are there, now get over here.'

I walk over to the table and stand behind Thorkell's shoulder, between him and my Earl. Harold half turns and looks at me kindly. For now, I have his approval, it is our secret that I have avenged the death of his cousin Bjorn.

'Sar,' he says, 'Tell these men how you and your friends captured Hereford.'

'Jesu Mawr,' I muttered under my breath as twenty odd pairs of malevolent eyes glared at me.

Ralph the Staller half rose, his left hand on the table, his right, finger pointed in my face, his mouth twisted in fury, 'Harold, are you saying this stripling is one of the men who pillaged and burnt an English city, our King's city?'

Earl Harold, grinned good humouredly and nodded.

'You fought with foreigners against your own country,' spluttered Ralph sitting back down in astonishment.

'I was hardly the only Englishman there was I,' I retorted, 'Aelfgar had an army of his own.'

'He was serving with my friend Faelen,' said Harold.

'Faelen, that Irish adventurer who you used to threaten your King not that long ago.'

'Ralph, my father and I were negotiating with the King, nothing personal.'

The other Ralph stuck his oar in here, 'And now instead of being executed for your temerity you have become the most powerful man in the Kingdom after my uncle the King.'

It was now his turn to be stared at by the Staller, 'You might be the King's nephew but I am the King's man. You would do better to stay quiet,' he bellowed.

Earl Ralph reddened and shrunk in his chair, torn between his authority as an Earl and his recent disgrace as a warrior. 'It's not so important how they got into the town but how we're going to get them out,' he muttered.

'You would say that,' said the Staller, 'Though, to be fair, you are right.'

'Sirs, Lords, may I speak?' Again, those malevolent eyes. 'I don't think they'll want to stay anyway.'

Go on.'

'Speak up young man.'

'Tell your boy to shut up Harold.'

'No,' said my Earl, 'Let's hear him out.'

Now I wished I'd kept my mouth shut, 'Two things; first everyone has got what they wanted. Second, the Irish are to sail round Wales to Deverdoeu to get paid, but I don't know when.'

Harold spoke first, 'So the Irish will want to leave and they will want Gruffud in Deverdoeu to meet them.'

I nodded.

'That leaves your first point,' said the Staller, 'Explain.'

Saint Diw, these are the people that run the country, I thought, 'Gruffud, is now King of all Wales. He's conquered the southern Waelas and united them all by beating the English. A thing every Welshman loves. He'll claim everything beyond the Afon Guoy as his own.

'And Aelfgar?'

'Aelfgar has Hereford to bargain back for his Earldom.'

'And the Irish and their Dyflin Viking friends?'

'They'll get their pay, any loot they've kept and quite a few slaves.'

'You think we'll be offered Hereford and peace in exchange for Aelfgar's Earldom?'

'And the King's acknowledging Gruffud's as the King of all Wales. He's a brute but he's not stupid. He'll know he won't be able to hold onto the town forever but he'll get himself recognised as the Welsh king and at very little cost.'

Most of the malevolent eyes turned back to Earl Ralph.

Harold rapped his cup on the table, 'Now Sar, show us how Hereford was taken. The river goes down the western side as I remember.' He dipped his finger in his wine and drew a line on the table top.

I leant forward to add to the picture when my heavy bag of coin hidden behind my short cloak bumped into Harold's upper arm. He drew his elbow back and for a moment weighed the leather bag in his hand. He looked at me with narrowed eyes.

'Carry on Sar, use this wine.'

I dipped my finger in the cup and sketched the rough half circle of the town, and a wavy line from each end of the crescent to show the river. 'All the town on the landward side was walled. Stone and timber. There was a gatehouse, here, on the town end of the bridge. Along the riverbank the wall was much lower and made of rammed earth.'

'But protected by the river?' said the Staller.

'Yes, fine for an attack by the Waelas, but we had longships full of warriors. The wall was lightly manned. They threw a few spears at us but the wall was low enough for us to throw them back alongside a barrage of our own spears and darts.'

'Darts?'

'Like short spears but with leather flights like arrows have feathers. Some of the Irish favour them. So, we're assaulting the walls while Aelfgar rams his huge longship into the bridge and his men climb straight up on to it. We're on the wall. Then after a short fight we attack the gatehouse from the flank. Aelfgar's men are facing both ways on the bridge. A wall of spears facing the routed horsemen forcing them to go north and ride through the ford.'

The Staller, clearly eager to understand asked, 'Then they couldn't get back into the town?'

Earl Ralph was shifting uncomfortably.

'Not the way they went out. They could, those that survived, have gone in one of the landward gates.'

'So why didn't they?'

'I don't know sir. Mostly we worked all this out later. I was one of those who scaled the wall and attacked the gatehouse.' I shuddered as I remembered stabbing a young man in the face before tumbling him into the waiting warriors below.

'And then?

'And then we were in the town where nobody was there to defend.'

A tremulous voice came from further down the table, 'You were with the Irish?'

It was the blind old bishop.

'Yes, with the Irish and the Dyflin Vikings.'

'First into the city.'

I wondered where this was going.

'Yes.'

'At the minster.'

The penny dropped. 'And everywhere else,' I answered evasively.

'Where my priests were hacked down in cold blood?'

'I did hear something about that,' I lied, 'but I didn't see anything.' Truth was his priests had acted like idiots and brought their martyrdom upon themselves.

'Hmmm, I can't see you boy, but your tone tells me you're lying.'

'No, your worship, I'm not,' I lied again.

'You burnt the minster down.'

'Not me, I think that was an accident. Aelfgar was furious.'

'I should hope he was. And you stole all the vestments and all the gold crosses and chalices. Your sacrilege brought on my Bishop Tremerig's death. He was a Welshman did you know that?'

'No Father, I'm just an ignorant foot soldier, sir.'

The Bishop's blind eyes started to weep. His aide tried to comfort him. It looked to me that he would soon be following Tremerig to his holy reward.

Good luck to him, I thought as I became conscious that Leofgar had been staring at me for quite some time.

'That's a very fine sword you're carrying. Did you steal it?' he asked aggressively.

'No,' I shot back just as hard, 'I killed an Englishman for it.'

'You what?'

'Aelgar's men were English. Your enemies. Still are, Father.'

'Sar, behave yourself. This man is my personal chaplain. If you can't respect his priesthood you can, and will, respect that. We will speak later.' Said Harold, forcefully.

It was clear that I was dismissed so I resumed my hungry wait at the back of the hall. Not long after wine was brought in and along with it the bard. It was my old friend Candalo, whose fingers, broken by Oslaf, could no longer play the harp. Morwed, his beautiful daughter played for him while he sang. There she was, her long black curls, her brilliant blue eyes. I felt weak at the knees and although she hadn't even seen me, my face burned bright red.

Eventually all the powerful men got up and, taking their musicians with them, went, leaving the housecarls and other retainers to sit at the boards and eat. Not curds but a filling barley and root stew with a wheaten bannock. No sooner had we started to eat when Thorkell came in and called Gyric and I out.

We followed him into a small house behind the cathedral. I'm still trying to stuff the bannock into my mouth as we walk when we came face to face with Harold, Ralph the Staller and Leofgar. Father Leofgar as I suppose I was to call him.

The three of them are sat on stools around an upturned barrel. Thorkell walks to take his accustomed spot behind Harold's right shoulder. Gyric and I, after leaving our weapons by the door, stand, side by side in front of them.

It was Ralph who spoke first, 'You two were at the battle of the Seven Sleepers, yes?'

We both nodded and shuddered. It had been a truly horrific day. Many great men had died and many, many more ordinary people too. The lucky ones violently in the battle, the unlucky in fever and delirium from gangrenous wounds in the days that followed.

'Why do you think you won? There were as many, if not more enemies arrayed against you on ground of their choosing and in their own country.'

'Earl Siward was a great commander, Sir,' I said. I knew no one would be unhappy with that answer.

Gyric, after pausing for thought spoke up, 'I think it was Burgric's planning.'

'How so?' asked Ralph.

'We were well supplied, sir. Even in Alba, so we didn't have to raid for food and there were always spare shields and other weapons, like the angons.'

'Angons, what are they?'

The others exchanged glances, equally mystified.

'Sar, knows best. He had to throw them,' said Gyric.

I was surprised they didn't know, 'They were throwing spears with a thin metal shaft behind the head. When they stuck in a shield or hit the ground they bent, sirs.'

Earl Harold asked, 'To what purpose?'

Always hard to explain to your betters what to you seems bleeding obvious. I squirmed a bit and said, 'Cos they were bent, they couldn't be thrown back and if they stuck in a shield, it became unusable.'

Burgric told me that they used them in the old days,' added Gyric.

'Your foster father isn't he, Burgric, I mean,' asked Harold.

Gyric nodded assent.

'Clever man. Liked his history, eh?'

I wasn't so sure. The horror of standing out in front of our army to throw those cursed weapons and my companion's foul death was still strong in my mind.

'A terrible number of fine men died that day,' I chipped in, sharply.

'Heroes, all of them,' said Father Leofgar.

Sibhyrt wasn't a hero. Didn't want to be one either. Just wanted to look after his oxen, not to die in a foreign country. I glared at Leofgar but held my tongue.

'They fought long and hard, all day long. It was horrific,' said Gyric, 'horrific.'

I could see he was starting to shake. Gyric had been deeply affected by the events of that day. He'd fought in the front line of the shield wall for hours.

'As for me,' said Leofgar, 'I'm surprised it took quite so long to beat a bunch of savages.'

I nudged Gyric with my elbow, and spoke up, 'Sir, some of them were very savage, sir. Fierce warriors fighting on their own ground.'

Leofgar's grey eyes turned to mine, 'You look like a savage yourself. I've seen you strutting around with a targe, throwing spear, your long hair. And you speak with a Welsh accent. So, what have you done? Just run around on the edges throwing things?'

Harold laughed, 'You should be careful here Leofgar my friend. This lad killed the shipmaster Eardwulf while he was still a pup.'

'Ah, this is the boy, I heard about that. A freak moment when you attacked a distracted warrior,' said Leofric.

'I killed his son too. It's his fine sword I carry.' I retorted; suddenly aware I might have said too much.

Harold saw this and said, 'Don't worry Sar. Leofgar is my chaplain. He hears my confession and Thorkell is privy to all such matters.'

'This, then, is the young man who avenged your cousin's murder. No doubt you had allies.'

'Come, come, you both serve in my household, put aside this squabble,' said Harold, 'Here, Sar, show him your scars and he'll know you for a fighting man.'

Now, don't get me wrong. Harold is my master. I'm sworn to serve him, I owe my life to him and have fought for him more than once, but asking this if me I did not like. Reluctantly I started to strip off as if the marks on my face and my missing finger weren't enough. I tried to conceal my bag of coins in my short cloak as I took it off but it thumped as it hit the floor. My body is covered in scars. Old ones, a large one along my right side, and new ones. Barely healed leg and shoulder wounds that still made me hunch and limp at times. I already had the lattice of small scars up my forearms that all seasoned fighter carry.

Even Harold was shocked and he quickly bid me to get my clothes back on. Leofgar grudgingly conceded that I'd been beaten a few times. I was growing to hate that man, who had never fought a battle, but I could see it mattered to Harold to believe we'd get along so I hild my tongue and hurriedly dressed. For the second time that day my face was burning red.

Then Harold asked me about the bag, 'I noticed you carry a lot of coin Sar, let me see.'

I was very reluctant, although the original hoard had been split in four and much of it spent, it was still a sizable sum. I just didn't know what to do with it. I picked it up and took it to my Earl.

He tipped it out, 'By the Holy Cross! There are gold mancuses here, and a fortune in silver.'

'You stole this from the church in Hereford, didn't you?' said Father Leofgar.

I glowered at this priest with his tonsure and his warrior moustache, 'No, Father, I did not. I swear on the cross I did not.'

Earl Harold sighed loudly, 'You do need to account for this Sar. Where did you get it?'

Reluctantly I told the story. How Maelcolm of the royal line of the Strathwaelas had been sent up to join Earl Siward's army to be set up on the throne of Alba once MacBethadh ad been expelled. How he had run away in fear of his life and took all the cash in the treasury with him. I had found him skulking around and we had escaped to Ireland together. I implied that I left him there, which wasn't true. My reward had been this money.

'He's lying,' said Leofgar, 'Maelcolm Canmore is ruling over the Scots in Alba as we speak.'

'Hmm,' said Harold, 'In truth, that's not the same Maelcolm our King first sent north. The original Maelcolm did disappear. We all believed he'd been murdered by another of the Strathwaelan princes, jealous of his success. Tell me Sar, what did he look like? Remember that I knew him from his days as a hostage in the King's court.'

'Well, sir. He liked to joke, at first anyway. He could fight with a sword, but he was soft.' I paused for though, 'Oh, yes, he could still speak his native tongue though he'd been in England since he was a boy.' I thought some more and then laughed, 'He was going bald. He wasn't happy about that because he was still a young man. Said, it proved he was a prince because his grandad was Owain the Bald.'

'It does sound like him,' said Harold.

'Yes, but anyone could know that,' said Leofgar.

I stood silent.

'They could, but the money disappearing was kept secret. Only Siward, Burgric and a select few know otherwise. We swore to the

King to keep it in confidence. I'm going to keep this money for now, Sar. We'll talk more later,'

I was aghast, 'Jesu Mawr, I earned that money. I took care of Maelcolm from Alba to Dyflin. I earned every silver penny and gold coin. We made a deal.'

I'd actually left Maelcolm in Wales, but he didn't need to know that. Maelcolm had become my friend. He wasn't so soft now either.

'Don't shout at me Sar. I've said what I've said.'

I ranted on, 'I'm also owed my share of the northern campaign and Gruffed owes me for my part in taking south Wales for him. Don't suppose I'll ever see that. Do I get nothing for all these scars?'

'Get out, Sar. Get out the both of you.'

There was yet another embarrassment to follow. As he escorted us out of that were leaving that confusing meeting, Throkell asked me about my sword.

Can you fight with it, Sar?' he asked.

'I'll learn when I have to.' There's no point pretending to Thorkell. 'You'll start learning tomorrow. See me at dawn.'

About the Author

Simon's love of history and historical novels goes all the way back to his childhood when he discovered the novels of Rosemary Sutcliff and Mary Renault in junior school. Since then, he's led an interesting and varied life. At the tail end of a not very successful education he, aged 17, had an accident while changing scenery overnight for a local theatre. This left him permanently wheelchair bound.

Three years after this he co-founded a commune aimed at self-sufficient living which is where he first became involved in animal husbandry. After its anarchic nature became its own undoing, he went on to work on a city farm in Bristol, before buying a smallholding. Eventually living the life of a medieval peasant lost its appeal and he decided to get an education by completing an Access course. Then he studied the public understanding of science before going on to do a Master's degree in the History of Science, Medicine and Technology. Then, in another abrupt change of direction, he retrained as a counsellor and then as a counselling supervisor.

This has resulted in a character who knows how to skin a goat, ferret for rabbits, grow vegetables, write learned essays on science history and dissertations on 18th century electrical medicine and help traumatised people heal. During all this he has been married twice and has helped raise his own children, step-children and grandchildren. He believes this mixture of experiences informs his writing, his characters and the adventures they have.

After retiring from his counselling career, he now travels when he can and writes historical novels both to entertain people and in the hope of encouraging his readers to share his own love of history and the doings of our ancestors.

Milton Keynes UK
Ingram Content Group UK Ltd.
UKHW041852080823
426556UK00003B/76